ALSO BY SAYANTANI DASGUPTA

Debating Darcy

Kiranmala and the Kingdom Beyond
Book One: *The Serpent's Secret*
Book Two: *Game of Stars*
Book Three: *The Chaos Curse*

The Fire Queen
Book One: *Force of Fire*
Book Two: *Crown of Flames*

ROSEWOOD

A Midsummer Meet Cute

ROSEWOOD
A Midsummer Meet Cute

SAYANTANI DASGUPTA

SCHOLASTIC PRESS/NEW YORK

Library of Congress Cataloging-in-Publication Data available

ISBN 978-1-338-79772-5

10 9 8 7 6 5 4 3 2 1   23 24 25 26 27

Printed in Italy   183
First edition, March 2023

Book design by Elizabeth B. Parisi

For all my fellow firstborn immigrant daughters

Give a loose rein to your fancy, indulge your imagination
in every possible flight.

—Jane Austen, *Pride and Prejudice*

Awake, dear heart, awake. Thou hast slept well; Awake.

—William Shakespeare, *The Tempest*

Oh, you and your rules.

—Kate Sharma, *Bridgerton*

Dearest Aficionados of *Rosewood*:

Please be apprised that season two casting for non-principal actors will have one unconventional twist!

In addition to our usual casting process, young multicultural actors will be sought out at our first-ever Regency Camps for a plethora of minor roles!

Will you have the opportunity to play a rake, a debutante, or perhaps an unfortunate victim of a Murder Most Regency?

The camp experience will be a living audition to seek out new faces for our international hit Regency-era romance/detective program.

So, don your finest crinolines or breeches and get thee to a Regency Camp! (All period-authentic costumes will be provided.)

Best of luck to all you aspiring lords, ladies, and high-society corpses!

Yours, as ever,
The producers of *Rosewood* season two

CHAPTER 1

N O WAY THAT is Regency appropriate!" I said for the millionth time, my eyes transfixed on my sister's laptop screen. There, amid the well-groomed greenery of a twisty garden labyrinth, was a hot, brown-skinned lord of the manor doing seriously R-rated things to a milquetoast but moaning lady. I wasn't a prude or anything, but all those barely covered heaving bosoms were a lot to take on a school night. "Jane Austen would definitely not approve!"

"Don't be such a snob, Eila." Mallika threw a piece of popcorn in my direction without blinking her thick-lashed brown eyes. Her calling me by my name rather than Didi, or older sister, revealed the depth of her feeling. Mal probably wouldn't care if an airplane flew by in the background of her favorite new obsession, the implausibly sexy Regency-era romance-slash-detective-series called *Rosewood*. "What do you care? You hate Jane Austen anyway."

"I'm sorry, excuse you, please!" I protested. "I do not hate Jane Austen. I just prefer more literary writers, like Shakespeare!"

"Literary?" Mallika asked without taking her eyes from the gymnastics happening on the laptop screen. "Is that just a different way of saying dead white male?"

If there was anyone who knew how to push my buttons, it was my sister. I mean, who was the feminist in the family? Was it march-attending, postcard-writing, president-of-the-school-gender-equality-club me, or Mallika, whose primary extracurricular activities involved buying and/or making her own clothes, watching celebrity TikToks, and skimming library romance novels for all the smutty bits?

"I don't get how you're so into all the Austen movies," I said. "I mean, it's not like you've taken the time to read a single one of her books, but you own, what, *three* 'I heart Mr. Darcy' bags?"

"Well." Mallika's dimpled face was the picture of serenity. "I do heart Mr. Darcy! And, in all bisexual fairness, the future Mrs. Darcy too! And even *you* like it when I slow down the Colin-Firth-getting-out-of-the-lake-in-a-wet-shirt scene!"

I didn't respond because my sister wasn't wrong. I also appreciated it when Mallika reversed and replayed the scene in the Keira Knightley *Pride and Prejudice* where Mr. Darcy flexes and unflexes his hand after helping Keira into her carriage. But I wasn't about to admit that now.

"Plus, don't even get me started on those fluffy modern adaptations!" I said, pointing at the bedazzled pink self-designed T-shirt Mallika wore that declared: CHER HOROWITZ FOR PRESIDENT.

"Just because teenage girls like something doesn't make it less worthy, or serious, or *literary*!" Looking not particularly serious at all, my sister waved the fluffy pink pom-pom-topped pen she'd

2

made to go along with her shirt. "Plus, *Clueless* was way ahead of its time in terms of LGBTQ+ representation! And there's a whole theory that the main character, Cher, was actually queer herself—that even Jane Austen's *Emma* is about compulsory heterosexuality!"

"Okay, fine, whatever!" I squinted at my sister, annoyed that she had actually made an interesting point. "But what about those other modern adaptations, like *Bride and Prejudice?* Yes, hashtag representation matters, but just because we are Desi does not mean I have to give a pass to Aishwarya Rai's terrible acting!"

"Well, *Rosewood* isn't modern day." Then, even as the laptop lord and lady moaned some more, my sister clarified, "How can you argue with the Regency formula? A brooding and proud hero, a poor and possibly rain-drenched heroine, some interfering-slash-embarrassing relatives, goofy clergymen, amazing costumes, and sexual tension for days! How does that not do it for you? Not to mention the costumes?"

"You said costumes twice," I pointed out. "But other shows have already perfected that formula. *Rosewood* is like *Bridgerton* meets *Murder, She Wrote*! I mean, how many violent deaths could have really occurred at those Regency balls? And the fact that no one in that entire fancy-pants society—"

"The ton," my sister interrupted me in a hoity-toity voice. "The upper crust of English society was called *the ton.*"

"I stand corrected." I rolled my eyes. "As I was saying, the fact that no one in the *ton* realizes that the detective solving the crime every week is just Lord Rosewood in a fake mustache and glued-on sideburns? I mean, *come on!*"

3

"It's a very thick mustache!" Mallika protested. "And those muttonchops really change his face shape! Lord Rosewood is both a sexy but brilliant aristocrat and a master of disguise!"

On-screen, the aforementioned Lord Rosewood was nibbling at his lady love's earlobe while surreptitiously affixing some kind of wax onto her thumb to get her fingerprint. Then he progressed his earlobe nibbling down to some neck nibbling, much to the lady's very vocal delight. I reached out to turn the computer volume down. The scene was doing something upsetting to my equilibrium, and I found it easier to watch without all the groaning.

"I just don't get everyone's obsession with the Regency these days!" I said. "It's all so trivial! No depth! *Rosewood* has, yes, some random murder-y plot, but mostly just a whole lot of suggested bodice ripping and multicultural eye candy."

Both Mallika and I went quiet for a moment as the lord and lady on-screen did things that were definitely NSFW. Good thing Ma had been called into the hospital right after dinner.

"Clearly, people in ye olden times got it on as much as they do now," Mallika said, snapping her gum. I noticed her light brown cheeks were a little redder than they were before.

I tilted my head, taking in the complicated poses that the noble couple were now attempting to undertake. The woman had some shrubbery poking into her side in a probably painful way, but she didn't seem to notice. Plus, was it entirely ethical for a detective to be hooking up with someone who was also a murder suspect?

"That is seriously acrobatic," I observed. I wondered if I would have broken up with Brickson, my ex-short-lived-quasi-boyfriend from our local Young People's Shakespeare Company, if he had known how to do some of the things Lord Rosewood was doing on-screen. I thought of Brickson's clammy hands and even clammier backstage kisses and gave a little shudder. "You know, I'm no expert, but I don't think that position was invented back then."

Mallika, whose head was tilted in a similar direction as mine, snorted. "Ever heard of the *Kama Sutra?*"

"We Desis knew a lot of things the Angrez did not," I said, unable to keep the smile out of my voice.

"They were living in trees still while we were inventing astronomy!" Mallika said in a fair imitation of Baba's voice.

"Not to mention geometry!" I gave the words Baba's cadence. Years of performing iambic pentameter had taught me to hear and reproduce the rhythm and musicality of dialogue. "And have I told you about the history of the number zero?"

Abruptly, tears sprang to Mallika's eyes. She reached out and hit the space bar, pausing the murder-solving hottie Lord Rosewood in the middle of an alarming pose.

"I miss him, Didi." My sister's lower lip was trembling. I stared at her beloved, familiar face—her wide, dark eyes, her curly lashes, and her thick hair that fell like a velvet curtain down her back. Mallika may have quit the Young People's Shakespeare Company because she was too lazy to memorize lines, but she was the sister who looked like a movie star, even with tears streaming down her face. I felt a lurch of protective love.

I reached out and squeezed my sister's hand, feeling something squeezing even stronger in my heart. "I know, my bonti. I miss him too."

It had been three years since our father had died, yet the sting still pierced at unexpected moments. But unlike Mallika, I couldn't afford to show it all the time. After all, I had her to take care of. Since Baba had died, Ma had gone back to full-time patient care in her pediatric practice, leaving me increasingly in charge of my sister. There were a little more than two years between us, but sometimes, it felt like twenty. Mallika had been so small when Baba died, so hurt and lost. And with Ma at work, I'd had to step in and fill the breach. On paper, I was soon to be a rising high school senior looking ahead to the rest of my life, but inside, I felt like a mother hen afraid to leave her beautiful, fragile, and somewhat immature chick.

Now I felt a sense of growing alarm at Mallika's rapidly escalating tears. She was doing the little hiccuping thing that meant that a full-on torrent of upset was just around the bend. Clearing my voice, I tried to change the subject.

"I really shouldn't let you watch *Rosewood*, Mal." I used my best scoldy schoolmarm voice. "You are only just finishing ninth grade. You know Ma wouldn't approve."

As predicted, my attitude dried her tears. "Don't act like you're so much older than me, Didi!" Mallika wiped her drippy nose with the back of her hand. Inwardly, I sighed. Only my sister could look this good doing something that gross. "And anyway, what Ma doesn't know won't hurt her!"

"Come on, the show's a little trashy," I said, not because I really believed it but because I wanted to make sure that Mallika wouldn't slip backward again into any more boo-hooing.

"I thought you said you liked *Rosewood* for its multicultural casting." My sister held her lips in a stubborn pout. "I thought you said that it was refreshing to see people who looked like us for once on shows, instead of always being invisible and erased in popular culture."

"Dang, someone's been listening to my rants," I laughed. "Yes, all true, but I still think they go a little far with the sexytimes."

"The only reason they got away with casting the way they did is probably because of the sexytimes," Mallika pointed out. "Can you imagine that Regina Rivera-Colón, an Afro-Latina woman director, would have been allowed to cast more shows like this, or get a second season, if the first season of *Rosewood* wasn't a blowout success? People may come for the Regency, but they stay for the smut."

"Look, I'm not saying he's not pretty to look at." I pointed at the six-pack of the frozen detective-slash-nobleman on the computer screen.

"Just pretty?" Mallika eyebrows shot sky-high. "I know you said after the Brickson catastrophe you didn't have time in your life for romance, but come on, Didi, even you've got to make room for a fictional boyfriend, or girlfriend, for that matter."

"Okay, yes, he's very, very pretty," I amended with a snort. "Maybe you can design me an 'I heart Lord Rosewood' T-shirt."

"So what's your issue?" Mallika demanded.

I sighed. "I just think they could tell stories about petticoats and poison with less hedgerow humping. I mean, if I had any say in *Rosewood* season two, I'd tell them to trust the plot and the characters more, and rely on the bedroom factor less."

"Well, then, aren't you in luck!" With a mischievous look,

Mallika reached into her backpack and pulled out two thick-papered, old-fashioned envelopes, handing over one addressed to me.

"What's this?" I ripped the envelope carefully open and pulled out the heavy stationery. The script was a beautiful calligraphy that didn't look computer generated but handwritten.

"Your chance to tell the producers of *Rosewood* how to be more classy and literary or whatever." Mallika's face beamed with pleasure.

Dear Ms. Das,

The Hudson Valley Theater at Norland Manor
(formerly the site of Norland Shakespeare Theater)
is pleased to offer you a position in our first-ever
summer Regency Camp! Thank you for your
audition videotape; we found it both unique and
delightful.

Please be aware that Regency-appropriate attire
(which we will provide) and behavior (which we
will train for) is required throughout your stay at
Norland Manor, and that our no-cellular-devices
policy is nonnegotiable. A full schedule of
activities, packing items, and contract will be
enclosed in a separate letter.

You may have heard that the producers of the
international hit television program *Rosewood* will
be scouting for a host of extras and minor speaking
roles through our Hudson Valley Regency Camp.
While this is true, your acceptance in our camp is
in **no way** a guarantee of any casting in the
television program. Rather, this is an opportunity
to step back in history, into a time of manners and
civilities, attention to self-presentation, and
community making.

We seek only your affirmative reply that you will
join us!

Yours, as ever,

Lady Theodora Middleton

Camp Director

CHAPTER 2

WHAT IN THE actual heaving bosoms is this?" I held out the letter I'd just read to Mallika. "Is this why my Shakespeare summer academy at Norland Manor got canceled? Because of this Regency Camp set up by the *Rosewood* producers?"

"I thought you'd be happy!" Looking dangerously like she might cry again, Mallika sniffed. "I thought this could be fun, since you were so disappointed about your Shakespeare summer thing not happening. Plus, this is something we can do together."

"But this isn't anywhere near an equivalent alternative to the Norland Summer Shakespeare Academy! I mean, actors and directors from the Globe and the Royal Shakespeare Company come from England to teach during that summer session. I'd been looking forward to it all year!" I shook the paper agitatedly. "This Regency Camp isn't about celebrating art or literature or theater! It's some *High School Musical* version of *Austenland* where Regency-appropriate attire is required and cell phones are verboten! What the heck have you signed me up for, Mal?"

"Not just you!" Mallika pulled out an identical letter to mine with a sunny expression. "I applied for us both!"

I rolled my eyes. "Does Ma even know about this?"

"It was Ma's idea!" Mallika said, completely shocking me. "You know how she's been talking about selling the house, buying something a little smaller that's closer to the hospital and the practice. She thought it might be easier to show the house if we were gone for a couple weeks this summer."

This revelation was getting worse and worse. I didn't want to lose my childhood home, and I really didn't want to go to some cheesy camp specializing in crinolines and cravats, or spend my summer with a bunch of fame-hungry high schoolers vying for a meaningless walk-on television role.

But that was my logical brain talking, the part of me that had been forced to grow up fast and be practical. The part of me that was still young and hopeful and in love with acting was, I hated to admit, intrigued. Against my will, my heart started beating out a new question—what if, what if, what if? What if, among all the superficial fame-seekers, someone like Regina Rivera-Colón was to recognize my talent as an actress? What if she actually cast me in her show and that launched my acting career? What if this was the opportunity I'd always dreamed of, but never dared to hope for?

Of course, I couldn't tell Mallika any of that. With a sigh, I put my head in my hands. "How could you have done this without telling me?"

"I really thought you'd be happy." Mallika blinked her eyes, looking infuriatingly like a vulnerable fawn. "You love acting!"

"I love the theater!" I corrected her.

"How is that different?" my sister demanded.

I thought about how hard our immigrant parents had worked to make a life for us out of practically nothing, how Ma had to almost start again after Baba died, and was only able to support us because of her training in medicine. I knew most actresses didn't make it in the industry and, even if they had some success, had to make money in between auditions with various part-time jobs. I couldn't put that stress on my family. I knew what my responsibilities were.

"Look, I'm not stupid. I know a brown girl like me isn't going to be the next Dame Judi Dench!" I set my mouth resolutely.

"Just because our drama club director is a narrow-minded bigot doesn't mean everyone is!" Mallika interjected.

Her words hit a nerve. Yes, I loved performing with them, but another reason I'd joined our community Shakespeare company was because kids of color never got cast as leads in our school productions. Mr. Kutcher, the director, all but openly said that he didn't believe in color-blind casting. And since the only plays he did, like *Our Town* or *The Crucible*, were all white, nobody with any melanin ever had any hope of playing anything beyond a maid or Townsperson #2. I mean, he always said that thing about how there were "no small roles," but everyone knew the real score.

"Theater is my passion, my hobby, but it's not a real career choice." I shook my head at my sister, my tone firm. "Like how Baba loved Shakespeare, but he was still an engineer. All those people who say 'just follow your dreams,' it's a joke! Folks who can do that have family connections, or a big fat trust fund they

13

can rely on. I told you, I'm going to be prelaw, not set my sights on some dream that's never going to happen!"

But unlike me, Mallika wasn't worried about such boring things as making a living. Her face glowed as she asked, "What if you're wrong, Didi? What if you *could* be the next Dame Judi whoever? I mean, look at *Rosewood*!" She pointed at the screen. "Shows like that are proving that girls like you, girls like us, *can* be cast in all those amazing roles!"

"Whatever! Not the point!" My brain searched desperately for an explanation that my sister would believe. "If I *could* make it as an actress, I'd want to be play legendary women like Lady Macbeth and Beatrice and Queen Titania, not some possibly murderous lady groaning in the bushes whose entire character arc is about titillation."

"But she's gorgeous." Mallika sighed, her hand to her heart. "Plus, that outfit she gets to wear is total perfection."

Ignoring her words, I turned my attention back to the letter in my hand. "What audition tape are they talking about here? Please don't tell me you've sent them a tape of me acting without my permission!"

"Well, I knew you wouldn't want to apply." Mallika shrugged in a blasé way.

I shook the letter at my sister again. "But how did I audition for this thing without knowing it?"

"Easy!" Mallika opened her doe-like eyes wider than should really be humanly possible. "I just uploaded onto the audition site a recording of you and me in that all-female *Taming of the Shrew* adaptation you wrote last year."

I felt my head about to explode. "That was a scene for an experimental student-run theater festival! I didn't write that for public consumption!"

"Granted, it was a little weird. I mean, you setting the whole thing outside a Planned Parenthood during a reproductive rights rally with everyone in *Handmaid's Tale* red cloaks and hoods was a *choice*." Mallika pursed her lips, and I felt a surge of embarrassment. Okay, yes, it had been a little heavy-handed, but at the time, I was sure I was being super radical.

"Katherina and Bianca are the classic feminist and anti-feminist characters." I sniffed defensively. "I mean, the shrewish and smart sister, the pretty and vapid sister? Each whose fate is tied to the other's? It made sense to me they'd be on either side of an abortion protest."

"If you say so, Ruth Bader Steinem!" Mallika singsonged. Then she narrowed her eyes. "Wait a minute, what do you mean classic feminist and anti-feminist characters? You better not be talking about you and me! I may be pretty, but I am not . . . whatever that other word was!"

"Vapid, which means airheaded," I said, adding quickly, "But of course I'm not talking about you and me! I'm just drawn to stories about sisters. Plus, I thought *The Taming of the Shrew* was ready for a feminist reinterpretation."

"As I told you at the time, why mess with perfection when *10 Things I Hate About You* is already out there in the world?" Mallika tossed her thick hair over her shoulder.

Her critique of my playwriting skills got me annoyed. "Well, the Regency Camp people obviously enjoyed the audition tape of my play. We got in, didn't we?"

"Exactly my point, dear didi of mine." Mallika smiled like a cat.

"Don't think I don't see what you did there." I pointed at my tricksy sister. "But forget it, I'm not going."

"Why is no the only thing you ever say?" Mallika demanded with a pout. "I mean, I was just talking to Emily and Joon at lunch about why you are always so afraid of saying yes!"

"Why were you psychoanalyzing me with your goofy friends?" I felt my temper flare. "And in the cafeteria of all places?"

"But am I wrong?" my sister asked, unfazed by my irritation.

I made a noncommittal grunt. Okay, maybe my sister wasn't entirely off base about the me-hating-to-say-yes thing. It was the same reason I didn't like improvising scenes in my Shakespeare company. The one rule in improv was, you had to go with whatever a scene partner said. You had to say, "Yes, and . . ." So if they said there was a green dinosaur in the room with you, or that it was raining fireflies from the sky, you had to say yes, accept that was the case, and then build on the scene, reacting to that dinosaur or those fireflies or whatever. The problem was, since Baba had died, that kind of leap of faith just felt too scary to take. Trusting someone else to alter your reality? No thanks. I preferred to stick with the safety of a script, the security of what I knew I could control.

Mallika's eyes were getting watery again. "Don't be so negative, Didi! Ma said that the only way she'd let me go was if I could convince you to go with me."

Ha ha. And there it was. The truth of the matter. "I thought this was all her idea, so she could show the house!"

"Well . . ." My sister twisted her delicate fingers around each other. "I might have suggested that idea to her, but when I did, she was totally on board."

"But she's not going to let you go if I don't agree, right?" I sighed, rubbing at my neck. Of course this was just like every other extracurricular activity in the last few years—if I didn't go, Mallika wasn't allowed. Because I was the responsible one, the serious one, the one who was supposed to keep my little sister out of trouble when our mother was busy. "What, can't your friends do it?"

"Em has soccer camp and Joon is going to Seoul with her family." Mallika's lip trembled and the water works began, slowly but surely. "Didi, you *have* to come with me! Imagine—both of us being cast as extras in *Rosewood* season two! Or maybe getting to be murder victims! And dressing in all those fabulous outfits! I mean, what's the worst that could happen?"

"I could hate it!" I grumbled, crossing my arms in front of my chest. "Everyone there will be superficial and the whole thing will be deeply inaccurate and farcical."

"But what if this is your last chance to give acting a try?" Mallika's eyes grew bright. "Before you go off and bore yourself at college preparing to be an accountant or whatever?"

"A lawyer," I corrected her, even as I felt my defenses begin to crumble.

"Same difference," Mallika sniffed. "And hey, this could even be a great topic for your personal statement: My two weeks at a historically inaccurate Regency Camp!"

There it was, the face-saving excuse I could present to my mother and sister, not to mention to myself, as to why I was

17

agreeing to go to Regency Camp. I didn't have to admit I still dreamed of being a professional actress. I could simply say I was there to be a good big sister and to bolster my college applications. Not to mention I *had* been trying to think of a personal statement topic for my applications, and really didn't want to write about Baba's heart attack, which was what my college counselor at school kept hinting I should write about.

"Well?" Mallika asked.

I studied her familiar face. Mallika was beautiful enough to catch the eye of some producer looking for pretty, multicultural extras. She'd be over the moon with happiness to get dressed and made up to be in the background of some ball scene, or maybe even get to be a gorgeous corpse whose murder Lord Rosewood could solve. And who was I to begrudge her that? Plus, it wouldn't look bad on her résumé when it was *her* turn to apply to college.

"I'm not going to kiss up to any producers!" I finally said, trying to convince myself as much as her. "This is only material for my personal statement! I'm seriously not interested in getting cast for anything!"

Mallika's expression became suddenly wistful. "Just remember how many wonderful times we had at Norland Manor before Baba died. Maybe we can be that happy there again!"

Now I felt my own eyes filling with tears. Even though we hadn't been there since he'd died, our family had visited the Hudson Valley manor's grounds to see outdoor Shakespeare productions almost every summer since we were little girls. It was an additional reason why I'd been so disappointed when their summer Shakespeare academy had been canceled. But maybe, just maybe, this Regency Camp being held at the same location was a sign. Maybe Mallika was right. Maybe this was my last chance to be young and carefree and full of dreams again, like I'd been before Baba had died.

"So?" Mallika said softly, her arm on mine. "Are you in?"

I felt something like hope flutter to life inside my chest. But I pushed it down, lest it get stronger and crack all my carefully built defenses wide open.

I made my voice gruff as I touched my curly hair, which, unlike Mallika's smooth and straight locks, tended to get frizzy at the slightest provocation. "Look, there's no way I'm wearing a bonnet, no matter what!"

"Don't worry!" My sister grinned. "Haven't you noticed? *Rosewood* has a strict no-bonnets policy!" Then she jumped on me, practically crushing me in her enthusiasm as she swept me into a giant hug. "Oh, Didi, this'll be the greatest summer *ever*!"

Dearest Attendees of Hudson Valley Regency Camp,

Please be apprised that costuming will be the first order of business when you arrive. It is imperative that no modern clothing is visibly worn during camp, in order to create the Regency experience for yourself and your fellow attendees. Our team of professional dressmakers will outfit you in true Regency style, allowing you to authentically feel yourself in a different time and place.

After costume fittings, all camp attendees must hand over their modern communication devices. The administrators have phones that may be utilized in case of emergency, and intermittent updates will be sent to your families to apprise them of your activities.

Your first day at camp will be capped off with a court presentation to *Rosewood*'s very own queen, Her Majesty Regina Rivera-Colón herself! So be on your best Regency behavior! Our queen will be back to meet you at the end of the camp session, when all campers will be invited to perform for her during a showcase—music, theatricals, and the like—right before our end-of-camp ball, which will be a grand and breathtaking affair!

Yours, as ever,

Lady Theodora Middleton

Camp Director

CHAPTER 3

I T WAS BIZARRE to be back at Norland Manor without Baba. But boy, had it transformed now that it was the home of Regency Camp. No way you could miss that the place had something to do with the show *Rosewood*. It was like someone had taken one of those thickly flowered backgrounds from a Kehinde Wiley painting and brought it to life. Except maybe with slightly less artistic flair.

"I've never seen so many roses in my life," I breathed, feeling a little dizzy from the heavy scent as Mallika and I left our bags below a rose-covered archway, from where they would be transported directly to our room.

"It's like a rose rave!" Mallika enthused. "A riot of blossoms! A veritable floral orgy!"

"Okay, okay. Calm down there, Countess Descripty-Pants," I laughed.

But I couldn't disagree with my sister. Since our mother had dropped us off at the main gate, we had passed dozens of varieties of roses—small, large, clustered on bushes, and trailing down trellises. And the colors were wild—from reds so deep they looked almost black through oranges, purples, pinks, yellows, and even some that looked green and blue. I wondered if those were natural or helped along by some dye-wielding set designers.

On top of the already over-the-top flowers, there were candy-colored sofas scattered over the grounds. Plus, there were other Regency-era oddities randomly placed—a sculpture here, a barouche carriage there. I sneakily took a few pictures of these pieces with my phone. You never knew what might be useful to inspire my personal statement. I was surprised when my Insta-loving sister gave me a scowly look.

"You know we've got to hand our cell phones in, right?" she said as we made our way from the luggage area over to a long line of attendees going into the costume tents.

I bristled. "I know. I know."

But I couldn't say anything more because of the ridiculously loud camp administrator at the front of the line yelling out instructions.

"Bonnets to the right, breeches to the left! Just a metaphor, of course, just a metaphor, no bonnets will be hurt in the costuming of this camp!"

The Amazon-like woman with the clipboard was, true to my sister's observations, not wearing a bonnet herself, but had her unnaturally blue, ringleted hair piled so high she seemed even taller than she was. And into that cartoony bouffant was tucked—what else—a bright pink rose. Despite her fussy hairstyle and

23

cotton-candy-colored, flouncy dress, she looked formidable—piercing eyes and a voice as sharp as a battle-ax. I mean, she'd be a completely plausible murderer on the show. But that only made me itch that much more to challenge her authority.

"The question of bonnets versus breeches is only upholding the gender binary, isn't it?" I asked. I projected my voice but kept well out of the woman's sight. I was outspoken but not stupid. "Pretty oppressive, if you ask me!"

Mallika stepped on my foot, hard. "Come on, you promised you'd give this place a chance," she hissed. "I mean, we haven't been here half an hour yet and already you're picking fights."

Unlike my sister, Tall Clipboard Lady seemed unfazed. "Regency Camp is a place where all are welcome. Choose whatever costume tent feels right for you," she said in a deadpan voice before continuing with her *Newsies*-style hawking of "Bonnets to the right, breeches to the left!"

"Doesn't resolve the problem of the imposed binary choice." This follow-up wasn't said by me, but by a dark-haired, broad-shouldered, posh-voiced person in line ahead of us.

Tall Clipboard Lady didn't seem interested in answering any more questions, just keeping the line moving.

"Look at that." Mallika nodded toward the person with the British accent. "You have a gender studies soul mate up there in line."

"Nah. Just another lemming in it for the fame and fortune," I muttered, even though I was impressed someone had spoken up to support me.

Per the blue-ringleted, clipboard-holding Valkyrie's directions, Mallika and I went right. Costume fitting was the first

24

thing on our schedule for the day, and my clothes-loving sister was predictably thrilled at the prospect. Me, not so much.

"They better not be expecting us to wear Regency-appropriate underwear," I complained as we got shown to a little screened-in changing area inside the "bonnets" tent.

We caught glimpses of half-dressed girls everywhere as we walked to our area. There were frills, laces, bows, and blouses as far as the eyes could see. I saw a couple of girls sizing us up from behind their changing screens. One of them, a tall, tawny-skinned model type, gave Mallika a seriously shady look, getting my protective older sister hackles up. I pulled our screen closed with a snap, protecting my sister from what our aunties in India would surely call the other girl's evil-eye nazar.

"You're supposed to wear corsets under gowns at camp, but these ones we have for you are nowhere near as uncomfortable as actual Regency-era corsets would have been," said a tiny little costumer who buzzed into our changing area, her arms full of crinolines and ribbons, dresses and petticoats. "And of course, you can wear your own underwear."

The girl had dark hair, ruddy cheeks, and an infectious smile, and wore what looked like Regency-era glasses with her rather fetching floral-printed Regency-era outfit. I particularly liked the watch pinned to her dress, which made her look a bit like *Alice in Wonderland*'s white rabbit.

"I'm Annie Park!" she said, the multiple hair ribbons in her perky, braided updo bopping as she talked. "At your service!"

"They let you be a costumer?" My sister was never the most subtle of people. "I mean, aren't you a high schooler?"

25

"I'm a rising junior," Annie laughed, making her ruddy cheeks look even ruddier. "I'm interning with my aunt, who's the head costumer here. In exchange, they're going to let me be a camper too and do activities and everything when I'm not needed to help my aunt's team! But I really want to follow in Auntie's footsteps—apply to one of the fashion design schools in the city for college."

I couldn't help but like the girl. She seemed smart and upbeat, and like she could be a cool friend while I was here. Just as I was thinking this, though, my sister suddenly presented a whole new side of herself.

"Those Greek-style dresses of Jane Austen's era didn't need as many petticoats as earlier times," Mallika said with an unexpected air of authority. "I think they only wore one petticoat underneath those Empire-waist dresses, right?"

I stared at my sister in confusion. How did she know that? Had she watched some show about European historical clothing with Emily and Joon? Surely this wasn't the kind of thing her TikTok celebrities were blabbing about on social media?

"Totally!" agreed Annie as a thinner, more imposing version of her sailed into the area.

It was her aunt, Ms. Park, who had obviously heard Mallika's comment as she came in. The woman beamed at my sister. "What a pleasure to meet someone with an interest in historically accurate dress!"

It was small of me, I know, but I had to suppress the desire to yell out that Annie and her aunt had it wrong. Mallika was the superficial one; I was the one who had interests in history and literature. *I* was the one with a life of the mind, not a life of the mall.

But of course, I didn't do any of that. I just stayed quiet as Ms. Park handed us both modern-looking corsets that were somewhere between a tank top and an exercise bra. Then Annie handed us each a white camisole-petticoat thing.

Turning to Mallika, Annie said, "You know, sometimes the material of those dresses was so thin they were practically transparent!"

"I read that Regency ladies would spill water on themselves on purpose to make their dresses even more see-through!" Mallika's eyes were round and sparkling as she said this.

Annie gave Mallika an appreciative look before nodding in agreement. "I read that too!"

Mrs. Park smiled at both girls, making me feel seriously left out. "The wealthy could afford something called Dhaka muslin, a material so fine and fluid, you could put an entire bolt of fabric through the center of a ring!" She nodded to her niece. "Looks like you have this under control, my girl. Let me know if you need me!"

As the older woman swirled out of our changing area, Annie wheeled in a rack of gowns with Mallika's and my names on it.

"The costume team preselected gowns for everyone's day-to-day wear," the girl explained. "I'll do a quick fitting of a few of them, just to see if they need any extra tailoring, but that's why we asked every attendee to send their measurements and a photograph."

I raised my eyebrows accusatorily in Mallika's direction. "I had your measurements from when I made you that dress for the junior formal," she admitted guiltily. "The one you went to with octopus-hands Brickson."

I scowled at her, deeply regretting my every life decision.

Regency Fun Fact

Most Regency ladies wore only a chemise but no underwear under their beautiful gowns. Although drawers, the precursor to modern underwear, were invented in Europe in 1806, this early version of underpants still only covered the legs, like chaps, leaving the middle quite exposed. Drawers were also only secured with a drawstring waist, and so would sometimes slip off while a lady was walking. A scandalous occurrence!

CHAPTER 4

ANNIE HELD UP one dress to Mallika's lighter brown face and another to my darker brown, before rejecting the choices and digging through the rack some more.

As Annie fussed about with Mallika's fitting, I looked up the phrase Ms. Park had used. "Huh! The art of spinning and weaving Dhaka muslin came from Bengal, where our family is from!" I exclaimed as I read off my phone screen.

Annie nodded as she helped Mallika into a vivid green dress with tiny white embroidered flowers that made my sister look like a blooming spring garden, and then pinned and tucked the material so it fit her shape perfectly.

"Auntie says Napoleon's wife Josephine, and maybe even Jane Austen, wore dresses of Dhaka muslin. European ladies loved the stuff! But eventually, there was a push to make cheaper textiles." The energetic girl speed-talked as she worked. "Indian muslin was too much in competition with British cotton, so the Brits boxed the artisans out of the market, and the knowledge of weaving the fine muslin got lost."

"Which only goes to prove that colonizers ruin everything," I muttered as my sister stepped back out of the green dress. Annie laughed in agreement.

Then Annie was helping me into a dress of bright pink, what in Bengali we would call "rani color"—the color of a queen. I studied myself in the standing mirror. It was brighter than something I would normally wear, but the material actually made my dark brown skin glow.

"So what do you want to do after college?" Mallika asked as Annie pinned and prodded my dress to fit my form. "Can your aunt help you get a job as a costume designer on *Rosewood*?"

"What a dream that would be!" Annie adjusted and pinned the fabric on my poofy sleeves so that they fit me properly. "I mean, I've got tons of ideas for how to make Regency gowns that are inspired by global, not just European, designs! Maybe I can bring by my sketchbook later and show you!"

"I'd love that!" Mallika beamed at the girl with such a look of open attraction, it made me pause. Even though my sister was, as she always said—loudly and to anyone who would listen—someone with equal-opportunity attractions, she'd never really dated anyone of any gender. I wondered if Regency Camp would change that.

With the initial fitting of our day-to-day dresses done, the costume intern now pulled in a different rack, this one with only two gowns hanging on it. Carefully, she shook out the folds of two pure white gowns with lacy overlay.

"Wow, those are iconic!" Mallika touched the overdress of one of the gowns. "Is this hand-beaded?"

"Absolutely!" enthused Annie, pointing out different parts of the dresses. "Look at that stitching work! And check out the sleeve embroidery!"

"Why are we wearing those fancy white gowns?" I suddenly had a bad feeling, a flashback to the sections of the long camp welcoming letter I hadn't read all that carefully.

"Well, for the presentation to the queen, of course!" Mallika frowned at me. "Did you forget?"

"Oh, for the love of Meghan Markle! What queen?" I groaned.

"Regina Rivera-Colón, the producer-director of *Rosewood*!" Annie helped Mallika gingerly step into her gown, then began to do on-the-spot tailoring to fit the bodice, this time sewing the fabric as my sister wore it. "I can't think of a better way to start Regency Camp than with a court presentation to the queen of must-see streaming TV, the reigning royal of *Rosewood*!"

"Did you actually not read the full schedule?" Mallika stared suspiciously at me. "It was all right there in the information packet! Day one—costume fittings and presentation to Queen Regina Rivera-Colón!"

"It's nothing to be stressed about, just a small walk up an aisle on the arm of one of the boys, and then a curtsy to her." Annie snipped off a thread from Mallika's newly tailored bodice. She leaned toward my sister in a conspiratorial whisper. "I think she's just doing a preliminary scouting out of potential extras. Plus, I hear she *adores* any excuse to get dressed up in *Rosewood* costumes!"

"It's so fun picking her out of the background in those ball scenes!" enthused my sister. "I love that she sneaks into shots of her own show!"

Annie handed my sister a pair of snow-white stockings as well as the old-fashioned garters to hold them up. She explained how to put the things on before coming over to me and helping me into my diaphanous gown. "You know those things are off-limits, right?" she said, looking at the cell phone in my hand. "You're going to have to hand it in at the front door before they let you into the manor building."

At my grim look, Annie added, "I don't make the rules, but I also don't want to get kicked out of Regency Camp, or worse, get my auntie fired."

"No, that's understandable!" said Mallika, who was still fumbling with her stockings and garters. In her beautiful low-necked gown, her brown skin glowing against the white of the dress, she looked like an absolute angel. "Of course we'll hand in our phones, right, Eila?"

This again felt like an infuriating reversal of our roles. Usually, I was the rule abider, not Mallika. But in this particular case, I knew this was a rule I was going to break. No way I was giving up my phone and losing that control, that connection to the outside world. Like committing to an improv scene, giving up my phone felt too scary, too much like taking a trust fall and believing this Regency Camp would catch me.

"Let me just keep my cell while I'm in here?" I said in what I hoped was a sweet way, channeling my inner Mallika. "Like a security blanket?"

Annie laughed, making a little touching-her-nose gesture. "Sure. You got it. Asian American solidarity, yo."

I gave the costumer a fist bump of appreciation that made me feel only a little guilty for lying to her.

And then, unexpectedly, two no-nonsense hairdressers crowded into our dressing area, armed with ribbons, pins, and enormous white feathers. They seated Mallika and me down and began roughly combing and braiding our hair, even as my sister and Annie kept up a nonstop stream of chatter about costumes.

"What do you think of this for daily wear?" Annie was holding up a white-and-blue-striped dress for Mallika's inspection.

"What about that one?" As her hairdresser combed her hair, Mallika pointed at a yellow dress with capped sleeves. "It looks kind of like something a socialite murder victim would wear!"

"Grim but true!" Annie agreed. "You have a great eye! And think about how awesome it would look covered with blood!"

Both girls giggled, launching into a conversation about all the different ways various lords and ladies had been murdered on the last season of Rosewood. As the two kept chatting, though, I started to feel nauseous. And it wasn't just because of their gruesome descriptions of poisonings, strangulations, and stabbings.

I'd agreed to come to Regency Camp because I'd thought it was my last chance to immerse myself in the world of theater. But what I loved about acting was the beauty of a well-written speech, the joy of transforming into a different character. Acting was something that happened on the inside, something that fired up my mind and heart. I hadn't counted on all this attention to superficial things like costuming and appearance. Baba had always said theater was about opening up parts of your soul to the beauty of the universe. What would he think of me preening and prancing around for stardom and limelight?

My right eye started throbbing. The warm summer afternoon

was making sweat pour from my hairline and down my back. Also it didn't help that a grumpy older woman sadist was scraping and pulling my hair into a series of complicated braids, then jamming bobby pins into my scalp like she was mining for oil.

"I'm getting a headache," I said, rubbing my stiff neck. I turned to the sadist in question, who looked like some kind of steely-mouthed cannibal because of all the bobby pins sticking out of her yellow-toothed maw. "Can I take a break to get some air?"

Bobby-Pin Mouth looked like she was about to protest, but Annie stepped in. "Come on, Dolores, give her a five-minute rest. You can sneak in a smoke break without anyone noticing!"

Tobacco-fiend Dolores grunted at this suggestion, and held up her hand in a five-finger splayed gesture that she ominously shook in my direction. But thankfully, she let me up.

"I'll be right back, Mal," I told my sister, who looked dazed and half-asleep in her chair at this point. Her stylist, a young man with dandified style, looked like he was giving her a scalp massage even as he gently twisted and plaited her hair into a stunning updo.

"Just be very careful with your dress, please!" Annie warned. "And don't get lost!"

"I won't! We used to come here all the time as kids with our parents." I pointed out of the tent, down toward a blue body of water in the distance. "Our dad would take us boating right on that lake!"

Mallika looked over at me, misty eyed, as Annie smiled. "Well, don't go near the manor! Auntie says no campers can go in there unless you are completely historically transformed!"

"Of course not!" I reassured her.

Annie smiled, convinced. After all, I was a pretty good actress, if I said so myself.

Because as soon as I ducked out of the tent's back flaps, I headed straight for the side doors of Norland Manor, breathing hard. I needed to get away from this land of artificial Regency make-believe and get back some semblance of control.

Damn the consequences.

Regency Rules of Etiquette

A Regency lady should never be in the company of an unrelated gentleman without a chaperone. She must never speak to any gentleman without being properly introduced first, and even then never use his first name. Apart from allowing a gentleman to place her shawl about her shoulders, help her off a horse, or offer an arm over an uneven walking path, a lady should never be in physical contact with a gentleman! Who knows what might transpire from such an encounter!

CHAPTER 5

s I LEFT the costume tent along one of Norland Manor's cobbled walkways, I took in the familiar fruit orchards where Mallika and I had wandered as elementary schoolers, the craggy trees in endless rows like magical spirits frozen mid-stretch. And of course, there was the small lake on which Baba had once taken us boating, right next to a picturesque vine-covered white gazebo. I remembered even now the unsteady feeling of being on the water, the comfort of the sun on our faces and our seemingly invincible father steering the little metal boat. And then there was the vista off the back of the manor, overlooking the cliffs on the other side of the Hudson Valley, and the mighty river below. Being back at Norland was like being magically put inside a painting. It was like walking into a memory.

I sighed. It was strange to be both so sad and so happy to return to a place that was not your home. As secretly as I could, I took a panorama shot—telling myself it was for the future essay I would write.

Hearing the rise of voices from the costume tent behind me,

I rushed on. I had to get away from all the chaos and confusion back there. Not to mention nicotine-toothed Dolores and her evil bobby pins. Lifting my delicate skirts high so I wouldn't get grass stains, but also so I could take normal-length strides, I walked swiftly up the hill and toward the manor house. I wasn't sure the side door I tried first would be unlocked, but it was. Quickly, I ducked inside.

The long corridor was dim and cool, a relief from the frenetic heat of the tent. I hadn't taken five steps down the hall when, to my left, I saw it: the ballroom—empty, cavernous, and waiting as if just for me.

Stepping into the high-ceilinged space with its ornate mirrored walls, I breathed in for what felt like the first time all day. The room smelled like dust and glass cleaner. Above me hung heavy chandeliers, their gleaming facets reflecting the streaming sunlight in stained-glass patterns across the floor. I took picture after picture with my phone camera, feeling myself calming down with each click.

I don't know why I had found the dressing tent so confusing, so suffocating. It wasn't that I was jealous of the attraction between Mallika and Annie. It was something even more petty. Something about how Mallika had so easily demonstrated her knowledge about Regency dress made me uncomfortable. I wasn't used to her being the one who knew more about, well, anything in any particular situation.

And then there was this ridiculous presentation to the "queen"—where I would obviously be graded for my appearance and not my accomplishments. Like Shakespeare's Katherina,

I'd never been valued for my looks—I was dark skinned, frizzy haired, and passably pretty. It was my sister who, like Bianca, was the beautiful one, the sweet one, the doe-eyed one. My entire identity was built around being the clever older sister—not the shrew, maybe, but the wit. And now I was going to be judged by some Hollywood types solely on what I looked like? Wasn't this what we women had been fighting *against* all these years?

I took a big breath, feeling like I'd come home only to find the furniture rearranged and all the pictures on the walls upside down. To me, Norland had always been a place of higher culture and beauty, not the superficial culture of stardom Regency Camp seemed to be.

I closed my eyes, remembering how Ma and Baba had always made a big deal of coming to Norland Manor's summer Shakespeare productions, packing a picnic basket feast we'd eat before the show on the grassy hill overlooking the river. Ma would lay out an old Indian bedspread and there would be homemade egg sandwiches and sometimes potato and tuna fish chops, cut fruit and cucumbers with black salt. There was a thermos full of homemade lemonade Baba would pour into tiny paper cups for us. The memory of its sharp tartness on my tongue brought pinpricks of water to my eyes. Mallika was usually doing cartwheels or making dandelion crowns or complaining about how boring Shakespeare was, too young to appreciate the magical experience. But I always remembered those picnics and plays as golden moments—my parents glowing in each other's presence, unaware of how little time they had left, like the glorious, setting August sun over the rushing river.

I put my arms out and twirled around the ballroom, catching a breeze from the open French doors. With each turn, I felt as if I was turning back the years, going back to being a little girl, holding Baba's hand as I entered the open-air performance tent not far from where the Regency costuming tents were now. Like magic, the Shakespearean actors would come up over the grassy lawn to thunderous applause, like sea spirits rising from the river itself. I loved how Baba would bend down to whisper in my ear, explaining the plot or language when it was too complicated for me. Too soon, I wouldn't need him. Like mastering a foreign language, I learned to understand the Shakespearean words tripping off the actor's tongues, the dialogue becoming easy and light to my ears. It was why I'd later joined my local Young People's Shakespeare Company. I wanted so desperately to be a part of that magical world of theater, that striving for something beyond ordinary human existence.

Lost in my memories, I twirled faster and faster across the length of the ballroom. The skirt of my delicate white gown lifted away from me as I did, and my halfway-done hair flew loose of several dozen bobby pins, which scattered on the floor. I laughed at the poor fallen pins, like lost souls, telling them, "Alas, our revels now are ended!"

I was startled when a posh British-accented voice continued, "These our actors, as I foretold you, were all spirits and are melted into air." Then the voice paused, adding, "Or, in this case, fallen randomly onto the ballroom floor."

I turned to the intruder, and felt the heat rush to my dark cheeks as I realized that there was a boots-and-breeches-wearing,

Regency-suited boy watching me. He was my age, but his golden-brown skin gleamed as if it would never dare to break out. His dark blue jacket fit his broad shoulders perfectly, nipping in at his waist with precision. At his throat was a neatly tied white cravat, and his dark hair was coiffed in styled waves from another century. There was something about his part-arrogant, part-humorous expression that told me he knew exactly how good-looking he was, and maybe even the effect his appearance was having on me.

"Who are you?" I blurted out. Then, unnecessarily defensively, I added, "How long have you been standing there watching me? Stalker much there, son?"

"Honestly, I didn't mean to startle you," the boy said, bending down to pick up my scattered bobby pins like he was picking flowers from a meadow. He handed them to me with a self-confident, cocky smile as if presenting me with a real bouquet and not one that was just pretend.

I accepted his offering, staring at the tiny black pins. I felt my hair loose against my shoulders, and wondered how chaotic it must look. It was a marvel how little there was holding up any one illusion.

Like he could read my mind, the boy went on with Prospero's famous speech from *The Tempest*, holding his arms out like he was an actor upon a stage. "The cloud-capped towers, the gorgeous palaces, the solemn temples, the great globe itself, shall dissolve."

You would think a boy in old-fashioned clothes who could comfortably recite Shakespeare would seem foppish or strange, but this guy was anything but. Maybe it was the twinkle that danced in his eye as he spoke, like everything was all a grand and hilarious joke.

Even as I thought this, more of Prospero's monologue spilled out of my mouth like water from a spring. "We are such stuff as dreams are made on."

I looked up from my bobby pin bouquet, feeling flustered by the expression in the boy's eyes. With an aggressive randomness, I started sticking the pins back in my hair, hoping that I wasn't making myself look like a scarecrow.

The boy studied me, raising a cocky eyebrow. "So do you make it a habit to recite Shakespeare all alone in abandoned ballrooms? Is it some sort of online trend I haven't heard about yet?"

"*The Tempest* was the last play I saw with my father—at the summer Shakespeare festival they used to have here at Norland Manor—before he died a few years ago," I blurted out, not even sure why I was revealing such a thing to a complete stranger. Maybe it was wearing the delicate gown. Maybe it was standing in the ornate ballroom. Maybe it was being in this place, this place that held so many special family memories. "Being back here feels like coming back to Prospero's island, only with the magic, and the magician, gone."

The confident expression slipped a bit from the boy's face. "I'm so sorry," he said simply, making my heart squeeze beneath my corset. "I lost my mother a few years ago too."

"I'm sorry for you too, then." We stood for a moment in silence, the mirrors lining both sides of the room reflecting multiple versions of him, multiple versions of me. Each of our selves stared at each of the other's selves, recognizing something of our common loss. Finally, I felt the need to fill the awkward quiet.

"You know Shakespeare." It wasn't a question but a statement of fact.

"I had a pain-in-the-arse teacher who made us all memorize significant passages," the boy admitted, his self-confident swagger back in place. "I suppose I didn't realize at the time just how much was being stored in long-term memory."

"My parents took me to so many summer productions here at Norland, I ended up joining a local Shakespeare company in my town." I was rambling, uncharacteristically revealing too much about myself, but couldn't seem to stop. "There's something about his plays that just seem, I don't know, *nobler* than day-to-day life."

"All the crass jokes and sexual innuendos notwithstanding, of course?" the boy quipped.

We both laughed, and some of the awkwardness floating between us seemed to dissipate, like spirits into the air.

"You know, the speech you were reciting, it's the bard himself warning that it's all just a performance, a magical spell, an illusion." The boy raised that cocky eyebrow again.

Then it occurred to me why his accent and voice were so familiar. "Wait a minute. You're the one who supported me when I was giving Tall Clipboard Lady a hard time this morning! About bonnets and breeches, the gender binary!"

"Like the great detective Lord Rosewood, you have found me out." The boy bowed low, as if he had already received the full series of comportment lessons that they advertised in the Regency

Camp brochure. How did a teenager learn to be so elegant? Must be a British thing.

"You're from England?" I asked, realizing I was still being socially awkward.

"From all over, really." The boy shrugged, a gesture that made something shiver inside my bones. "I grew up in Singapore and then Hong Kong, before moving to London for a few years, and then New York."

As he said all this, the boy walked over to the French windows to look out at the beautiful Norland Manor grounds. Without thinking about it, I followed, my beaded dress making a soft shushing sound as I walked. "Sorry, I didn't mean to be nosy. You just startled me."

"I know I must have done, but I can't be sorry I met you." He smiled in such a disarming way that I smiled too. "I just needed to get away from all the action out there and take a breath. I didn't realize there would be anyone else here."

"I don't think I'm supposed to be." I indicated my disheveled hair. "I was warned not to enter the hallowed halls of Norland Manor before being entirely historically dressed."

"Never fear, your secret is safe with me!" The boy's eyes sparkled. Then, in an odd coincidence, he made the tapping-the-side-of-the-nose gesture that Annie had made earlier. "Anyway, those ringleted Regency styles are a bit much, aren't they? And those high feathers I've seen some of the girls wearing around the grounds just now look so uncomfortable. I much prefer your hair this way."

I wanted to respond indignantly, say that he had no right to prefer my hair in any way, shape, or form. But his words made me glance again in one of the room's many mirrors, and instead of seeing myself as I normally might, a fright of frizz, I saw myself as he must see me: flushed and bright-eyed, my hair wild, curly and thick about my shoulders. My dark skin was striking against the white of the elaborate dress. It made me feel like I'd never truly looked in a mirror before.

So instead of firing off a witty barb, I did something unusual, at least for me. I accepted the compliment gracefully, feeling as if I had dropped into someone else's story line, someone else's fairy tale. It was one in which, for once, I got to be the beautiful, desired, and carefree heroine.

A Regency Vocabulary Lesson

Rake: (noun) short for "rakehell."
A Regency-era term for a charming scoundrel
of a man, witty, roguish, and, of course,
handsome. Often wasting his money on
gambling or drinking, the rake is an immoral
character, but potentially reformed by love—
at least in stories. As many modern-day
historical romances insist, "A reformed rake
makes the best husband!"

CHAPTER 6

PPROACHING ME WITH one hand behind his back, the boy made me another formal bow. "Allow me to introduce myself. I'm Rahul. Rahul Lee. A somewhat good Bangladeshi Chinese Singaporean British boy, at your service."

"I'm Eila. An entirely good Bengali American girl." I smiled. "You're Bangladeshi! Do you speak Bengali?"

Rahul shook his head. "Only a few lullabies, and of course the scoldings I got when I was naughty."

"And what is a naughty Bangladeshi Chinese Singaporean British boy like you doing in a place like this?" I asked with a laugh. "Did you just wake up one morning and say to yourself, you know what? I think I'll go to Regency Camp!"

"Something like that." He grinned. "The truth is, I'm a sucker for people who know what they're doing with words. Like Will Shakespeare. Like Jane Austen. I can't get enough of it."

I groaned. "Oh no! Another Janeite!"

Rahul raised a dark eyebrow. "I take it from your tone you aren't a fan?"

"My sister is addicted to every Regency-era movie and show, like *Rosewood*. I mean, so much swooning and so many lingering looks . . ." I began, then trailed off.

"And so you were forced to come to Regency Camp against your will by your sister?" Rahul narrowed his eyes. "And, let me guess, she's made you watch some of the movie adaptations, but you yourself—a lover of Shakespeare and the beauty of the written word—haven't actually read Austen's novels? Maybe because you think they're too fluffy and romantic for you?"

I stared. How did he guess all that?

"Yes, maybe. But don't tell on me! I'm sure it'll get me kicked out of Regency Camp!" I paused. "That and the illegal use of my cell phone." I indicated the phone still in my hand.

Then, on impulse, I held up my phone and snapped a picture of the boy. His reaction was so strange. I mean, I'd met people who didn't like to have their picture taken before, but he looked downright spooked, like I'd stolen a secret piece of him.

But as soon as the expression came on his face, it fell off it again, and he was his suave and confident self once more. Which only supported my long-running theory: Boys could be seriously weird.

"It is a truth universally acknowledged that whatever happens at Regency Camp stays at Regency Camp." And with this, Rahul held out his hand and said in an extra-aristocratic voice, "May I have this dance?"

"I'd be honored, kind sir!" I said, a giggle rising in my throat.

"No, no!" Rahul protested in a fake-gallant way. "The honor is all mine!"

I don't know what got into me. I mean, it's not like I knew anything about ballroom dancing, in this century or any other. I looked at his held-out hands. From all the actresses I'd seen do it in Regency movies, I knew I had to pick up my skirt with my left hand, only that would give me nowhere to put my phone.

"Here, I got you," Rahul offered, tucking my phone into his pocket before I had a chance to protest.

Picking up my skirt with my now-free hand, I put my other hand in his. Then I lowered my voice. "You know, I really don't know how to dance."

So softly I almost didn't hear him, Rahul replied, "From what I saw when I walked in before, I'm going to have to respectfully disagree."

I had no idea where to look, or what to say, but I didn't have to come up with anything because, with a smile, Rahul twirled me easily around the floor. He danced without self-consciousness, holding me with more than comfortable ease. Up close, he was even more handsome than he'd been on first meeting. And he smelled absolutely wonderful: a little bit, I realized, like roses.

Dancing so close together, I should have been embarrassed. I should have been nervous. But I wasn't. It was the easiest thing in the world. It felt like I'd been dancing with him forever.

"'What happens in Regency Camp stays in Regency Camp'?" I asked as he gave me a slow spin and a dip. "A *Pride and Prejudice/ Fight Club* mash-up? Really?"

"I hate to contradict, but I'm afraid you're wrong." Pulling me up from my dip, Rahul led me across the floor once again. "That was actually a *Pride and Prejudice*/Las Vegas tourism mash-up."

"How dare you correct me, young man!" I raised my voice to imperious levels and fanned myself with a pretend fan. Then, placing my hand dramatically on my head, I wailed, "Oh, whither my fainting couch? Where are my smelling salts?"

Rahul's eyes twinkled, and he took a moment to twirl me around. Then, returning to our easy dance steps across the floor, he clarified, "If I were going with a *Pride and Prejudice/Fight Club* mash-up, then I would have said: The first rule of Regency Camp is that you do not talk about Regency Camp. The second rule of Regency Camp is that you do not talk about Regency Camp."

I narrowed my eyes, grinning in spite of myself. I poked him lightly on the shoulder, a shoulder that felt seriously muscle-y under my touch. "Tell me the truth. Will there be unseemly basement fistfights between bonneted ladies? Bruises, blood, teeth knocked out?"

"No Jane Austen Fight Club, I'm afraid! Although I do think you should give Austen's novels a fighting chance," said Rahul, taking a step closer to me. His mouth twitched with good humor. "Despite your prejudiced first impressions, I think you might be surprised at how much they appeal to your, em-ma, sensibility."

"I don't sense so." I took a step closer to Rahul myself. "But then again, I might be persuaded."

Rahul twirled me around again and again, three times in succession. When I came to a stop before him, we weren't dancing anymore but standing close, very close, staring at each other.

"Eila . . ." Rahul began, reaching out a hand to smooth a hair away from my face.

"Will you escort me?" I blurted out before my brain could

tell me not to. My heart was beating a million miles an hour and I swear my bosom was heaving beneath my gown. But unlike in Austen's time, I was a modern woman. I lived in an era when it was no big deal to ask a guy out. Right? "I mean, will you escort me to the presentations to 'the queen' this afternoon? I hear it's a big, fancy deal."

"Oh!" Rahul frowned, dropping his hand from my hair as if my locks were suddenly on fire. "I'm sorry. I'm not sure I can."

"Why not?" I asked, confused. My breath was still a little uneven from the dancing, or maybe just the company, but Rahul's breakneck change in mood was screeching me back to my senses.

"It's just that—well—" Rahul looked angrily at his shining boots, like they'd done him a wrong. "I'm already supposed to escort someone else."

"Oh?" I frowned at this, and how it contradicted the way he'd been acting toward me this whole time. "How did you meet someone already? Didn't we all just get here?"

"Lucy is someone I know from home, a family friend." Rahul cleared his throat, running a careless hand through his hair. "Kind of. Sort of."

I tried not to let my hurt feelings be too obvious as I took a few steps away from him. After all, we'd just met. He owed me nothing, really. But then what had all this been about—the flirty banter, the dancing? I knew I hadn't imagined the attraction between us.

I made my voice as arch and theatrical as I could. "You, sir, are obviously what they call a rake!"

Rahul stared at me for a moment, his face twisting into a

regretful expression. But what was he regretting? Admitting to me he had a girlfriend, or forgetting he even had one?

Finally, he spoke, his light tone mimicking my own banter-y one. "If by rake you mean wealthy ne'er-do-well, you're probably right."

I felt something harden inside me. Of course he was rich and privileged. Which meant that unlike me, he had all the choices of the world probably laid out at his feet. Which was why he could dream of being an actor without worrying about the consequences, or flirt with one girl while dating another.

"Well, I'm glad you warned me." I looked away from him, and out through the French doors. I suddenly wanted to be back in the dressing tent with my sister, anywhere but here. I tried to make my next words artificial and playful, but they came out with a bit too much truth to them. "You know, I could have lost my heart."

Rahul's expression got more serious. "Oh, your heart wouldn't have me."

"Why not?" I gave a forced and somewhat artificial laugh, feeling totally out of my depth. I wanted a script, something clear in black-and-white writing, but this—what Rahul and I were doing—felt way too much like improvisation.

"Soon, the illusion would be shattered." Rahul's face was almost grim. His already low-pitched voice lowered even more until it was a husky growl. "The magician's staff broken and book of magic drowned."

I wasn't sure what to say, but that's when we heard the voices coming down the hall.

"You better go, that sounds like Lady Middleton," Rahul said, glancing over his shoulder.

"Who?" I repeated, even as I scrambled toward the French doors that opened onto the lawns. The voices in the hall were getting louder every minute.

"The blue-haired hawker with the clipboard. Bonnets and breeches. From this morning." Rahul was half pushing me out the door. "She's a real stickler for the rules."

"But you should come with me, won't you get in trouble too?" I asked. The voices sounded like they were right outside the ballroom now.

"Is there anyone in here?" an imperious voice asked from the hall.

"You said it yourself, I'm a rake. I can take care of myself," Rahul said.

The last sight I saw before I picked my skirts up and ran across the lawn was Rahul's wistful face, closing the French doors behind me.

It was only after I returned to the tent that I realized he still had my cell phone.

Regency Fun Fact

For the elite daughters of the Regency, coming out into society started with one's presentation at court. Young Regency ladies would make their curtsies to the queen, and often have large balls thrown by their families in their honor. Being presented at court to the queen was an important affair that announced the young lady was now eligible for marriage. Young women wore elaborate, hooped gowns of white to court that were larger and more cumbersome than actual Regency formal wear, along with heavy jewels and feathered headpieces. After making her low curtsy to the queen and any other royalty present, a young lady was expected to back out of the room (you don't turn your back on royalty!), praying she did not trip, fall, cough, or sneeze!

CHAPTER 7

BEFORE THE COURT presentation that afternoon, we all had to practice our curtsies and bows. The guys had it easy. All they had to do was walk straight-backed up the aisle without falling, while escorting a lady on their crooked arm. Then they had to pause in front of the throne and bow from the neck, short and sweet. We ladies in our elaborate dresses and feathery Big Bird headgear were way worse off. We had to make it up the aisle before the throne without falling over our skirts. Then, once before the queen, we had to tuck one foot behind the other and kind of do a low plié, then manage to stand back up again.

"We're being shown off like they were back in Regency times, when women were nothing more than heifers in a breeding market," I muttered as Lady Middleton took us through a round of practice curtsies after we were all appropriately costumed.

I was feeling edgy and irritated not only from the tight costume and heavy headdress but my whiplash-inducing encounter with Rahul. And of course, the fact that I'd lost my phone. No, *lost* wasn't right. The fact that I'd voluntarily given over my phone to a boy I barely knew, and then been so thrown off by his hot-and-cold attentions, I couldn't even remember to ask for it back!

"Chill, Didi," my sister whispered, even as she performed a lovely, deep curtsy. "It's all just pretend. We can take what we want from those bygone times, and leave what doesn't suit us."

I frowned at Mallika, not irritated with her, of course, but Rahul. Only, he wasn't here, so I unfairly snapped, "But why even play this sort of make-believe? Shoving ourselves into other people's oppressive stories?"

My sister gave me an impatient sigh. "Because—oh, I don't know—beauty! Because fun! Because joy? Not everything has to always make perfect political sense, you know, Didi."

I gave an exasperated snort. "Or is believing that just how we waltz into a gilded cage?"

"We're wearing gowns and feathers, not handmaids' hoods and cloaks, if you hadn't noticed." Mallika swept into another deep curtsy on Lady Middleton's command, giving me a confused look. "Are you all right? You don't have to make everything so difficult all the time, you know."

I didn't answer. I wished Mal would understand, for once, how much more weight I had to carry in the family because I was the big sister, the oldest daughter of an immigrant family. Life had never been just fun and games for me. But I guess she, the beautiful, perfect younger sister, the baby, would never know just how much more baggage I carried so that she wouldn't have to.

At the end of all the curtsy practice, and before the actual event, there was tea and little sandwiches brought around on trolleys, along with some giant napkins so we didn't spill on our perfect gowns. As I sat down to nibble on my crustless prawn sandwich, I rubbed my aching temples. What was it about Regency Camp that unnerved me so much? Was it all the froth and frills, my confusing encounter with Rahul? Or was it being so close to something—acting—I had loved for so long and yet convinced myself I could never have?

Later, as we stood outside Norland Manor in a snaking line of ladies waiting to be presented, I felt strangely calm. Mallika, on the other hand, had a serious case of the jitters.

"I hope I don't trip." Mallika fussed with her long white gloves.

"Whatever happened to beauty, fun, joy?" I asked. "Not to mention make-believe? Who's taking all this too seriously now?"

We were coming from the bonnets tent, to the right, while the guys were coming from the breeches tent, to the left. In the middle of us was a red carpet with gold trim that had been placed up the center of the Norland Manor steps. I squinted at it, wondering if it was giving Regency, or old Hollywood, or a little of both.

Whatever its inspiration, the carpet was in keeping with all the other over-the-top decorations. Even beyond the roses, there was a riot of color everywhere. There were overflowing vases of flowers on both sides of the steps, as well as (obviously not period) fairy lights wound up the manor's tall columns and cleverly threaded through the nearby trees. The staff was not only historically dressed, but spoke with Regency manners, only once in a while breaking character with a modern expression or the flash of a clearly-not-historic tattoo. We could identify them also by the roses they all wore—tucked in their hair or on their lapels, or even embroidered into their livery. All the beautifully dressed, multi-cultural campers only added to the lushness of it all.

"Don't be mean, Didi." Mallika bit her lip as she always did when she was scared. "Since we lost Baba, everything has been so hard and bleak. Sometimes, don't you want to just go through the wormhole, find Wonderland, fly on the back of a tornado to Oz? And here's our actual chance to enter a world like *Rosewood*—where everything is beautiful and colorful and everyone belongs."

Mallika's words made me remember how, back in the ballroom, I'd tried to do exactly what my sister was talking about—dream my way into a different world. But the truth was, no good came of such dreaming. If Rahul's answer to my asking him out hadn't been a sign of that, I didn't know what was. I took a deep breath, folding myself like a piece of origami back into the persona I'd carefully constructed since Baba had died. I was the responsible one, the serious one, the one with my feet on the ground. I knew my responsibilities. One of them being taking care of my sister.

"You won't trip," I assured Mallika firmly, meeting her nervous gaze with what I hoped was steady reassurance, even as I tried to surreptitiously look around for Rahul in the boys' line. I wanted to see who this girl was he had all but forgotten about when dancing with me. Plus, I wanted my phone back. "You got this."

"I would hate to ruin this beautiful beadwork," said Mallika, admiring her skirt's delicate overlay.

"You won't." Then I took in my sister's appearance, from the one delicate feather that curled from her majestic hairdo down to her cheek to the way the dress she wore seemed like an ethereal fairy gown on her. "You will blow Regina Rivera-Colón, and everyone else, away. You're the real queen here."

"Whenever life gets you down, remember whose daughter you are and straighten your crown," muttered Mallika.

"Did you get that from a Target housewares department? Like next to one of those *Live, Laugh, Love* signs?" I asked with a smirk.

My sister snorted in a very un-Regency fashion. "Shut up, Didi," she laughed. "You're the worst. You haven't got one romantic bone in your body."

I tried not to look hurt. Was Mallika right? Was I so unworthy of romance and love that Rahul had sensed it and run away? Maybe I'd spent so long pushing away all joy and frivolity that I didn't even know anymore how to be young and free.

"Next!" called out a wigged and liveried footman, ushering the next lady-and-gentleman pair into the main hall of Norland Manor.

As opposed to the excited chitter-chatter of the costuming tent, all the girls seemed nervous as we waited to go in, like lambs awaiting the slaughter. I caught a lot of them giving Mallika appraising looks, like they were sizing up the competition and not liking their own odds. I remembered the tall girl who had given Mallika the stink eye back in the tent, but didn't see her nearby.

"If I throw up on Regina Rivera-Colón, do you think that will blacklist me as an extra in Hollywood?" asked a tiny, round redhead with a face full of freckles who was in line in front of us. Her name was Penny O'Toole, she told us, and the green look around her gills suggested she might not be exaggerating about the whole vomiting thing.

"Have a ginger candy," said Annie helpfully. She'd gotten dressed herself in a white outfit, had pearl-studded ribbons threaded through her dark hair, and had ditched her glasses for contacts.

"Is that some kind of mean joke?" wailed Penny.

When Annie looked blank, I filled in, "She thinks you're making fun of her red hair."

"I'm not making fun of you. I just don't want you to throw up on me!" Annie laughed, holding out a candy. "Ginger is very good for the digestion. Lots of cultures use it as a natural remedy!"

The poor girl barely had time to take the candy and stick it in her mouth before it was her turn to go inside. Penny's escort from the boys' line had his hat perched on his curly hair at a jaunty angle and somehow made his entire outfit look fashion-forward, even though he was wearing the same dark coat and light breeches as everyone else in his line.

"Come on, Ginger, we're up," he said cheerfully, holding out his elbow to a candy-sucking Penny.

The tiny redhead scowled at Annie, as if to say "See?" before she was whisked off up the stairs and into the main hallway by the laughing boy with the jaunty hat.

"You look great," said Mallika to Annie, looking uncharacteristically bashful. The flush was rising up her light brown cheeks.

"You too! That gown's amazing on you!" burbled the little costumer before she was whisked off.

Moments after Annie was escorted away, it was Mallika's turn.

"I'm Brandon, milady," said a dark-skinned boy in a red military uniform as he held his elbow out for Mallika to hold.

"Charmed, I'm sure," said my sister in a terrible British accent before turning to me to whisper, "Here goes nothing!"

"Next!" called the footman.

I was about to take the arm of a tall blond boy with light brown skin when, out of nowhere, Rahul appeared.

A Regency Vocabulary Lesson

❧ **FIEND SEIZE IT** = *damn it*

❧ **SWELL OF THE FIRST STARE** = *fashionable man*

❧ **WELL-INLAID** = *rich*

❧ **HIGH IN THE INSTEP** = *proud or haughty*

❧ **BLUESTOCKING** = *intellectual woman*

❧ **BEFOGGED** = *confused*

❧ **FUSTIAN NONSENSE** = *rubbish*

❧ **HIGH DUDGEON** = *bad mood*

❧ **SWALLOW HER SPLEEN** = *hide or control her anger*

USED IN CONTEXT: Fiend seize it, the swell of the
first stare was well-inlaid, but clearly high in the instep.
The lady might be a bluestocking, but he had her temporarily befogged with his fustian nonsense. Now, although
she was in high dudgeon, she had to swallow her spleen.

CHAPTER 8

SORRY, MATE, I promised I would escort this lady in," Rahul said, stepping in front of the other boy.

"Hey, no cutting, dude!" the tall blond protested, and for a moment I was afraid the two would get into it. Rahul looked as dashing as ever, shooting me a secret look from beneath his lashes, like this had been our plan all along.

Then I heard a feminine voice from a bit back in the line. "I never!"

I whirled around to see the tall girl, who looked more like a Hong Kong supermodel than a high schooler. She had a British-adjacent accent that matched Rahul's, and the evil look she had once given my sister back in the dressing tent was now transferred to me. I realized she must be the girl from his childhood Rahul had told me about. His girlfriend. Or date. Or whatever.

"What are you doing here?" I turned on Rahul, not even trying to hide my irritation.

"You asked me to escort you." Rahul raised an infuriating eyebrow.

"And you said you had promised another girl." I pointed in the direction of the statuesque model.

"In cases such as these, a good memory is unpardonable," Rahul answered with a grin, adding, "That's an Austen quote, in case you were wondering."

I wanted to kick him. I wanted to tell him exactly where he could stick his rakish charm and unsolicited literary quotes. I wanted to refuse to be escorted in by him. But then the footman repeated, "Next!" and it was our time to go up and in.

"That girl looks like she's plotting painful ways to kill you!" I muttered, looking over my shoulder. Then I looked at Rahul's placid, confident expression. "You know, I should probably let her."

"This is a camp sponsored by a romance-slash-detective show," Rahul agreed with a grin. "So it would be in keeping with the overall theme."

I didn't want to, but I had to hold on to Rahul's arm as I tried to gracefully climb the stairs without tripping over my skirts.

"I would hire a taster for my soup posthaste if I were you." I didn't look at him, so concentrated was I on not tripping. "Sleep with one eye open, that kind of thing."

Rahul let out a snort. "Lucy always looks like she wants to kill everyone. It's just her resting murderer face."

I tried to imitate his coolly uninterested tone. "How do you know I was talking about her killing you, not me killing you?"

Rahul looked surprised for a second, before his expression relaxed back into his usual overconfidence. "You clearly don't know the depths of Lucy's murderous capabilities or you wouldn't say that."

I wanted to argue with him, about how it was the misogynist patriarchy that pitted women against one another in the pursuit of men, and how he shouldn't belittle her to me, and more, but we were at the top of the stairs now in the earshot of a bunch of crooked-wigged camp footmen. So I dropped the Lucy issue and muttered out of the side of my mouth, "Did you even bring my phone?"

"Phone? Don't you know that modern contraptions like cell phones are forbidden at Regency Camp?" Rahul asked, and for a minute, I felt a freak-out coming on. Then, as smooth as you please, he slipped my phone down into one of my gloves.

"I thought maybe you took it on purpose!" I said accusingly, even as I wiggled the phone into a less obvious position.

"Oh, I did! I did!" Rahul said dryly, his face in a fixed, serious expression. "My entire agenda of coming here to Regency Camp was as an undercover phone thief."

"Well, you clearly have a lot to learn about thievery, since you just returned it." I narrowed my eyes. "Maybe you should consider a different profession?"

"And maybe you should consider dating me," Rahul answered smoothly.

It was all I could do not to yelp, or trip on my dress. "What?"

"It doesn't have to be real, we could just pretend," Rahul amended with a smile. "But seriously, you'd be doing me a huge favor. It would help me get rid of Lucy without having to explain to my not-particularly-understanding dad why I blew off his best client's daughter."

"Dude, you are completely delusional!" I whirled on him, not caring about the footmen or maids, not caring who else could hear me. What was wrong with this guy? "Are you seriously asking me to fake date you so you can blow off your murder-y vibed girlfriend?"

"Well, it was just a thought," Rahul said, calm and cool in the face of my fury. The only sign of his possible discomfort was a little fiddling thing he did with his cravat, like it was suddenly too tight and choking him.

"Clearly, not a great thought," I pointed out.

"From your violent reaction, I can see that you think that." Rahul stopped fiddling with his collar and cleared his throat. "Anyway, Lucy's not my girlfriend, just someone my father wants me to date. Although I think you're selling yourself short. You really could give Lucy a run for her money in the murder-y vibes department."

I stared, out of words. This guy was making sweaty-hands Brickson look like a serious Romeo.

"All right, all right," Rahul said appeasingly. "No fake dating. I've got the message, loud and clear. No need to shoot poison daggers at me with your eyeballs."

We had just made it to the top of the red carpet and into the cool, marble-floored foyer beyond. I could see a throne-like seat at the end of the room, and the sea of nervous teenage courtiers in between. Ornate marble columns dotted the long space and there was a balcony from the second floor all around. There were gilt mirrors on the high ceilings overhead, and on the walls, giant paintings of old white dudes on horses and reclining white ladies in fancy gowns being fanned by children of color.

"What am I even doing here?" I muttered, not sure if I was more annoyed at the gross paintings or at Rahul. "I mean, I had relatives who died fighting for freedom from the British Raj."

Rahul looked around, then at me. "Remember, it's all just pretend," he said. "Think of it as a subversive act. How Queen Victoria would squirm to see two brown ex-subjects like you and me here doing this."

"For a phone-thieving rake, at least you have a sophisticated understanding of imperialism," I muttered.

"I didn't take your phone on purpose, but the truth is, I did consider deleting that picture of me you took." Because the staff was giving us dirty looks now, Rahul waved his arms as he talked like he was admiring the many paintings of dead white guys on the walls.

I pointed inanely at a painting of an out-of-place-looking zebra. "Why would you do that?"

Before Rahul had a chance to answer my question, we were being prepped by some footmen and maids. Someone straightened the feathers in my hair; someone else brushed an invisible crumb from Rahul's lapel.

"Smile!" said a maid in my ear. I was so occupied fighting with Rahul that, like an obedient robot girl, I did as the woman asked.

"Well?" I hissed through my plastered-on smile.

"I'm very vain," said Rahul in an over-the-top voice I almost laughed. "Very, very vain. In fact, I would have deleted the picture, if you'd just been a darling and told me your little password."

"Well, then, good thing I'm not a darling—yours or anyone else's." I was trying hard not to laugh at his antics. The guy really did make it hard to stay mad at him.

In front of us were Mallika and her escort, making their way up the aisle toward the raised dais at the end of the room. As red-coated Brandon and Mallika approached the throne, they stopped, bowing and curtsying as we'd all been instructed.

The elaborately gowned and wigged woman at the throne stood up, with help from her two fawning attendants. I knew what Regina Rivera-Colón looked like, of course, from all her television interviews and magazine profiles. She was a tall, sharp-featured woman with long braids that must be tucked under her elaborate gray-white wig now. The gown she wore was bejeweled with multicolored three-dimensional roses that duplicated the sculptural roses tucked into the top of her hairdo. Her eyes twinkled and she looked inordinately pleased with herself, as if she was having an absolute blast playing dress-up.

"All must stand when the queen stands!" intoned a footman. And all the white-dressed girls and dark-suited boys sitting on either side of us, the ones who had already been presented to Queen Regina, obediently stood up.

Regina Rivera-Colón let out a deep, bell-like laugh. "I do love being sovereign!" she declared.

I watched her with interest. Regina was not only one of the most powerful women in Hollywood, but a trailblazer who had made the way that much easier for other female directors of color coming up behind her. Mallika had made sure to tell me all about the filmmaking scholarships she gave out, as well as the mentorship institute she'd created for women of color hoping to break into the film industry. Despite all my criticism of her show—at least the sexy bits—I couldn't help but like her. She looked smart and charming and brimming with good humor.

As I was thinking all this, Regina Rivera-Colón made her way down to Mallika, lifting her chin up delicately with her fingers. "What is your name, child?" she asked in regal tones.

Keeping in character as well, my sister smiled, murmuring, "Mallika Das, Your Majesty."

"Well, Mallika Das, you are a lovely creature," said Queen Regina to my sister, her face a bouquet of generous smiles. "And I most heartily welcome you to Regency Camp!"

The entire room seemed to become electric, big-eyed fellow attendees looking with a mixture of envy and excitement at Mallika. As usual, my sister didn't notice, but just gave another graceful curtsy to the queen and allowed herself to be led to a waiting chair.

Then it was my turn. "Well, here goes nothing for real," I muttered.

Rahul squeezed my hand. "Remember what Prospero said, and that the magic is all just make-believe."

I gave him a hard look. "Yes, I suppose it is."

At this, he at least had the grace to look guilty.

Regina Rivera-Colón was still standing below the throne as we approached her. Which gave me an up-close view of her expression as she saw us. It was—was it?—one of shock and confusion. I stopped, trying to make sense of it all when Rahul spoke up from my elbow.

"You must be remarking on the similarity between these two ladies, Majesty," he said smoothly. "No wonder, as this is Mallika's older sister, Eila."

I saw Regina Rivera-Colón's gaze snap from Rahul to me and then Mallika, now seated to the left of the throne. "Of course," she said with a smooth smile. "Welcome, young lady!"

But was it just my imagination, or did the queen have to cover up her surprise at something else? Something that had nothing to do with my sister or me?

I was still pondering this as Rahul escorted me to our chairs. After a few more presentations, Queen Regina stood up again from her throne, expansively gesturing to us all.

"Not all of us, growing up, were allowed to dream of beautiful things," said the famous director, her eyes shining. "Not all of us, growing up, were allowed to think of ourselves as heroes and heroines, not the sidekick, but the protagonist of the story. And that is why the Rosewood Foundation has decided to sponsor this magical Regency Camp, with plans to open more in the years to come throughout this country and England. Because all of us deserve to be a part of the fantasy. All of us deserve to celebrate the magic that has always been there, inside ourselves."

She went on like this, speaking of representation and inclusion, the importance of role models and the necessity of multicultural casts in mainstream media.

As she talked, Rahul leaned toward me. "Pretty inspiring,

huh? Does she change your mind, make you willing to give this place a shot?"

I met his inquisitive eyes with my own skeptical ones. "Perhaps," I said, unable to stop myself from both liking and disliking him. "Perhaps."

Dear Aficionados of *Rosewood*:

You already know that season two extras casting is happening in an unusual way, through a Regency Camp sponsored by the Rosewood Foundation.

But the secret that the producers don't want you to know is that one of the newly cast principal actors will be there among you so that producers can judge his chemistry with any potential leading lady.

Who will the incognito actor be? Will you be able to spot him? More importantly, will you be able to secure his affections?

Best of luck to all you aspiring lords and ladies! (Well, particularly you, ladies!)

Your faithful insider and whisperer of truths,
The Heir of Allenham

CHAPTER 9

THE PRESENTATIONS TO the queen were old news. Instead, all anyone could talk about during the next morning's croquet game was the illegally viewed Insta post from someone called the Heir of Allenham. Within an hour of the post going up, all the camp knew that the poster was new to the platform, was following almost no one, but somehow, magically, had amassed several thousand followers with just his first post. His misleading photo—a still of almost all the *Rosewood* season one cast—didn't give clues to his identity, except to establish him as a *Rosewood* insider. Was he telling the truth? Was he stirring up trouble? Who knew. But we all knew that the identity of the secret principal actor was the main topic of conversation through every segment of the camp.

Clearly, I wasn't the only person who had stashed an illegal cell phone down her gown.

"Who is this Heir of Allenham?" Mallika whispered to me as we were instructed by Lady Middleton on how to hold our mallet and hit the colored balls over the grass through the wire hoops.

Mal was wearing the green sprigged dress that Annie had tried on her the day before, and the color made her light brown eyes glow. "Everybody's gossiping about him! I mean, Regina Rivera-Colón, the veritable queen of Hollywood, paid me a huge compliment yesterday, but no one seems to remember! Everyone's just talking about the Heir of Allenham!"

"Be grateful they have something else to distract them!" I adjusted a curl on my sister's forehead, remembering the vicious looks the others had given her when Regina Rivera-Colón had singled her out. "Otherwise, these fame-hungry vultures would have been tearing you apart by now!"

We were on the grassy knoll near the gazebo and lake, where a morning croquet game had been set up for eight people. The other campers were at other similar games set up around the grounds. I wasn't sure if I was disappointed not to see Rahul among those at our site.

Mallika and I were awkwardly holding our mallets as we tried to understand the rules of the game. Around the edges of the playing area were some jewel-toned sofas in teals, pinks, purples, and blues that had been brought outside, as well as a random assortment of outdoor tables, shaded by trees from the sun. On each table was a tiered tray of tea sandwiches and pastries, scones and cream, along with a tea set, and there were rose-liveried footmen circulating among the tables, refilling our food and drink. But as we hit our balls across the grass, stopping to drink tea or nibble a cucumber sandwich, the gossip spread like wildfire.

"Surely that Insta post was written by the principal actor himself," said a posh-accented someone near my shoulder. I turned to find myself face-to-face with Lucy Suwannarat—Rahul's girl/friend! Acting as if she didn't recognize me, she continued in her Hong Kong–British twang, "I'm absolutely positive he's leaking information to get everyone in a tizzy about him!"

"But can we trust this anonymous poster?" said Penny, the red-haired girl we'd met the day before, adding earnestly, "You can't believe everything you hear online, you know."

"Oh, there's an actor here, don't you doubt it." Lucy imperiously handed the smaller girl her mallet, then flicked a tiny piece of cucumber sandwich from her diaphanous blue skirt. "I am in possession of inside information confirming that fact."

"How do you all know about this? My sister and I handed in our cell phones!" Mallika wrinkled her brow. "Oh, *why* did we hand in our cell phones?"

Freckle-faced Penny nodded in agreement. "We all handed them in. So how did so many people find out about this Allenham person?"

"Oh, you sad, naive children!" Lucy reached out a gloved hand to pat Penny on the cheek in a patronizing way. The shorter girl made a face, but didn't do anything else to stop her. "Did you all actually believe that any of us aspiring actors would give away our one connection to the outside world?"

"My sister always makes us play by the rules!" said Mallika, the color rising in her face. "But, Eila, do you see why it sometimes pays to play dirty?"

Lucy raised her eyebrows at me, and I felt myself squirm inside. I really had to talk to the girl privately about Rahul and explain that I'd never intended to come between them.

"Well, Mal, it's not like you didn't find out about this Insta post soon enough." I felt my cell phone, which was tucked down the bosom of my blue-and-white-striped gown, burning against my skin.

"Still!" argued my sister, her eyes flashing. "To know that one of the principal actors of *Rosewood* is here among us, acting like an ordinary human! Isn't it dreamy?"

"Dreamy," deadpanned Lucy, eyeing Mallika a bit like I imagined a predator might eye tasty prey. The girl raked my sister up and down with her eyes, her lip curled the whole while in a sneer. I felt my defensive instincts humming into the on position, but then wondered if Lucy's attitude was actually stemming from her hurt feelings about me and Rahul. Which then, of course, made me remind myself there *was* no me and Rahul.

"But to meet the actor! To see if you might be the one to have chemistry with him!" Mallika gushed, and I could see Penny's eyes light up at my sister's enthusiasm. "But even so, why would the person himself leak that kind of information?" Mallika continued, picking up on Lucy's earlier suggestion. She pursed her lips as she distractedly hit her croquet ball with an earsplitting thwack, sending it far off in the wrong direction. "I mean, the producers will be able to judge who has the best chemistry with him if we're all acting naturally, not running around trying to impress this actor!"

"Ladies keep their voices even and gentle at all times, even in the midst of competitive play," said one of the footmen who was circulating by our croquet game. He was wearing not only the rose-embroidered livery but a terrible white powdered wig that stood in sharp contrast to his dark skin. He'd obviously heard Mallika's excited, rising tones, and come over to admonish her non-period behavior.

"My apologies, that was me," I said, smiling coolly at this ridiculous piece of sexism. "I was upset at missing the hoop. I'm so sorry, it won't happen again. I will keep my feminine voice meek and docile at all times."

The footman looked confused even as he bowed. Then he wandered off to assist Penny, who appeared to be digging a hole into the earth with the force of her misdirected mallet swings.

Lucy gave me a curious look, as if she couldn't fathom why one sister would cover for another.

I took a tentative step closer to the girl, not knowing where to begin. "Lucy," I said in a low voice, "I wanted a chance to talk to you about . . . yesterday."

I studied the girl's face, but couldn't see any traces of hurt or anger in it. What I could see was that her cheekbones were perfectly contoured with some obviously non-Regency makeup.

"You're feeling bad that Rahul decided to escort you into the court presentations yesterday rather than me. Well, don't." The girl gave me a little conspiratorial wink. "He and I have a bit of a *tempestuous* relationship, you might say."

The warmth in her tone as she said the word *relationship* made me feel a little queasy, but I studiously kept my expression neutral. Just because I didn't particularly like the girl didn't mean I shouldn't be honest with her. Dividing and conquering women was a trick of the patriarchy, and I wasn't here for it.

"He and I only just met yesterday," I explained. "When I asked him to escort me, it was kind of spontaneous."

"Don't worry, darling. I've seen girls come and go in Rahul's life." Lucy reached out and squeezed my arm. "We're old family friends, as I'm sure he told you. In fact, our family corporations are about to go into a huge venture together, and I'm sure our families expect *we'll* eventually go into a huge venture together, if you know what I mean."

"Sure, okay," I backpedaled, both verbally and physically. Clearly, Lucy didn't need reassurance from the likes of me. I mean, had she just told me she was planning on marrying Rahul? "I just wanted to be clear with you that there was nothing going on between us."

Lucy gave me a look so cutting I could feel its sharpness on my skin. "Oh, I know there's nothing going on between you and Rahul."

Annie, who had just walked over to join us, must have overheard this last comment from Lucy, as well as her tone. The costume intern raised a curious eyebrow in my direction, saying nothing verbally but a whole lot with her expression.

Lucy turned away, as if dismissing me, then raised her voice so that everyone could hear. "The truth of the matter is, in the blink of an eye, the Heir of Allenham has made sure the game's changed."

"What do you mean?" Annie asked as she hit her bright pink ball. It bumped Lucy's green striped ball, making it roll a distance away. I seriously wondered if she'd done it on purpose as I watched her nonchalantly smile first at me, then at her mallet like it was in on the scheme.

"Oh, just that any of us gentlemen could be the principal actor in question!" It was the serious-looking boy named Brandon who had escorted Mallika to the presentation ceremony. He was once again wearing a bright red British army uniform with shiny gold buttons. "So you ladies better be nice to us!"

Lucy, who was already looking irritated at her ball being bumped out of place by Annie's, looked poor Brandon up and down, her gaze full of scorn. The pimple-faced boy squirmed under her study.

"I don't think so," Lucy concluded finally, adjusting the wide yellow ribbon that wound under her bustline like it was her sword belt. "But nice imperialist lackey costume, Brandon. I mean, isn't your family from Antigua, a former British colony?"

Brandon looked so uncomfortable, it made me immediately feel protective of him.

"It's not like any of us are off the hook in that regard," I snapped. "I mean, my sister and I are Desi. And here we are acting like lords and ladies in make-believe Regency dress when most of our ancestors were oppressed by those very same lords and ladies."

"Even our imaginations are colonized beyond repair," sing-songed the jaunty boy who had escorted Penny yesterday. His name was John Santos, but he'd introduced himself earlier as "Sir John" in such an over-the-top and funny way, I'd immediately liked him. His words now made me like him even more. "Our very fantasies are the stuff of our own subjugation."

Mallika and Annie gave Sir John a little round of applause with their gloved hands even as Penny looked confused and Lucy irritated.

"True enough," I agreed. "And yet, here we all are. At Regency Camp."

John looped his arm through mine. "We are the stuff that contradictions are made of."

"I hope you don't mind me asking, but, um, which costumer picked that outfit for you?" asked Mallika of John. He was wearing a purple velvet coat, yellow breeches, and a green hat placed at a rakish angle on his head.

"This old thing?" John self-consciously straightened his jacket, grinning. "I picked it out myself!"

"I can tell," said Annie dryly as she hit her ball, sending it flying almost straight into Sir John's ankle. The boy sidestepped the missile just in time.

"I think it's wonderful. Very self-conscious and self-deprecating at the same time." Mallika touched John's sleeve. "Fashion shouldn't take itself too seriously, I think."

"I utterly agree, beautiful lady!" John gave Mallika a deep bow.

"Fashion is the most serious thing there is!" protested Annie, her face strangely flushed. "It's not frivolous or simply functional, it's art, reflecting not just our own personal choices but the values and priorities of any era!"

The rest of us kind of smiled uncomfortably at Annie's fashion rant—she was, after all, the niece of the head costumer—but I could see that Mallika was taking her words seriously.

"But I don't think what you said contradicts me at all!" my sister protested, shading her eyes from the sun. "Can't fashion be all those things but also about personal self-expression and whimsy?"

There was a moment of odd tension between the two, which Penny stepped into breathlessly. "But I thought we were talking about the Heir of Allenham? Lucy, can't your father find out who it is?"

I looked curiously at Lucy. "Your father?"

The girl didn't even have the grace to look uncomfortable. She nodded. "He's a multi-award-winning Hollywood producer. Not involved directly with *Rosewood*, but very high up in the same studios."

"I thought your family owned a company?" I asked.

"My mother owns a company," Lucy said, a breeze ruffling her dark hair about her shoulders. "But my father works in the biz, as they say."

"It's why, unlike the rest of us, Lucy has her own room here," muttered Annie with a snort. "Her daddy couldn't bear to have her slumming it with us proletariat."

Lucy turned to Penny. "Alas, my father has more important things to do than follow up on Insta posts."

"Well, I imagine whoever the real Heir of Allenham is, he doesn't want to go public," Brandon said. "Wouldn't do to have all you ladies throwing yourself at him left, right, and center."

"Oh, don't you worry, I think I know who the Heir of Allenham is," said John with a wicked smile.

Dearest Aficionados of *Rosewood*:

It has come to our attention that someone calling himself the "Heir of Allenham" is posting outrageous falsehoods about our Regency Camp.

Although we will be scouting for non-principal actors, there is no subterfuge at play.

We categorically deny that there is any principal actor hidden among the campers!

Please disregard any such rumormongers and bad actors (ha ha) who seek to undermine the success of our camp!

Best of luck to all you aspiring lords and ladies!

Yours, as ever,

The producers of *Rosewood* season two

CHAPTER 10

Who's the Heir of Allenham? Who! Tell us, Sir John!" Mallika's eyes were sparkling with curiosity, her face bright in the sunshine.

I saw Annie sneaking an appreciative look in my sister's direction. Turning her head, Mallika caught Annie's look and smiled warmly back. I felt something soft and indulgent bloom in my chest as I wondered if the two girls even realized how obvious their attraction to each other was.

Our little group waited while John took his croquet shot—which went ridiculously wide, then rolled down the little grassy incline, landing with a splash in the lake.

"Oh well!" the boy sighed, clearly unbothered. He lowered his voice to a conspiratorial whisper. "This incognito *Rosewood* actor is my roommate, Will. I'm sure of it. He hasn't just smuggled one cell phone into camp, but two. And he's been getting texts and calls nonstop. And he wears a rose in his lapel, just like the people who work for the camp."

"Does that mean anything, though?" Brandon asked,

fidgeting with the collar of his thick British regimental uniform. The poor kid must be hot under there. "Anyone can wear
a rose."

"But by any other name smell as sweet," I murmured.

Lucy rolled her eyes. "Pretentious much?"

"Funny that you think so," I snapped. "Since Rahul seems to
enjoy Shakespeare as much as I do. More, I dare say."

Someone in the group went "ooh" and I felt my cheeks warm,
annoyed that Lucy had made me stoop to petty mean-girl behavior. I cleared my throat, turning away from her purposefully and
toward John. "Tell us more about this roommate of yours."

Lucy was looking at me in a murderous way, but I tried my
best to ignore her.

"Well, riddle me this: Where did a regular high school boy
like him get the money for all that Prada he wears?" said John,
waggling his eyebrows like he was Sherlock Holmes, or maybe
Lord Rosewood, solving a mystery.

"From Lucy's daddy?" muttered Annie, making me laugh.

"More likely he's an about-to-become-famous star who's here
undercover?" said John with a smirk. "Not to mention he's absolutely the most gorgeous thing I've ever seen." Then he lowered
his voice. "Plus, he's white."

Our entire group, all people of color except Penny, gave
knowing nods. "What?" Penny asked, her voice shrill and face
reddening. "Why does that matter?"

We all exchanged glances, wondering who was going to try to
explain this to the girl. In the end, it was Mallika.

"Well, *Rosewood* is a very multicultural show, but the couples are always mixed," explained my sister. "At least until now, you never see two people of color who are involved with each other."

"Which is a critique a lot of BIPOC folks have about mainstream shows," I added.

Mallika nodded. "That it's usually always one white partner and one partner of color."

"Appealing to the viewership," muttered John. "Wouldn't want to show any of us happy with our own people."

"As if white viewers can't relate to something if they don't see someone who looks like them," added Annie. "As if the rest of us haven't been consuming media our whole lives, being forced to relate to people who look nothing like us."

"Anyway, just percentagewise of who's here, and the fact that the producers made such a big show of saying they were casting for multicultural extras . . ." I let my sentence trail off.

Penny looked like she was going to cry. "So my chances are terrible, huh? At getting picked and cast?"

The rest of us exchanged looks of frustration. "Do you want to take this? Explain the history of who's been included and excluded in media representation?" Annie said to John. "You *are* the one who brought it up."

John looked like he didn't want to touch Penny's comment with a ten-foot sedan chair pole. Luckily, he was saved from having to do so by the appearance of the roommate in question himself.

"Look, speaking of the Regency star, there he is!" said Sir John, pointing.

And there, as my entire croquet party watched, over the crest of the small hill on the opposite side of the lake, like Aphrodite rising from the foam, arose the most handsome boy I'd ever seen. His locks? Windswept. His shoulders? Broad. His breeches? Tight. No—very, very tight.

"Hubba-hubba!" muttered Penny, making us all laugh. Her blush crept up under her fair skin like a rash. She might be clueless, but the girl was sweet.

"Aren't you going to drop your handkerchief and make him pick it up?" Lucy asked, a hint of aggression in her voice. I could tell she was being mean to Penny, but the poor redhead seemed not to notice, drinking in Lucy's comments with wide eyes. "Or better yet, you should faint and have him catch you!"

"It's kind of far; he is all the way across a body of water," pointed out Brandon doubtfully. He too seemed to be missing the fact that Lucy wasn't being serious.

"Then you should scream!" Lucy wiggled her fingers at Penny like she was casting a spell.

"I should?" Penny took a deep breath, as if preparing to do just that.

"Don't!" exclaimed Annie, throwing out a hand to stop Penny, like a mom braking too hard at an intersection. Then, by way of explanation, the costume intern went on quickly, "It's not like we're not all here for the next umpteen days. There are teas, and horseback-riding lessons, and archery parties, and picnics, not to mention comportment, dancing, and elocution lessons. And then of course the showcase and final ball. You'll have plenty of opportunity to meet John's roommate—if he's the actor in question or not."

"But Lucy's not wrong. The first one to charm Will does have a serious advantage," John said thoughtfully. "It does make sense to try to get a jump on meeting the guy."

Unfortunately, that was when Mallika, my impulsive, don't-think-the-consequences-through sister hit her croquet ball with such ferocity it flew off the grass in a wide arc and into the lake with a loud plunk.

"Oh no! My ball! I must get my ball!" she shrieked in staccato, almost-deafening tones. "My ball! My ball!"

"Is she saying the word *ball* an unnecessary amount of times, or is that just me?" quipped John.

Before I could anticipate what she was doing, or try to stop her, Mallika took a leaping run down the little hill, and then, whether on purpose or by accident I couldn't tell, caught her foot in a hole and fell the rest of the way down.

"Mal!" I yelled, trying to get to her.

But I was too late. Obviously intending to get the attention of Sir John's roommate, Will, my sister did just that. In the process, she also got the attention of the entire camp. Because not only did she tumble down the hill, shrieking all the while, but she did so until she fell with a loud splash right into the murky lake.

A gentleman ... was passing up the hill ... when her accident happened. He ... ran to her assistance. She had raised herself from the ground, but her foot had been twisted in her fall, and she was scarcely able to stand. The gentleman offered his services; and perceiving that her modesty declined what her situation rendered necessary, took her up in his arms without farther delay, and carried her down the hill.

—JANE AUSTEN,
Sense and Sensibility

CHAPTER 11

ALLIKA!" I YELLED, running down the hill after my
fallen sister. Now, if you've never run down a hill in
tiny Regency boots and straight skirts, I don't recommend it. Because the next thing I knew, I'd tripped and would
have fallen right down the hill after my sister, like a Jill to her Jack,
had Brandon and Annie not stopped me.

"Careful!" Brandon caught my hand in his surprisingly strong
one. He might look like a pimply beanpole in a red uniform, but
clearly there were muscles in there somewhere.

"Watch it, or you'll fall in just like your sister!" Annie looked
upset, and I wondered if she was mad that Mallika had ruined her
costume, or that my sister was literally throwing herself at some
random guy she hadn't even met yet.

"Well, clearly, *some* people don't mind making a show, creating an exhibition of themselves," sniffed Lucy, pulling at the
ribbons of her dress like they'd done her a wrong.

"Attention, attention!" said a voice through some kind of hidden speaker system. We all looked around, confused. "We have a lady-fallen-into-the-lake incident at the north lakeside croquet station!" The voice then changed in tone, going on, "All other croquet players, please wrap up play and make your way indoors for table lessons, which will commence in thirty minutes. Confused about your salad fork? Always wondered which direction to drag your spoon while eating soup? Discover all these secrets and more at table lessons!"

This announcement was made with such casualness, it made me wonder if gowned and gloved ladies falling into bodies of water was going to be an everyday occurrence at Regency Camp.

As we all watched, Mallika flailed about in the lake. At first, I panicked, thinking that her clothes were somehow caught on something, because my sister was a strong swimmer. I mean, her butterfly stroke could use some work, but this was not a girl who should be flailing about in any sort of body of water. That's when I realized she was doing it on purpose.

"Assistance! Please, someone lend me their kind assistance!" she wailed while making the most enormous splashing with her flopping arms. It sounded like she was trying to approximate a British accent and failing in the process. "Oh dear, oh dear! Woe is me! I've fallen all kerploppy into the lake-y!"

Our entire group looked over at me as if Mallika was speaking an unfamiliar foreign language and I was the tour-appointed translator.

"'Kerploppy'?" Brandon's bushy eyebrows were raised high like a pair of perplexed caterpillars.

"'Into the lake-y'?" asked Annie, her voice thick. "Really?"

I wasn't imagining the look of upset on the little costumer's face, and felt a squeeze of sympathy. Honestly, Mallika could be such a ninny sometimes.

"Is your sister simply treading water with her feet as she waits for someone to rescue her?" Lucy sounded furious that she hadn't thought of the idea first. "Or standing on a rock or something?"

"No, of course not," I lied baldly. "She's just . . . flustered."

"She doesn't look very flustered." Sir John adjusted his jaunty hat to an even jauntier angle.

I shaded my eyes, looking out at my sister in the middle of the lake. Mallika was projecting entirely in Will's direction and had managed to get her hair smoothed off her face even as she "drowned." And were my eyes deceiving me, or did she actually have a tube of lip gloss in her hands she was trying to apply while in the water?

"She's so pretty." Penny's blue eyes were wide like saucers. "Like a real-life damsel in distress from a story!"

"I think that's the general idea." Lucy's top lip curled in disdain.

"Never fear, dear lady, never fear! For Will is nigh, Will is near!" shouted the boy in question, removing an alarming number of articles of clothing as he ran from his side of the lake. As he shed each piece, like a tree shedding leaves, there arose collective sighs and gasps from onlookers of all genders on all sides of the water. His jacket—gasp! His cravat—shriek! His vest—whoa! He had just flung aside his white shirt and dived into the lake when there rose the loudest collective exclamation from everyone watching the scene.

"Did you see those abs?" breathed Penny, bright pink and

fanning herself with the back of her hand. "What was that, like an eight-pack? A ten-pack? A twenty-two-pack? How is that even humanly possible?"

"Are you feeling faint?" Annie asked, reaching into her purse for more ginger candies.

When the little redhead shook her head no defensively, John jumped in, drawling, "Well, if you did faint, none of us would blame you. I'm not ashamed to admit that I'm feeling a little light-headed too."

Wordlessly, Annie handed the ginger candy she had been about to give Penny to John, who popped the thing in his mouth.

"Go Wi-ill, go Wi-ill!" John began chanting through the candy. "Save the gi-irl! From the wa-ter!"

"Absurdist patriarchal rescue narratives, yo," I muttered under my breath, unable to contain my embarrassment.

"Not to mention heteronormative," added John, lightly hitting his riding boots with his own mallet. "But still, I do enjoy a spectacle!"

Will, in the meantime, had swum confidently through the water and reached my sister. He did that thing where he kept his head above water, tossing it dramatically side to side with each stroke. Then, instead of dragging her from the lake, lifeguard style, Will just picked her up in his arms and stood up, making it obvious how shallow the area was. As they made their way toward the shore, water streaming from their clothes and hair, the two seriously looked like something out of a movie.

There arose wild clapping and cheering from all those who had witnessed the dramatic scene.

"Are you all right, miss? I mean, respirationally?" I heard Will ask, far too loudly. "Do you need me to do the Heimlich?"

Annie gave a snort. "I think he means mouth-to-mouth resuscitation."

"Thanks to you, I am well, dear sir!" Mallika sang out. She was rapidly blinking her long-lashed eyes and I wondered if it was for dramatic effect or if she'd lost a contact lens in the water. "Had you not come, what fate would have befallen little old me?"

"To whither safe haven shall I betake you?" asked Will, again way too loud. He added, kind of bizarrely, "Whither, sirrah? By George, and blimey and all that?"

I cringed in embarrassment. It was like the two of them were performing lines from a Regency-era script written by a precocious middle schooler.

"Thither!" Mallika pointed in my direction. There was a lot of sighing and fluttering of handkerchiefs as Will sloshed out of the lake, Mallika firmly ensconced in his arms, and then headed toward us on the opposite bank without putting her down.

"Dude is seriously strong," said John appreciatively.

Annie gave a snort. "So was Gaston from *Beauty and the Beast*."

"I have to say, I'm impressed," muttered Brandon.

"By that ghastly acting?" Lucy was twirling her croquet mallet in her hands like she was considering hitting my sister with it.

"Jealousy is an unflattering look on you, Lucy," I snapped, unable to stop myself.

Okay, yes, I was a little embarrassed by Mallika's over-the-top behavior, but I'd never admit that to the likes of Lucy Suwannarat.

In fact, I was beginning to understand why Rahul had suggested he and I fake date so he could get rid of Lucy. If I were him, I'd chew off a limb to get away from the nasty girl.

"That was weirdly reminiscent of the Colin-Firth-coming-out-of-the-lake scene." Annie took off her glasses and polished them on her dress as she spoke. "But if Colin Firth had hella more muscles."

"Oh, yes! Colin Firth!" Penny's guttural sigh, so low and full of sexual innuendo, made us all laugh.

"Will and Mallika do make a beautiful couple," observed John dryly. "They would look great together on-screen."

Annie made a harrumphing sound and gave him a withering glance, but said nothing.

"What is the meaning of this?" shrieked a loud voice from behind us. It was the blue-haired and pink-gowned Lady Middleton, who seemed to have acquired a few more roses to tuck into her hairdo since I'd last seen her.

"A rescue of a damsel in distress!" Will had arrived by now on our side of the shore and gently deposited a sopping Mallika at my feet. "By myself, verily!"

"Thank you so much for saving me, kind sir!" simpered Mal, making me not sure if I wanted to laugh or shake her.

"It was my honor, my lady!" announced Will, adding, "An honor that is all mine, my lady . . . of honor!"

That made me out-and-out guffaw.

"No one's slick like Gaston," Annie sang under her breath. "No one's neck is incredibly thick as Gaston!"

Lady Middleton, who had seemed on the verge of yelling

some more, now looked around at all the cheering and delighted onlookers and reconsidered her initial position. She waved at her wigged and liveried assistants.

"Get Mr. Allen some appropriate clothing, someone, will you, please?" she said in an artificially saccharine tone.

"Your name is Will Allen?" I asked my sister's rescuer.

"Indeed, fair lady mine. That is the name my parents have given me anon, name-wise," said the shirtless boy, giving a little bow. He seemed completely unbothered by the fact that he was naked from the waist up and dripping wet. He put out his hand to shake mine. As I put mine out, however, he didn't shake it, but bent over it in a formal bow, looking like he was about to kiss my hand without actually doing so. "Will Allen, at your service, milady."

"Allen?" repeated Annie, her clever eyes sharp. "As in, Allenham?"

"Yes, verily, that is so!" Will agreed, his hands placed on his hips like a superhero. As he was still shirtless, it was hard to know where to look. I mean, the guy really was built like a statue.

Annie's lips twitched as she muttered, "He simpers, and smirks, and makes love to us all."

"But he is very pretty," I murmured, remembering Lord Rosewood's similarly remarkable abs. Will would honestly make a good *Rosewood* hero. I was beginning to think that John might just be right about him being the incognito actor.

One of the footmen draped a way-too-small towel around Will's shoulders and another waited nearby with a shirt. A white-capped and aproned maid had appeared at Mallika's side with a similar set of towels for her.

"Come, my lady, I will help you up!" said the rosy-faced maid. As my sister rose to her feet with the assistance of the woman, Will turned back, his face a caricature of alarm.

"No! She shall not walk!" he intoned with all the solemnity of Gandalf telling the underground fire monster Balrog he shall not pass. "Do you not see that Miss Mallika has hurt her ankle, orthopediatrically!"

"I have?" asked my sister with surprise, before sinking gracefully once again to the ground. "Kind sir, you are right, I have injured my ankle!"

"I will thusly carry you inside, verily!" declared Will, drawing the approval of the admiring crowd now gathered all around the lawn.

By this point, Will was wearing the new shirt that the footman had supplied but neglected to button it up all the way. His still-wet hair was curling around his ears and shoulders, and his wet breeches were clinging to his legs dramatically. He really did look for all the world like the dashing hero.

But the next thing he did clinched it for me that he wasn't just a generic heartthrob but very possibly the actor from *Rosewood* hiding here among us undercover. Because Will plucked a red rose—not from a bush exactly, but rather from the lapel of a passing, and rather disgruntled, footman—and tucked it into Mallika's hair.

"A rose for my rose," he murmured, before lifting my sister into his arms like she weighed no more than a feather.

"My hero!" sighed Mallika, intertwining her arms prettily about his strong neck.

Without another word or a look back, Will strode off toward Norland Manor, Mallika in his arms and the maid scurrying to keep up with them.

The sigh elicited from the crowd by this action was practically ear-damaging. Even the maids and footmen looked moved, and I noticed Lady Middleton fish a large handkerchief out of her sleeve to dab at her eyes.

"Did I or did I not tell you it was him?" John singsonged, and the rest of us nodded in agreement.

True Politeness:
A Handbook of Etiquette for Ladies (1847)

Table napkins are indispensable at the dinner table; and silver forks are now met with in almost every respectable house.

It is usual to commence with soup, which never refuse; if you do not eat it, you can toy with it until it is followed by fish; of either of which never take more than once.

Always feed yourself with the fork; a knife is only used as a divider. Use a dessert spoon in eating tarts, puddings, curries, &c., &c.

If what you are eating before the dessert has any liquid, sop the bread and then raise it to the mouth. For articles of the dessert having liquid, a spoon is usually provided.

Fish must be helped with a fish slice: you may carve it more dexterously by taking a spoon in your left hand.

Soup must be eaten from the side, not the point of the spoon; and, in eating it, be careful not to make a noise, by strongly inhaling the breath: this habit is excessively vulgar; you cannot eat too quietly.

CHAPTER 12

I N THE WAKE of Will and Mallika's dramatic departure, the rest of us walked back toward the manor from the croquet area. I'd been walking quickly, hoping to catch up with my sister, and so lost my new group of friends.

I was halfway across the wide lawn when I heard a familiar voice to my right say, "That was quite the dramatic rescue."

I turned around to find Rahul's amused face. I wasn't entirely sure if I was happy to see him or not. So I made my words sharp even as I looped my arm through his. "Your girlfriend, Lucy, certainly didn't seem to enjoy it."

"I can imagine she didn't." Rahul smiled, looking pleased that my arm was in his. "Also, as I think I've said before, she's really not my girlfriend. Just a girl whose family my business-minded father wants to do a deal with."

"So you say, so you say," I murmured, enjoying the feeling of the sun on my face as we walked across the green expanse overlooking the sparkling Hudson. "And yet, she seemed to suggest you and she were heading toward a merger of a different sort."

"She didn't!" Rahul groaned. "Come on, Eila, save me from my family's machinations. Won't you please reconsider my offer to fake date me? I promise I'll be the best fake boyfriend you've ever had!"

"Only because I've never had a fake boyfriend," I noted, as if making a point in a debate round.

"Precisely!" Rahul grinned, counting off on his fingers. "There will be fake flowers, fake love letters, and I'll even see if I can throw in a fake Jane Austen Fight Club. Emma taking down Lizzy with a fake right hook, that kind of thing."

"Oh, you do make my fake heart go pitter-pat when you talk such sweet nothings," I burbled, batting my eyelashes at him as if my life depended on it.

"Is that a yes?" Rahul asked. "Or should I throw myself into the lake now and be done with it?"

"That is a tempting offer, I must admit. The throwing-yourself-into-the-lake part, I mean." I dropped his arm, making my way into the building alone. "But I think I'll have to pass!"

I waved my hand airily without turning around, leaving Rahul laughing behind me even as I felt my own face widen in an uncontrollable grin.

My sister wasn't in our room. In fact, she didn't reappear until I made my way downstairs toward the grand dining hall of Norland. Will had her on his arm, and even though they both looked a bit squishy around the edges, they shone with radiant good looks and charm as they strolled toward the hall. Will was whispering something into my sister's ear as they walked, and she kept tossing back her head in merry laughter. In turn, he beamed at her, like she was the only girl in the world.

I should have been irritated with them, and with my sister in particular, for having made such a ridiculous scene earlier. And then disappearing when I was looking for her. But at that point, I was still buzzing from my brief flirtation with Rahul, and everything seemed rosy and good.

"Never fear, Wallika is here!" Will announced to the crowd of our fellow campers as Mallika tossed back her head and laughed again.

I caught Rahul's eye across the room and smiled, shaking my head as he grinned and moved away to find his group.

"Wallika?" repeated Penny, her face a round moon of innocence.

"I think that's their couple name?" Brandon was fiddling with the buttons on his military jacket. "Will plus Mallika?"

Still surrounded by her admiring fans, Mallika gave another sparkling laugh.

"You know, in Regency times, only loose women laughed out loud in public. And only trollops showed their teeth," said Lucy, suddenly at my ear. I felt my good mood sour, like she was a cloud that had decided to open up and pour rain down on my picnic.

I spun on Lucy, ready to let her have it, but luckily, I didn't have to. Because my band of new friends was there to do it for me.

"Shut up, Lucy, you're just jealous she got to the Heir of Allenham before you did," said Penny, her flushed face betraying how much her brave words cost her. But the short redhead wasn't backing down either.

"'Trollop'?" snorted Annie, looking Lucy up and down. "Takes one to know one."

"Just because your father donated so much money to the Rosewood Foundation and Regency Camp doesn't mean you get to have everything go your way," said Sir John, arching a shapely eyebrow.

"Yeah, what they said!" agreed Brandon, sounding nervous.

I smiled at all of them in appreciation. It was nice to have my own Jane Austen Fight Club in my corner.

"You had better keep your sister out of my way, Eila." Lucy pushed roughly past me and farther into the dining hall. "Or else she might find her ankle broken for real this time."

"You're a real charmer," I said in a loud enough voice for Rahul to hear across the room.

By the time we picked up our assigned seating cards, we realized Lucy had gotten herself seated in a different group, which was a relief. Still, her words pricked at me, like nettles caught under my skin. I wished Mallika didn't always leap before she looked, whether into lakes or iffy social situations.

"What in the Regency romance ridiculousness were you thinking, Mal?" I complained under my breath as my sister sat down next to me in the grand dining hall. Having deposited her in her seat, Will now joined his own group at the other side of the wide table.

"What are you scolding me for now?" asked Mallika. Her hair was still damp and curling delicately around her face.

"Oh, I don't know, for falling into the lake on purpose? Exposing us to the ridicule of awful people like Lucy?" I twisted the napkin in my lap like it had done me a wrong.

"People like Lucy are going to be awful no matter what we

do," Mallika said, putting her hand on my own to still its agitation. "Don't worry about her, Didi. What she thinks doesn't matter."

Mallika wasn't wrong, of course. But even as Lady Middleton began a complicated lecture about the proper Regency-era use of napkins, spoons, forks, and knives, I realized that I wasn't the only one in our little group who was feeling some kind of way about Mallika and Will.

"So that was quite the sweeping romantic spectacle, huh?" Annie leaned over John to ask Mallika.

Mallika looked uncomfortable at Annie's disapproval. "It's all just a bit of fun, you know?"

"I don't actually know," said Annie, sounding miffed. "But I guess you've gotta do you, girl."

"And I guess Will's gotta do Will," John added, staring at Will across the table with a wistful expression.

"Awkward," muttered Brandon to Penny as Lady Middleton droned on about the direction that we were to move our soup spoons and the importance of not dragging the utensil noisily across the bottom of the bowl.

My stomach was seriously growling by the time we all dug into our first course, something called white soup. The veal-and-cream-based glop had apparently been quite the delicacy back in ye olde times, but to my modern—not to mention Desi—tongue, it was an oily and nasty mess.

"No wonder the Brits colonized India." John plunked down his spoon so loudly he received a horrified look from Lady Middleton. "They needed y'all's spices for real."

"Not like they did anything with them." I drank big gulps

of water, hoping to wash the taste of the soup from my mouth. "Have you *had* modern-day British food?"

"Only chicken tikka masala," said Annie with a laugh.

"That's British?" asked Penny, her blue eyes round. "I would think that's Indian."

At that, we all exchanged amused glances but said nothing.

We had a few more courses of equally odd-tasting food, all beautifully plated. There were jellies and ices and minced things and other not-great-tasting courses. Then it was time for the elaborately decorated pheasant pie.

"It looks a bit like a hat," observed Annie as a footman placed the huge square thing in front of us.

"Not a very nice hat," Mallika offered hesitantly, looking obviously relieved when Annie grinned.

"A truer word has not been spoken," quipped the little costumer. "That is some poor millinery."

"What's it made of?" Brandon squinted at the pie like he was afraid four and twenty blackbirds were going to fly out of it.

"Peasants," John said dramatically, wiping a nonexistent crumb from his lip with the napkin that was tucked, Regency style, into his front shirt buttons.

Poor Brandon looked like he was going to pass out, or vomit on the snow-white tablecloth. "Did you just say *peasants?*"

"He's joking!" Penny reassured him as she threw John a dirty look.

"We're all starving, please don't tease him, John!" I begged. "Maybe this pie will actually be edible."

"No, no, ladies, we mustn't keep the brutality of the European feudal landowner system from innocent Brandon here." John's expression was utterly convincing, like the practiced actor he clearly was. He'd told us that he'd been doing commercials and things since he was a kid, and it definitely showed. "Yes, my friend, I am sorry to say it, but back in the day, if you didn't produce enough wheat for the lord of the manor at harvest time, the only option was being thrown into a pie."

"You're joking!" Brandon practically yelped, pushing the pie away from him.

"Oh, for goodness' sake! Pheasants are a kind of bird!" Annie explained in an exasperated tone. "The ingredients of the pie aren't serfs, or farmers working for landowners, but birds!"

Penny smiled more kindly at the flustered-looking Brandon. "They were always galumphing around their manors, shooting birds, so had to do something with them!"

Like the white soup, the pheasant pie was not as glamorous tasting as it sounded. I barely forced down a few mouthfuls before groaning in a decidedly un-Regency manner. Unfortunately, my stomach groaned even louder. I wished not for the first time that I'd stashed some Cheetos in the little satchel purse on my wrist.

Tikka Masala
FUN FACT

Claimed to be the British national dish, chicken tikka masala was supposedly invented in the 1970s by a Bangladeshi immigrant restaurateur who added a cream-based tomato sauce to a dish of chicken tikka kababs to satisfy the palate of a British customer. (The Brits apparently like gravy with all their meats.) Weirdly, Britain also celebrates "National Curry Week" during the month of October. While none of this seems to have anything to do with Regency England, remember that Desi influence on Britain, and Desi immigration to Britain, was secondary to the British Raj colonizing the South Asian subcontinent for over two hundred years. Even though British crown rule wasn't established until after the Regency, in 1858, the influence of the East India Company began during the Regency era. In fact, Jane Austen's family had ties to the East India Company, and she mentions it in at least one of her novels. And all that from a plate of tikka masala!

🌹 CHAPTER 13 🌹

ENOUGH REGENCY GROSSNESS! I could really do with some chicken tikka masala about now," I sighed. I wondered if there was any way to get a delivery service to bring takeout to an isolated mansion.

Far down the table, Rahul must have heard my comment. He let out a bark of a laugh, which only inspired Lucy to shoot me one of her special murderous looks. I barely controlled a childish impulse to stick my tongue out at her.

"Ooh," said Mallika, ignoring my silent but deadly visual interchange with Lucy and focusing all her attention on Rahul. "Is that the boy you walked in with at the presentation? What's his name?"

"I didn't catch it." I frowned at my sister, which only made her grin broaden. "Okay, fine, it's Rahul."

"You li-ke him, you really li-ke him," Mallika singsonged as she pointed at me.

"Shush! He'll hear you!" I batted at her dancing fingers. I wondered how to explain my confusing feelings about Rahul to my sister. "Look, I don't like him, not like that. I mean, he has some kind of weird history with Lucy that I don't entirely understand. But he's nice, I suppose. I guess I enjoy his company."

"Oh, golly gee, how wonderful! You enjoy his company!" At these words, Mallika gave a big, fake yawn and pretended to fall asleep on the back of her chair. She even gave a couple of snores, eliciting a disapproving look from Lady Middleton.

"Get up, drama queen!" I swatted at my sister.

Mallika opened her eyes with a grin. "Enjoy his company! Didi, could you be more insipid!"

I picked up my fork and poked at the jelly desert thing in front of me. It wiggled in a disturbing way, like one of those slime specters from *Ghostbusters*. "Well, what am I supposed to say?"

"You're supposed to say that the ardor of the soul is never satisfied by concealed affections." Mallika flung the back of her hand dramatically to her forehead. "That to love is to burn, to be on fire!"

I gave a snort of laughter. "Is that how you feel about Will?"

My sister and I simultaneously turned our heads to look at Will, seated across the table. The giant bohunk was eating his mutton as if auditioning for strange caveman play to an audience of one. Never breaking his gaze from Mallika, he took huge He-Man-type bites of meat. Then he licked each of his fingers, slowly and deliberately, in what I supposed would pass for a sensual fashion.

"To love is to burn, to be on fire," I deadpanned.

But my sister seemed unbothered by Will's manners. Instead, she tossed back her head and laughed in an over-the-top dramatic way, like an old-timey actress. Or a GIF of an old-timey actress, at least.

Then, without missing a beat, Mallika turned back to our conversation. "I don't know, maybe I am in love with Will! Or maybe I'm just acting! Does it matter?"

I rubbed my temples. "How can it not matter if you're acting on real feelings or fake ones?"

"Look, Will's gorgeous and sweet and a blast to hang around with." My sister laughed, her eyes sparkling and cheeks blooming bright. But I did notice she kept her voice low, so that only I could hear her words. "So who cares? We're having fun together! I mean, did you think it would be any different if you had gone to your precious Shakespeare camp? That would just be playacting too, right?"

I wanted to grind my teeth. Every word out of Mallika's mouth just made me feel more muddled. Of course acting was a chance to try on different roles and characters, to dive into different story lines and time periods. But then why did the whole dramatic scene my sister and Will had staged feel so different?

"How can you be sure Will is the actor who they're talking about in that Insta post anyway?" I asked.

"Have you looked at him?" Mallika smirked. "Even you must admit he's the most handsome guy here, the guy who most looks like an actor from *Rosewood*."

She wasn't wrong. But I didn't have a chance to say this to her, because right then, without warning, the anachronistic speaker system—which appeared to be hidden within the huge floral display centerpieces stretched along the long table—crackled to life once again.

"Will Miss Mallika Das and Mr. Will Allen please report immediately to Lady Middleton?" asked the voice. "Miss Mallika Das and Mr. Will Allen!"

As if our heads were attached to mechanical devices, everyone's necks swiveled around to look at Mallika, beside me, and Will, across the wide table.

"Oh my goodness, what could this be about?" Mallika rose gracefully from her chair and handed me her used napkin. Only, because she wasn't really looking, she ended up flinging the dirty cloth in my face. I took the thing from her, only a little irritated.

"My lady, anywhere I am with you is an honor!" said Will, making a dramatic hand gesture and knocking over his neighbor's water glass in the process. "Wallika is called and Wallika will answer!"

As others cleaned up the messes they had made, my sister and Will swept from the room, leaving the rest of us to wonder what exactly they were getting summoned to do.

"Well, I might as well go start packing," I said as Penny patted my hand. "Obviously we're going to get kicked out because of that stunt Mallika pulled."

"What, the whole dramatic lake rescue? I doubt it!" Annie laughed not a little bitterly. "That is exactly the sort of thing that the *Rosewood* producers love—it's precisely the kind of over-the-top thing that happens on that show!"

"They're probably getting called into Lady Middleton's office to get contracts on the spot!" John's voice betrayed a hint of jealousy, and I wondered if the birth of celebrity couple "Wallika" had broken more than one heart. "Don't worry, this is a good thing."

"You really think so?" I asked my new friends, and they all nodded. All with the notable exception of Brandon, who was suffering a one-on-one knife-holding lesson from one of Lady Middleton's wigged and breeched lackeys.

Due to Brandon's knife- and fork-holding problems, our group was the last to rise from lunch.

"Nice job, Brandon," grumbled John. "Now I have to go see where I stashed those illegal protein bars in my room."

"I'm sorry, everybody." Brandon squirmed uncomfortably, pulling at the collar of this red coat. "Regency knife and fork rules were complicated."

"Don't worry, we don't blame you," said Penny, cheerfully linking her arm through his.

"Don't listen to her, we actually do blame you," Annie said, but the venom in her words was diluted by her grin, and the playful punch she landed on Brandon's arm.

"Ouch!" He rubbed his arm as we all finally left the banquet hall.

Only when we were already out of the dining room and heading down the front stairs of Norland Manor did we see Mallika again.

"What happened?" I grabbed her arm as I climbed down the stairs, my worry making my voice sharp. "Did you get in trouble?"

"Trouble?" Mallika's laughter made the tension I'd been holding in my shoulders melt away. I hadn't realized how upsetting the thought of being kicked out of camp was. "Hardly."

"So what happened?" Annie demanded. The early afternoon light bounced prettily off her dangling earrings and dark eyes. "Did you get to audition for Regina Rivera-Colón?"

"No, we didn't see Queen Regina, but we did see one of the *Rosewood* casting directors!" Mallika was practically giddy with excitement.

"Where?" breathed John enviously. "Are there casting directors milling around the camp too?"

"I'm not sure about that, but they took us up to the second floor, up that staff-only staircase," explained my sister. "There are offices up there where they took some headshots and even had Will and me do a scene for the camera!"

I tried not to sound judgy as I asked, "And how did that go?"

"Great." Mallika bit her lip a little. "I think, anyway."

"I bet you blew them all away!" enthused Brandon as he took the steps down from the manor two at a time.

"Well, I was a little nervous, and fumbled some lines at first," Mallika admitted. "But that's to be expected, right?"

"They made you memorize lines in that short of an amount of time?" Annie looked horrified.

"No, we were reading them off a script." Mallika nibbled even more nervously at her poor lip.

"And so you fumbled them . . . how?" Penny's sweet face was wrinkled in confusion.

"Well, Will kept trying to improvise lines, which was silly of him, but I guess he was just trying to pretend that he wasn't the actor already cast," Mallika said with a shrug. "But then I had trouble seeing the printed lines . . ."

"Because you didn't put a new pair of contacts back in after you lost the ones you were wearing in the lake?" I guessed, my voice rising. "Oh, Mal, how could you?"

"I didn't think I'd need them!" Mallika's pretty face was a picture of not really regretful regret. "But Will and I definitely had a lot of chemistry."

"Of that I'm sure," I agreed dryly.

"Wallika is called, and Wallika will answer," said John, making us all laugh.

Regency Drama Fun Fact

The history of "racebent" casting in Regency
dramas, with people of color playing roles
originally written for white actors, can perhaps be
linked to similar practices in Shakespearean
productions. In Elizabethan times, where men
played women (as women were not allowed
onstage), stage audiences became accustomed to
actors in Shakespeare's plays who did not match
the original description of the character.

CHAPTER 14

MALLIKA AND I had just gotten to the bottom of the stairs when I realized I had to go back.

"I forgot my purse on the table!" I turned to go back into the manor.

"Just leave it!" Mallika pulled at my sleeve. "I want to tell you about the audition! Anyway, we don't have much down time before dance class; don't you want a break?"

"Someone will find it and get it to you!" Penny said. "Let's go take a walk! Get some fresh air!"

"Let's take a turn about the grounds!" Brandon offered his arm to a blushing Penny. "It's so refreshing!"

"No, I really should go get it." The anxiety at someone finding my purse was making my stomach turn.

"Because there's something in your purse you'd rather folks not see?" Annie guessed, examining my face.

"Nothing like that, I just don't want to lose it." I could feel the heat rising in my cheeks at the lie.

Because of course, Annie was absolutely correct. I'd stashed my cell phone inside that little cloth satchel and couldn't afford to have someone find it. I really had to talk to Annie and her aunt about getting more pockets sewn into some of our day-to-day dresses.

"You guys go ahead! I'll catch up!" I called, darting up the stairs as fast as my long skirts and tiny boots would allow.

I was nervous as I entered the dining hall, but the staff mostly ignored me as they cleaned up the plates, cutlery, and glasses from the unappetizing meal.

"May we help you, miss?" said one older liveried gentleman as he cleared up used silverware on a tray.

"No, I just left this! Silly me!" I chirped, holding up the satchel, which was still lying on my chair, right where I'd left it.

The staff went back to their work, and I was about to turn and walk back out of the room when I heard the familiar, shrill voice. It was Lucy, berating someone or other nearby.

So, naturally, rather than leaving her to her private conversation, I turned back toward the side alcove from where her voice was coming. I tried to justify my nosiness by reminding myself the girl was a menace, and that I didn't trust her as far as I could throw her. Plus, I wondered if the person she was talking to could actually be Rahul. I hadn't seen him leave the dining hall, and wondered if that was because of Lucy.

"My father is not going to be pleased to hear that I have spent almost no time with the new leading man," Lucy snapped. "He is going to hold you directly responsible!"

"Why would he do that?" sputtered the person to whom she was speaking.

It was clearly not Rahul. I leaned in closer, trying to figure out who Lucy was yelling at.

"He's going to hold you directly responsible because I will tell him you are directly responsible!" Lucy declared, her words sharp like a dagger.

"No, please, miss, please don't do that. Also, you must apologize to him—deeply, sincerely—on behalf of the entire Regency Camp team," begged the woman she was speaking to.

It took me a minute to realize who it was, because the person was usually so bossy and imperious. Now she was being meek and obsequious as a peasant in a pie. Just that fact made my Spidey-sense tingle. How could Lucy, a mere camper here, threaten an adult in such a way as to make her sound like she was afraid?

I pressed myself against the far wall of the dining hall, wedging my body behind a giant flower display so that I could hear Lucy and Lady Middleton's conversation without them noticing me. I was far enough away from the dining area as to be out of the view of those clearing the table as well. I had to admit, it made me feel a little bit like Lord Rosewood on the case. Minus the mustache and sideburns, of course.

"Lady Middleton, if that is your real name," Lucy was sneering in an imperious tone that probably would have made a Kardashian cringe, "my father isn't interested in apologies; he is interested in results. We are very close, he and I, and he will be very disappointed if I do not have the opportunity to demonstrate to Regina Rivera-Colón why I'm the perfect new multicultural face for the second season of *Rosewood*."

"Miss Suwannarat, I understand. But there's really nothing

I can do. Please try to appreciate the delicacy of my position," said Lady Middleton. "Rules are rules. In order for me to ask you young ladies and gentlemen of the ton to obey them, I must as well. There's really nothing I can do!"

"Nothing you can do? Are you joking? You've got to get rid of that girl! I can't have a little nobody like that stand in the way of my chances to get cast!" Lucy's words made my heart freeze. She sounded so vindictive, I wondered if she was actually capable of doing my sister some kind of harm in her quest to get close to Will. And it also made me realize something else. If Lucy was this hot and bothered to spend time with Will, she clearly didn't have very strong feelings for Rahul. Hm. I stored that little fact in my brain, not sure right now what to make of it.

"I can try to make sure they are not thrown together, but beyond that . . ." Lady Middleton trailed off. I could imagine the poor beleaguered lady twisting her hands as she spoke. She certainly sounded like she was twisting her hands.

"You will find some excuse to get her kicked out!" snapped Lucy. "I'm sure you will come up with something, and I'm sure you know my father will make it worth your while."

"But my position with the Rosewood Foundation," murmured the older woman. I did notice, however, her tone was sounding less upset and more wheedling now. "I couldn't cross Ms. Rivera-Colón."

"She's not actually a queen, you do realize that, don't you?" Lucy snapped. "Regina Rivera-Colón is a newcomer, today's fashion. My father has been a film executive for decades. He knows everyone in the business. If Regina Rivera-Colón fires you, he'll get you another position. A more powerful and better-paying position."

There was a pause, as if the older woman was considering her words, and the options Lucy had put before her. Finally, she sighed. "I'm sorry, miss, I cannot betray Ms. Rivera-Colón in that way. She is a good and fair employer and I owe her better than that."

Lucy made a frustrated grunt. I could almost imagine her stomping her foot. "You're making a big mistake!"

"Don't do anything rash, please, miss," Lady Middleton said. "I know your father's generous donations to the Rosewood Foundation are part of the reason I am even here, but I must be fair to all the other attendees as well."

"Fine, if you don't do anything about that little upstart, I will!" Lucy's voice was hard as iron. Or maybe diamonds was the more apt comparison, since the girl had obviously grown up with a sense of privilege stuck in her mouth the size of a giant, sparkly spoon.

"I really must go now, miss," said Lady Middleton in a tired voice. "Please try and remember what I said."

"There's no way I'm going to let that nobody get cast in *Rosewood*, no matter what chemistry she has with what lead actor!" snarled Lucy. "If you're not willing to do something about it, I am!"

They sounded like they were going to come my way, so I beat a hasty retreat out of the dining hall, my heart thumping like a hunted pheasant in my chest. Lucy had been trying to strong-arm Lady Middleton to kick Mallika out of camp, and now that the woman had refused, Lucy was obviously going to try and do something herself to prevent my sister's chances at being cast. But what could she do?

That's when it hit me. Of course. The audition tape. Lucy could tamper with or lose Mallika's audition tape. I had to find that thing before Lucy did!

I just know that any time I undertake a case, I'm apt to run into some kind of a trap.

—CAROLYN KEENE,
Nancy Drew 11: The Clue of the Broken Locket

CHAPTER 15

LIFTED MY SKIRTS in a seriously unladylike way and raced down the main corridor of the manor, hoping that Lucy and Lady Middleton wouldn't see me. I took a hard left before the ballroom, my feet silent on the smaller hallway's heavy carpet runner. When I finally reached the side staircase, the one with the red tasseled rope strung across it and a sign that read STAFF ONLY BEYOND THIS POINT, I ducked under. Taking a quick look behind me down the still-empty hall, I tried to slow my breathing and climb the stairs in a way slightly less evocative of a Regency girl running from a serial killer. If I wanted to stop Lucy from tampering with, or destroying, Mallika's audition recording, I had to find the room in the administrative wing where she had done the audition in the first place. And then I had to hope that the camera they'd recorded the audition on, or the computer they'd uploaded it to, was there and accessible. But first, I had to avoid getting caught.

As I walked up the stairs, I concocted a story in my head if I was caught by one of the staff in their private office area. Should

I say I was lost? Not really believable, as the STAFF ONLY sign and rope were pretty obvious. Should I say I wasn't feeling well? But then why hadn't I just rung one of the staff to my room, like I'd been told by Lady Middleton to do? Plus, what would a bunch of Regency throwbacks do anyway if I said I was sick? I didn't exactly fancy having leeches stuck on me to drain bad humors, or some rancid-smelling salts stuck under my nose to treat the vapors.

I didn't have any more time to come up with a better lie, because only a few moments later, I turned a corner and came face-to-face with a wigged footman. I recognized him as the same person who had been helping teach us croquet. What was his name again? Oh yes. Thomas.

The stout man stopped short when he saw me, his bushy eyebrows drawing together in a frown. "What are you doing here, miss? No campers allowed in the administrative areas."

I gulped. In movies, they were always saying that lies with a generous helping of truth were the most believable. And so, that's what I went with. My hands tucked behind my back, I ad-libbed, "Well, actually, my sister, Mallika, left her purse up here in the offices while she and Will were doing the scene for the casting director. And you know how she hurt her ankle when she fell into the lake, so I offered to come get it."

My heart pounded, even as I felt proud of myself for coming up with an improvisation for once. But my worry was unfounded, because Thomas just nodded at my explanation, as if it was completely believable.

"In that case, she would have left it in here, miss," he said, opening a door to his right.

We stepped into a dark and cool manor bedroom that had been converted into an office. The same wackadoodle colored sofas that graced the rest of the manor were dotted around the room. There was an ornate wallpaper on the walls, an old-fashioned scene of gun-toting men on horseback and their hunting dogs. Every corner had potted plants and every table an overflowing display of roses. And then, next to a fireplace at one end of the room, was a decidedly-not-period camera tripod, only with no camera in it.

"What amazing wallpaper! That duck being shot midair is very, uh, realistic! I mean, look at that spurt of blood!" I gushed, and as Thomas turned to look at the gross scene, I tossed the purse in my hand onto the ground, and then pretended to pick it up again.

"Here it is! I've got it!" I said triumphantly, holding up the little satchel.

Thomas nodded noncommittally, then gestured me toward the door we'd just entered. I sauntered back out into the main hallway, my heart running a marathon in my chest. I couldn't believe I'd just pulled that kind of a switcheroo off. Hang Jane Austen and her tea parties, I had a feeling both of my childhood favorites—Harriet the Spy and Nancy Drew—would be very proud of me in this situation. Not to mention the hot Lord Rosewood. I felt well on my way to also becoming a sexy aristocrat and master of disguise.

I walked off toward the staircase, waving at Thomas. But as soon as he turned away, I tiptoed forward again, keeping my back close to the wall and senses peeled. I had to find that camera that was missing from its tripod! Otherwise who knew what mischief that no-goodnik Lucy could do with it.

There was a closed door to my right. I put my hand on the doorknob and gently tried to open it. Unfortunately, it was locked. As was the next. And as I got to the third doorway, I heard voices coming toward me down an intersecting corridor. Crap. All right, maybe this hadn't been the most thought-out plan after all. Wishing I had some leeches to throw at them, or at least a handful of smelling salts, I doubled back into the room I'd just been in with Thomas, letting out a relieved breath. That is, until I felt the person behind me grabbing my arm.

Despite all my planning, despite all my reading of detective and spy stories as a young girl, I was seriously not prepared for someone creeping up on me. Without meaning to, I let out a sharp scream. Only, the person behind me seemed to anticipate this, placing a heavy hand over my mouth and stifling the sound.

But Ma hadn't sent Mallika and me to all those community center self-defense classes for nothing. On instinct, I kicked out hard with my heel, making contact with my attacker's shin and hearing a soft whoosh of exhaled air. Seizing the moment, I spun, jamming my crooked elbow into his solar plexus. It was gratifying to hear him groan.

I whirled around, fists up, wishing I wasn't at Regency Camp at all but at Shakespeare academy, where I could confront my attacker with a sword or dagger. What in the world could Austen heroines fight their foes with, beyond witty repartee? A hatpin to the eye? A crochet needle to the armpit?

But the person I saw when I whirled around made me stop thinking about how to use a hatpin as a weapon. "You!" I breathed.

"Somebody's been training for Jane Austen Fight Club!"

moaned Rahul, alternately rubbing his shin and stomach with a pained expression.

I suppose I should have felt guilty for hurting him, but I didn't. "You scared me half to death! You're lucky I didn't have a weapon on me!"

"You seem to be doing just fine without one." He let out a big breath, looking rueful as he straightened slowly to stand. "That kick was absolutely not Regency appropriate! Not to mention that elbow to the gut! You have very sharp joints!"

"My mother will be glad to know I could cause some damage even in this prissy outfit!" I whispered, shaking off the fright he'd given me with rueful, if soft, laughter. I brushed straight my skirts with still-shaking hands. "Seriously, you should not sneak up on women like that! Do they not teach you that in how-not-to-be-a-creep school?"

"I'm sorry, I wouldn't have done in any other situation!" Rahul said. "But you could get in terrible trouble for being up here! They use this room all the time!"

"How do you know that?" I asked.

He didn't have a chance to answer, because the voices in the hallway were growing louder again, and this time I recognized Lady Middleton's sharp tones. She was berating someone who wasn't speaking.

"And make sure to keep her room pristine—nothing but the best! I don't want to hear any complaints! Her father is a very powerful man!" Lady Middleton was saying. Unfortunately it sounded like she was saying it right outside the door of the room we were in.

"I've got to get out of here!" I ducked down behind a brocade chair embroidered with horned sheep, like that would effectively hide me from the Regency Camp director.

"This way!" Rahul pulled me toward a door I hadn't noticed on the far side of the fireplace. It was hidden by the busy wallpaper and its handle was camouflaged behind a potted plant. Opening the door as quietly as he could, Rahul ushered me out, shutting the door behind him. And it was just in time too, because as he was easing the door closed, we heard voices in the room we'd just been in.

Lady Middleton was still ranting at her companion, probably about Lucy's rooms. "Fresh roses, no limp ones, every day! Freshly laundered towels and linens! No slacking!"

I looked around nervously, hearing even more voices in the hallway behind us. The administrative wing was downright bustling with activity. Maybe this hadn't been the wisest time of day to come spying. I shot Rahul a desperate look.

He grabbed my hand, whispering, "Come on!"

Sometimes you have to lie. But to yourself you must always tell the truth.

—LOUISE FITZHUGH,

Harriet the Spy

CHAPTER 16

WE RAN DOWN the carpeted hall, up a small connector staircase, and across the top floor of the manor. From my extensive watching of *Upstairs Downstairs* and *Downton Abbey* with Mallika, I knew we must be in the servants' quarters. The hallways were low ceilinged and plain, the doorways narrow and squished close together. It was the place that both Rahul and I would have been staying if we'd actually lived in Regency times. Because of course, brown people like us would have been servants, not guests. We jogged along without speaking. We were still in parts of the manor off-limits to campers, and needed to get away before we were spotted by Lady Middleton or her lackeys.

Finally, we were at the end of the servants' hallway and plunging down another mini-staircase, then through a door back onto the second-floor corridors of the manor. But this part was more familiar, a replica of the brocade-wallpapered, high-ceilinged hallway where Mallika and I were staying.

"In here!" Rahul breathed, pulling me through a doorway to the left and locking the heavy wood door behind me.

It took us both a few moments to catch our breath. Even though I wasn't sure how I felt about his methods, I was grateful Rahul had rescued me from Lady Middleton's rule-following grasp. The woman would definitely have kicked me out of camp if she'd found me up in the administrative wing. Then not just my but Mallika's chances of being cast in *Rosewood* would be ruined. And that would be awful. Not just for my sister, but me too. I wasn't sure where, when, or how, but during all the wacky high jinks of the last twenty-four hours, I'd gone from resenting Regency Camp to really having fun here.

"Thank you for your help," I said with as much sincerity as I could manage.

But the suave and carefree rake I had known was gone. Rahul, his hands on his hips, his hair kind of disheveled, looked more like a put-upon dad of a toddler than a romantic hero. "Eila, what in the bloody Regency romance were you doing up there in the administrative wing? Do you want to give Lady Middleton an excuse to kick you out?"

As an older sister, if there was something I really did not take well to, it was being scolded. That was my move on other people, and I did not enjoy have my own tricks turned on me.

"'You're welcome' is the more standard response when someone thanks you," I snapped.

"You're welcome," said Rahul sarcastically, splaying out his hands in an overexaggerated bow.

"There, was that so hard?" I twittered, dropping into a fake-sweet curtsy.

Ignoring his disapproving expression, I turned around, taking in the beautiful, sunny bedroom with its wide four-poster bed. Unlike the loud, hunting-themed wallpaper in the room we'd just been in, the walls showcased a soothing woodland scene whose delicate greens and blues were matched by the natural-colored drapes and bedclothes. There was a settee and chair to the right of the bed, and a dressing area behind a screen. There even seemed to be a connected bathroom.

Through the slightly ajar door of the standing wardrobe, I could see some shirts and jackets, most of them falling off their hangers, and a randomly piled stack of boots below. The bedside bookshelf was similarly disorganized, crammed to overflowing with books of beautiful leather binding. There was a stack of similar books upon the nightstand, next to a pitcher of half-drunk water and a half-full glass.

"This is your bedroom?" I guessed. "You're not exactly one for neatness, huh?"

Flushing a little, Rahul rushed over to shut the wardrobe, jamming a jacket in by force when it threatened to fall out. "I haven't had a ton of time to straighten up."

"We've only been here since yesterday," I remarked as I watched him go over to his bookshelf, attempting to stack the books there in some sort of order. "Also, isn't that a lot of books for a two-week stay?"

"I never know what I'll want to read," Rahul said defensively. "I like to be prepared."

It was hard not to smile at that. I wondered to myself what woman of intellect wouldn't be attracted to a man with such a big bookshelf?

After the same book slid over about three times, Rahul gave up on the bookshelf, standing with a sigh. "I've not brought you here for any nefarious purposes, you know. It just seemed the closest and easiest place to hide from Lady Middleton. But you still haven't answered my question. What were you doing in the administrative wing in the first place?"

His mention of "nefarious purposes" made something unexpectedly twist in my belly. Would I mind if he had lured me here for purposes that were "nefarious"? Defensively, I blurted out, "I was in the administrative wing trying to stop your girlfriend from ruining my sister's chances at getting cast."

"How many times do I have to tell you this?" Rahul made a frustrated sound. "Lucy's not my girlfriend. Our families know each other. My dad was putting a lot of pressure on me about her, but we actually haven't seen each other in a couple years. And now that I've met her again, well, I can see what she's become." Rahul looked down at his hands, then up at me again with a calculating expression. "And if someone would just agree to fake date me, maybe I could finally get her off my back."

"Well, I actually don't think that's necessary anymore. If you really don't want to date her, you might be off the hook, based on what I just overheard," I said, rubbing my aching neck. Sneakery really did make your muscles tense up.

"Here, have a seat." Rahul indicated the comfy chairs in front of what I now realized was a working fireplace. He certainly had a nicer room than my sister and I did. Rather than sitting near me, Rahul backed up, leaning against a small window that had light streaming through it. "So what did you overhear Lucy saying?"

"Oh, just that she had it out for my sister, and if Lady Middleton didn't kick Mallika out of camp, Lucy was going to do whatever she could to make sure Mal wouldn't get cast in *Rosewood*." The words tumbled out of my mouth airily, but they made me sick to say.

"Whoa. Has Mallika had time to make enemies already? Your sister doesn't seem the type." Rahul didn't add "unlike you," but I could hear it right there, under the surface of his words.

"It's totally messed up. It's because of Will—the Heir of Allenham, I mean," I began.

"The guy who made the giant scene, rescuing your sister from the lake?" Rahul asked dryly.

"Yes, him. I mean, since everyone's guessed he's the principal actor—the one who's already been cast in *Rosewood* season two—"

Rahul cut me off. "There's an actor here who's already been cast in *Rosewood* season two?"

"Come on, it was all over Insta! Someone calling himself the Heir of Allenham spilled the beans, said that there was an actor planted here among the campers, and that the *Rosewood* people wanted to see which lady he had the most chemistry with!" I said, recklessly showing him the evidence on my phone. "Where have you been, living in a social-media-free hole?"

"Apparently," Rahul said with a stiff smile. "I suppose you're not the only one, then, with an illegally stashed cell phone."

"Obviously." I brushed away an errant strand of hair from my face with an impatient gesture. "Anyway, I guess Lucy's transferred her affections from you to Will now that his identity has come out, because she sounded pretty adamant about getting Mallika out of the way so that she could spend more one-on-one time with Will."

Rahul grimaced as if the very thought of Lucy was painful to him. "She was really threatening Lady Middleton? About getting closer to Will?"

"Yes, really." I sighed. "Your girlfriend, or ex-girlfriend, or whatever, is a real peach. Lucy doesn't want Mal to get in the way in terms of vibing with Will. She was pretty clear on that fact."

"Vibing with him," Rahul repeated without looking at me. He had reached over and was flipping through one of the books on his bedside table.

"Establishing chemistry, whatever," I clarified. "How are you not aware of the commonplace use of 'vibing' as a verb?"

"I am woefully out of touch with not just social media but popular youth culture, I'm afraid." Rahul looked up from his page, his expression deadpan. "Having been brought up in a hothouse where I am forced to do very little but dance the minuet, debate obscure cricket rules, and, of course, bow to pictures of the queen."

I paused for a second, trying not to laugh. "British people are so weird."

"You have absolutely no idea," Rahul agreed, breaking into a grin. "I mean, just suet pie as a case in point."

"*Anyway*," I went on, rolling my eyes at him. "Lucy said she was going to ruin Mallika's chances of getting cast, so I figured she must be tampering with the audition recording that Mal and Will just did for some casting director."

"And so you went to the administrative wing to stop her?" Rahul asked. "Even though the audition was probably done digitally and is already uploaded via computer to wherever it needs to go?"

"I thought of that, but I still had to go up there, to be sure," I said. "What if it was done the old-fashioned way—on a tape or something—and Lucy's up there unspooling it as we speak?"

"I'm pretty sure Mallika's audition wasn't recorded on some old-time VHS tape or reel-to-reel." Rahul closed his book with a snap as if to emphasize his point. "And it's not like Lucy can launch herself into cyberspace with the force of her vindictiveness and stop it from uploading."

"Okay, yeah, I probably didn't think it entirely through, but I was just trying to protect my sister." Suddenly, I felt very tired. Or maybe it was that veal soup not agreeing with me. "Things have been really hard for her since our father passed away a few years ago. Being an extra on *Rosewood* is, like, her dream. I just don't want any nasty competitive rich girl to ruin it for her."

"Fair enough." Then Rahul tilted his head curiously. "What about you?"

"What about me?" I tossed my phone lightly from hand to hand, not wanting to look at him.

"Why are you here? It's not just to accompany your sister." Rahul's piercing eyes were studying me in a way that made me want to squirm. "I know you love acting. I've seen how much you love it."

I shook my head. "I don't know what I love anymore."

There was an awkward silence and then Rahul cleared his throat. "Well, either way, I think what's most important now is that you two walk the straight and narrow, not give Lady Middleton any excuses to kick you out. You might, for instance, turn in that phone of yours, like a good, law-abiding Regency lady."

He pointed to the phone I'd been playing with in my hands. On impulse, I unlocked it and took a quick picture of him, looking all otherworldly and backlit by the sun streaming through the window. This time, though, he saw me coming, and put up his hand to block his face.

"You're not vain, you're just shy," I said as I lowered the phone.

"You've found me out." Rahul's voice was a little husky. He narrowed his eyes, studying my face again. "But as much as you don't want to give Lucy an excuse to kick you and your sister out of camp, you're not going to turn in your phone, are you?"

"Are you disappointed in me?" I stood up and walked over to him, standing an arm's distance away.

Rahul stared at me as the sun hit my face, warming me up. "I don't think I could be if I tried."

There was another moment's silence, which I tried to fill with chatter. "So besides the phone, what else can I do? Do you have any ideas about how I can stop Lucy from trying to sabotage my sister?"

Rahul fidgeted with his collar for a few seconds. Finally, he said, "Lucy specifically said she wanted to get Mallika kicked out of camp?"

"She didn't mention my sister by name, but she wanted to get rid of the girl who was in her way of getting to know the incognito actor, who is obviously Will," I explained.

Rahul was quiet, looking down at the book in his hands. Behind him, the sunlight made what looked like a halo around his head.

"You know, I said before that I didn't know what I loved, but that's not true," I said suddenly.

"Oh?" I realized how my words must sound when Rahul raised a dark eyebrow even as he reached out to pull me closer to him. His fingers were warm against my wrist.

"I had been desperately looking forward to coming to the summer Shakespeare academy that used to be held here at Norland Manor," I explained hastily as he continued to hold my wrist. "That is, until Regency Camp kicked them out."

"This Regency Camp didn't kick out the Norland Shakespeare Theater." Rahul traced little aching circles on my palm.

My lips parted in surprise. I noticed Rahul's eyes flit to them as I asked, "It didn't?"

"No, the Shakespeare theater found a different, less expensive place to rent, down the Hudson River at a place called Barton Hall. Because of the move, their summer academy isn't in session, but they're certainly still having their outdoor theater performances."

"Oh!" I was trying to pretend that Rahul's fingers weren't on my wrist, that his touch wasn't sending little shivers up my arm. "I was really looking forward to attending the Summer Shakespeare Academy, and when it was canceled, I guess I assumed the worst, that the theater itself was canceled too."

"I understand why you were excited to go. It's a fantastic summer program—I went last year." A smile played at Rahul's lips.

"You did?" I grabbed his lapels and shook him a little. "I'm so jealous. Was it wonderful? Was it magical?"

Rahul closed his hands over mine. "The strong-based promontory have I made shake, and by the spurs plucked up the pine and cedar; graves at my command have waked their sleepers, oped, and let them forth, by my so potent art."

I smiled, thinking of the first time we had met, when we had first spoken Shakespeare to each other. "But this rough magic I here abjure," I said, continuing the magician Prospero's famous line.

Before I could go on, Rahul closed the distance between us, leaning his forehead against mine. "I have required some heavenly music, which even now I do."

"So I guess you enjoyed the Shakespeare camp, huh?" I laughed.

"Not as much as I'm enjoying this one," he breathed, a little shakily. "This is all the magic. All the time."

I realized I was feeling a little shaky myself. Plus, my temperature regulator was all off. I felt hot, then cold, then hot again. "Mallika had to convince me to come to Regency Camp when the Shakespeare academy fell through. But I'm glad I'm here."

"I am too," Rahul murmured, his eyes searching mine.

I felt the heat rising under my skin, making me feel near volcanic. "I mean, for my sister. I'm glad I'm here for my sister."

A little smile played on his full lips as he nodded. "Of course, that goes without saying. For your sister. Sure. Right. There couldn't be any other reason."

Feeling overwhelmed at the sight of those lips, so soft and so close, I turned my gaze to the view over his shoulder. Awkwardly, I blurted out, "You have a view of the lake! My father used to take Mallika and me boating there sometimes."

"I know." Rahul's hand reached up to tuck a strand of my curly hair back in place.

I couldn't help but shiver when his fingers gently touched my cheek. "You do? How?"

A funny look crossed Rahul's face. He cleared his throat, then seemed to forcibly readjust his expression. "A lucky hunch." He grinned. "The women in your family can't seem to resist that body of water."

I lightly punched his arm. "Stop. It's too humiliating. My sister is the most ridiculous."

"She's endearing and full of life and joy," said Rahul matter-of-factly. We were standing so close I could see the flecks of gold in his dark eyes. "Not unlike a certain character in a certain Austen book whose older sister also frets about her behavior."

Rahul handed me the novel he'd been looking at before, which I reluctantly took from him. "Tell me the truth, did you lure me into your bedroom for this exact nefarious purpose?"

"To make you actually read Jane Austen's novels, rather than judging her on her adaptations?" Rahul asked with a crooked smile. "Yup. You've caught me out. You did promise to give her a fighting chance."

I turned the book over in my hands, quoting Rahul back to himself. Or rather, I guess, quoting Rahul quoting Austen. "In cases such as these, a good memory is unpardonable."

That made him laugh, a sound that warmed me right up from the inside out. "Where'd you hear that?"

"Oh, just from an irritating rake of a boy I met the other day," I said.

"He sounds like bad news," Rahul observed, playing with the material of my sleeve.

"He seemed like he was at first, but now I'm not sure." I felt like I couldn't look at him directly, like he was a solar eclipse or something.

"Better stay away, though, just to be safe," Rahul said seriously.

"Not sure I can," I said in a low voice, immediately horrified by my words. To cover up my embarrassment, I studied the book in my hand, running my finger along the gilded pages. "Wow, it's really amazing! The binding is just gorgeous!"

"There are five more Austen novels bound just as beautifully when you finish this one." Rahul put his warm hand over the one of mine that was holding his book, so that we had it connecting us.

I looked up at him, understanding his meaning from his expression. "No way. I'm just borrowing this to read. I can't accept it as a gift."

"Why not?" One of Rahul's hands was still over mine holding the book, his other possessively around my wrist. "How about this: Read it, and if I'm wrong and you don't like it, you can return it. But if I'm right and you love it, then you accept it as it was meant, freely, as a gift?"

I looked up at him, my mouth dry. Unable to say anything, I nodded.

Our eyes met and Rahul leaned forward. I was sure he was

going to kiss me, and was also sure the experience would be nothing like kissing the slobbering Brickson. The sun was still streaming from behind his head, and it bathed my face directly in its warmth. I licked my lips, the anticipation of the moment making me a little dizzy.

"May I?" whispered Rahul, his hand reaching toward my cheek.

I was about to nod. I was about to just go ahead and kiss him first. I was about to do quite a few other things, but then we were interrupted in the rudest way possible. The screeching sound system came on, reverberating throughout the manor house and beyond. Rahul and I jerked back from each other as if stung by leeches—or electric eels, maybe.

Totally ruining the mood, the announcement system blared: "Will Mr. Rahul Lee please report to Lady Middleton's office for a personal phone call. Will Mr. Rahul Lee please report to Lady Middleton's office for a family call. Everyone, please report to the ballroom for dance class! Get your cotillion on the dance floor! Please report to dance class!"

True Politeness:
A Handbook of Etiquette for Ladies (1847)

If a gentleman presumes to ask you to dance without an introduction, you will of course refuse. It is hardly necessary to supply the fair reader with words to repel such a rudeness; a man must have more than ordinary impertinence if he was not satisfied by your saying, "I must decline, sir, not having the honor of your acquaintance;" and recollect that his previous rudeness ought to be punished by your refusing to be introduced.

Draw on your gloves in the dressing-room, and do not take them off during the evening, except at supper-time, when it should be invariably done.

Let your dancing be quiet and unobtrusive; let your movements in the dance be characterized by elegance and gracefulness, rather than by activity and complexity of steps.

Pay attention to the dance, but not so marked as to appear as if that attention was necessary to prevent a mistake. A lively manner harmonizes with the scene; but, to preserve this, it is not necessary to be boisterous. Refinement of manners has, in woman, an unspeakable charm.

Do not mistake affectation for refinement: it would be no less an error than confounding vice with virtue.

CHAPTER 17

REGENCY DANCE CLASS was held in the ballroom in which I'd first met Rahul. The grandeur of the room, the gilded mirrors on the walls, the open French doors letting in the afternoon breeze were all familiar, but with so many more people in the space, including a Regency-costumed orchestra, everything felt different. Still, being there so soon after our time together in his room, and our near kiss, made me feel almost giddy with anticipation. Rahul had gone off to the office for his phone call, but I couldn't wait until he'd be back.

Dance class was a surprise. Regency dancing was a lot less gliding gracefully around a ballroom in your partner's arms than I anticipated. It was a lot more prancing, skipping in lines, standing in squares, switching up of partners, and, to be honest, sweating than I had ever imagined. Annie had been asked by her aunt to help in the costume department, so our little group consisted of John and me, Brandon and Penny, and of course, the inseparable Will and Mallika. Despite how much of a show the two of them made, twirling dramatically into the center of the ballroom instead of staying in our little social square, I couldn't stay mad at my sister. Rahul was right. She was full of joy and life and making her own happiness.

Just like I was trying to do now too, after far too long. With Rahul.

"*One and two*, and one and *two*," shouted the dancing master, a white-wigged man with a heavy French accent named, improbably, Monsieur Florimond. He was affected, as if playing the part of a movie dancing master, but at the same time very exacting, not letting any of us get away with subpar footwork or hand gestures. Monsieur even had a little black beauty patch glued onto his face and a thin, swirling mustache.

"Non, non non, mademoiselle!" the dance master shouted at a girl who had a lot more boogie and a lot less glide in her steps than was historically appropriate. "Dances like this were social events to show your best aspects to others. To mark your family dignity. To meet potential partners. Not to shake your body like a fecund hippopotamus who has mistakenly found herself on the dance floor!"

I tried not to laugh. But being French, Monsieur's pronunciation of the word *hippopotamus* was so wonderful, I couldn't resist a chuckle.

"I love him," said John as we danced together, coming close before moving apart. "He's so over the top."

"Like everything else in this place!" I agreed.

Even as John and I danced, I couldn't help fixating on the entrance doors to the ballroom, waiting until I could see Rahul again. Sir John caught the direction of my gaze, grinning.

"There's a somebody I'm longing to see," crooned my dance partner in my ear as we approached each other again. "I hope that he turns out to be . . ."

We separated before John could finish singing the lyrics, but I finished them for him in my head: "Someone to watch over me."

As we came back together, joining hands in a large square, John grinned at me. "You're smitten with this dude Rahul, huh?"

"I don't know, maybe," I said with a laugh.

From the other side of the square, Mallika interrupted us. "Oh, she's smitten for sure! Don't you let her tell you otherwise!"

As the rest of the group smiled and teased, I caught John giving Will a longing look.

"I'm sorry," I said softly when we were dancing in such a way that only he could hear. "About Wallika, I mean."

John shrugged in a self-deprecating way. "It's okay. Your sister's a sweetheart. And Will likes who he likes. Besides, I've survived worse heartache."

We danced on, whirling and exchanging partners and making large and small circles as Monsieur Florimond instructed and yelled and exclaimed in exasperation. Mallika and I were clapping to the rhythm, as instructed by Monsieur, moving our slippered feet to the music. It was hard work, but after my encounter with Rahul in his room, I had so much electric energy wound up inside me, I welcomed the chance to use it. I remembered how he'd touched my hair, my wrist, how we'd almost kissed, and gave a little shiver.

Finally, after what seemed like an eternity, the ballroom doors opened, and Rahul arrived. I felt my heart filling up like a balloon as I tried to catch his eye, waving.

But something was wrong. A grim-faced Rahul glanced over in my direction once, but looked quickly away. Then, in an inexplicable move, he walked away from me, moving directly and purposefully toward Lucy at the other side of the ballroom. Before my amazed gaze, he bowed, and asked her to dance. Shooting me a triumphant look, the girl gave a little curtsy and then, just as he had once done with me in this very room, he took her closely in his arms.

"What's he doing?" Mallika had joined me to follow my shocked gaze. "Why would Rahul ask that awful Lucy to dance?"

"I have no idea." My voice felt wobbly and my legs weak. I felt stupid, like the world's biggest fool. How could he have changed like that, on a dime? Why had I gone back on my own instincts and said yes to him when the safer answer was always no?

The rest of my crew formed a tight circle around me, even as Monsieur Florimond commanded us to keep dancing.

We were learning the steps of something called the Allemande, but it was near impossible for me to pay attention to the lesson. There was nothing I could think about aside from Rahul and Lucy across the ballroom. Over John's shoulder, I watched them, my stomach tightening with emotion. Both tall, slim, and dark, they were a striking pair. And they had known each other forever, or had they gone to school together? I couldn't remember. Certainly, their powerful parents were in business together, and expected them to be in a different kind of business together too.

As the dance twirled me away, making me face the other direction, I lost sight of them. I wasn't sure what was worse. To be able to see Rahul dancing with Lucy, or not be able to see him and instead imagine them together in my head.

"I think they look like they're arguing," said Penny, during a moment when Mallika, she, and I were circling together. Both she and my sister were shooting me supportive looks, both squeezing my hands in sisterhood.

I didn't have the heart to look anymore. "But why would Rahul ask her to dance in the first place? He said he didn't like her! He even asked me to fake date him so he could be rid of her."

"He's a fool for choosing her over you," John said in a "buck up" sort of a tone, but his words made me feel worse, not better. Was that what Rahul had done? Chosen Lucy? But how and why? Then I remembered our first meeting in this very ballroom, how he'd blown hot then immediately cold, flirting with me, only to tell me he was escorting a girl from home. Was this the same sort of thing?

"I could challenge him to a duel," suggested Will, his handsome face serious and sincere as he approached me in the dance. "Or simpler, I could just beat him up."

I put my hand on the actor boy's enormous biceps, catching a glimpse of what my sister must see in him. He really was kind of endearing. "Thanks, Will. I appreciate that. But I don't think a duel will be necessary."

"Necessary or not, it might make you feel better," Mallika observed.

The dance had turned me around, so that I was again facing the direction of the ballroom where Rahul and Lucy were. I felt something tighten painfully in my throat. But I bit the inside of my cheek, determined not to cry.

"Rahul owes me nothing," I said as the dance ended and we all bowed and curtsied to one another. "Nothing at all. It's just a misunderstanding, I guess. A horrible misunderstanding."

And then, with my unshed tears threatening to fall like rain, I rushed out of the ballroom.

... in the acuteness of the disappointment which followed such an ecstasy of more than hope, she felt as if, till that instant, she had never suffered.

—JANE AUSTEN,
Sense and Sensibility

❧ CHAPTER 18 ❧

RAHUL CAME LOOKING for me after dance class, but I holed myself up in my room. My sister fended him off, and the rest of our crew helped run interference, even bringing me up dinner so I wouldn't have to go down. I didn't want to talk to Rahul, but I was really dreading seeing Lucy. I didn't think I had the strength to deal with her mean-girl comments and triumphant looks.

I had trouble falling asleep that night, so I stayed up reading the novel that Rahul had given me. I wanted to hate it, as I wanted to hate him. But unfortunately, I didn't. The novel, I mean. I actually loved it. It was funny, sharp, witty, full of social critique and insight about the unfairness of society. On the other hand, my feelings for the boy who had lent me the book were far more complicated and unclear.

The next morning, music lessons were the first thing on the agenda, and I knew I couldn't hide in my room anymore like a petulant child. So I dressed carefully and headed down, ready for battle.

Rahul sought me out right away. He was wearing a light brown coat that fit him perfectly, but his hair was messy, like he was a hero from a novel who had brushed off his manservant and stridden purposefully out onto his grounds without bothering with all the fuss of a hairbrush.

"Eila," he began, pulling me to the side of the music room, into a little unseen alcove behind a potted plant and a giant harp.

"You don't have to explain anything to me," I said by way of greeting. "Look, I'm happy for you and Lucy."

"What?" Rahul scratched at his already messy hair. "No, you've misunderstood. That's why I wanted to come talk to you right away. Lucy and I—yesterday—" He seemed at a loss for words.

I pulled away from him, trying to contain my emotions. "Seriously, I should get back to my friends."

"No, wait!" Rahul tugged at my elbow. "Listen, that phone call I got yesterday, it was from my father."

"Who is pressuring you to date Lucy because of some business merger with her family's company," I filled in impatiently. My eyes burned with tiredness. "I know, you told me."

"Yes, you're right, but there's more." Rahul fidgeted again with his collar. "I didn't tell you that my father's company is in some trouble, and it's going to be in a lot more trouble if this deal doesn't go through."

I couldn't help but feel some sympathy for him. "So your dad called to put pressure on you?"

Rahul nodded miserably. "Lucy apparently called her family, and they called my dad, who then called to scream at me."

152

"That doesn't seem very nice." I couldn't think of what else to say.

"My dad isn't known for being nice," Rahul admitted, pulling at an already out-of-place chunk of his hair. "But pimping out his son is a bit far, even for him."

I was a little shocked. I wouldn't have described the pressure he was under in that way, but I guess Rahul wasn't wrong either. On the other side of our alcove, I could hear music class beginning. "So what are you going to do?"

"That's what I wanted to tell you yesterday." Rahul grabbed my hand earnestly, but I pulled it away.

"What? You wanted to explain why you had to get back together with Lucy?" Feeling sympathy for his family situation was one thing, but that didn't mean I was ready to trust Rahul again.

"No, quite the opposite." Rahul sighed. "I asked Lucy to dance yesterday because I wanted to tell her what I thought of her being so manipulative. I wanted to tell her that no matter what she did, I wasn't going to be able to give her what she wants."

In silence, we both listened to the cacophonous tuning of instruments that was happening on the other side of our little enclosure. "What about your dad? And his company?" I asked finally.

"He's going to have to figure it out." Rahul was wrestling with his collar again. "I told him that if the deal was so flimsy it could fall through based on who his teenage son is dating or not dating, maybe it wasn't that strong to begin with."

"He couldn't have liked that." I couldn't help but feel impressed.

"He really didn't." Rahul grimaced, then made a funny sound in the back of his throat. "But I had no choice. Because I'm not interested in dating Lucy. I'm interested in dating somebody else."

I felt my cheeks warm with pleasure as I caught the way he was looking at me. But still, I felt awkward and unsure. Rahul and Lucy had looked so perfect dancing together yesterday. What if he really was the rake I'd teasingly labeled him as? Was I sure I could trust him?

"I don't know, Rahul," I began slowly.

"You don't have to tell me anything," he reassured me quickly. Then, tilting his head in that way he had, he asked, "But do I have a chance to hope?"

"To wish is to hope, to hope is to expect," I said, by way of an answer.

Recognizing the quote, Rahul's eyes lit up. "You read the book I gave you! Austen's first novel! Did you like it?"

"If a book is well written, I always find it too short," I said, quoting from Austen again.

"I knew you'd like it!" Rahul looked so pleased it was hard not to feel myself melting.

"We should probably go back to music class," I said, indicating the sounds coming from the other side of the giant harp.

As soon as I rejoined the others, Mallika grabbed me by the elbow. "Well? Kissed and made up?"

I rolled my eyes at her. I definitely wasn't back to the place I'd been when I was in Rahul's bedroom, about to kiss him, but

I also wasn't in that same state of despair and betrayal I'd been in yesterday. "Why don't I just say that I'm not ready to make him a victim of a Lord Rosewood murder mystery anymore."

Mallika gave a little snorting laugh. "Well, that's definitely a start."

I smiled at my sister's response. Yes, it was. Definitely a start.

Music lessons were tedious as we molded our mouths to imitate crisp British accents in song. But finally, when I was sure I would fall asleep from the silly lyrics we were learning, Countess Flemington, the ridiculously named music teacher, tapped her baton on her music stand, calling us all to attention.

"If you will, ladies and gentlemen!" she intoned. "Your attention please for the first performance of a new musical piece written by one of your own, Mr. Will Allen!"

"What's this?" I whispered to my bright-eyed sister. "Not another lake rescue?"

"Just wait!" Mallika was practically giggling with excitement. "This is going to be even better!"

Since pretty much everyone at camp was by now convinced of Will's secret actor identity, there was a lot of excitement in everyone's clapping. We settled into the gilded chairs set up in rows before the pianoforte as Will made his way up to the front. Mallika grinned in obvious delight even as I felt a little shiver of worry. Even better than the lake rescue? What did Will and Mallika have in store for us?

With an ostentatious flourish, Will sat down before the piano. For a moment, he bowed his head, and then, with a great dramatic gesture, tossed his hair back and put his long fingers to the keys. He was a good piano player, I had to give him that. Within seconds, the room was filled his seemingly effortless playing, the notes nimbly dancing across the room like invisible dancers performing a perfectly timed cotillion.

Then, in a beautiful bright tenor, Will began to sing. At first, it was pleasing enough, until I listened carefully to the lyrics. As I did so, I began to shrink more and more into my chair, until I wished I could just be swallowed up by it entirely.

"Your life I held within my arms!" sang Will, his face grave and dramatic. "From a watery grave you were reborn!"

It was ridiculous. It was corny. It was goofy to the extreme. But rather than laugh, the audience seemed to eat Will's song up. I heard a few sighs and even a little sniff from somewhere behind me. I turned around to see a shamefaced Penny actually wiping her eyes. I gave her a look, and she shrugged helplessly.

"It's just so beautiful and pure," she mumbled by way of explanation. Beside her, a besotted-looking Brandon patted at her hand.

"You are my life, you are my rose," Will sang on, his fingers flying over the keyboard and voice becoming deeper with emotion. He shook his hair as he sang, clearly aware of the Byronic effect. "Forever bloom, without a thorn!"

And then, as if things weren't bad enough with Will's terrible rhyme scheme, my sister stood up and joined him.

"Our garden blooms together free." Mallika added her voice to Will's, harmonizing the ridiculous words with pretty emotion. "I am for you and you for me!"

Almost everyone in the room was looking like they were

going to faint at all this. There were sighs, and quite a few sotto voce moans. It was all I could do not to laugh.

But as I saw Lucy shooting poison looks toward me across the room, my embarrassment and irritation turned to delight at Mallika and Will's ridiculous performance. I even started hoping they would keep going, ham it up more, and continue to torture the awful heiress. If it was painful to Lucy, surely I could tolerate it?

The worst line came next. "What do Will and Mallika make?" sang my sister.

Her flamboyant suitor answered with a little warble in his voice, "Wallika!"

"What do Will and Mallika make?" sang my sister again.

And then, to my utter surprise, quite a few people in the audience joined Will in singing, "Wallika!"

"Our names blend together, our hearts join as one!" sang Will.

"Our souls sing in harmony, our love is a song!" sang Mallika.

Lucy's face was so red I thought it would actually explode like an overripe tomato.

I'm quite ashamed to say that I put aside my sense of honor and dignity in that moment to simply feel joyous that Will and Mallika had so infuriated Lucy. They were ridiculous, but as long as they were making the heiress see red, I could hang with the over-the-top silliness that was *Wallika* the musical.

A Regency Vocabulary Lesson

❧ **TO MAKE A CAKE OF YOURSELF** =
to make a fool of yourself

❧ **TO MAKE A MULL OF SOMETHING** =
to make a mess of something

❧ **BROUGHT TO A POINT NON PLUS** =
in a situation without any options

CHAPTER 19

T HAT WAS RATHER charming," said Rahul, a deep laugh teasing the edges of his voice.

"That's one way to put it." I smiled, indicating the other campers, still clapping, shouting, and hooting after Mallika and Will's performance. "But everyone else seemed to enjoy it."

"Ladies and gentlemen!" Lady Middleton was bellowing from the front of the room. "Some decorum, please, in your applause! Hooting is hardly Regency-appropriate behavior!"

Next to her, poor Countess Flemington was so overcome— whether with pleasure at the song or horror at our rather twenty-first-century reception of it, I'm not sure—that she actually needed a footman to fetch her smelling salts. I was really hoping the leeches would come out next.

"Is Mallika entirely . . . enamored with Will?" Rahul was asking me, his face troubled.

"I think she likes him quite a lot." I nodded to the front, where Mallika was still making deep-kneed curtsies and Will was bowing to their adoring fans. "But I can't figure out how much of that is the glamour of him being the secret *Rosewood* actor, and how much is something more. But I think what I'm realizing is it doesn't really matter if they're having fun together—which I think they actually are."

"I wasn't implying she was anything but a charming and enthusiastic soul," Rahul said. "I was just asking if she would like Will quite as much if it turned out he wasn't actually the actor who's been cast. I mean, I wouldn't want someone to take advantage of Mallika's sweetness."

"I appreciate the concern, Rahul," I said, "but your point is moot, isn't it? I mean, we all know that Will is the actor who has been cast."

"Yes, we do." Rahul rubbed at his chin. "Don't we?"

"Look, it's sweet that you're worrying about my sister." I leaned toward him, feeling shy. All around us, the applause was dying down, but people were still enthusiastically chatting about Will and Mallika's performance. "But I think she's okay. Will loves the spotlight, just like her, but he does seem to genuinely like her."

Rahul laughed. "He seems like a giant puppy."

I was just about to agree with Rahul, when something unexpected happened. As everyone was clapping and standing up, moving chairs, and going to the front to speak with a beaming Wallika, Lucy made a beeline toward Rahul and me. Her face tight with concentration, her stride determined, she looked like an incoming missile headed in our direction.

Rahul saw her coming toward us first. "Lucy! What's going on?" he began.

"Don't even start!" She held up her hand. I expected her to

160

head past us, and say something mean to Mallika or Will, and so I moved across her path to intercept her. But Lucy wasn't planning on saying anything to my sister, apparently, because that's when she stumbled, obviously on purpose, and landed with her hands outstretched right on the chair where I'd been sitting. In the process, she pushed my partially open satchel onto the floor, sending the contents inside, including the phone, skittering across the parquet tiles.

That falling phone did what Lady Middleton hadn't been able to do with her scoldings—it got everyone in the room really quiet, really fast.

"Eila!" shouted Lucy unnecessarily loudly as she bent down to pick up both my phone and satchel, holding them up above her head so that everyone could see. "What horrors! I do humbly apologize for spilling the contents of your handbag. What is this modern device you had hidden therein?"

Her eyes twinkled with maliciousness even as she made sure that Lady Middleton, Countess Flemington, and all the other Regency Camp staff saw what she was holding.

I felt the blood drain from my face. Oh no. This was it. Lucy had just sealed my fate and gotten me, and probably Mallika, kicked out of camp. I was furious, with her but also with Rahul. If he hadn't provoked her yesterday, would she be being so vindictive to me today? I mean, she'd actually been focusing her sights on Will, hadn't she? That is, before Rahul had to step in and be all Mr. Noble Rejection Guy and piss Lucy off.

"Miss Eila Das!" bellowed Lady Middleton in a decidedly un-Regency manner. "May I see you immediately, please!"

My stomach in knots, I moved toward the front of the room. All around me, people were tittering, probably pointing with glee. But then another unexpected thing happened. Thomas the footman, who was standing near Lady Middleton, leaned over and whispered something in her ear.

At first, I couldn't understand what he could possibly have to say in the matter, until I saw Lady Middleton's face change expressions and her eyes flicker from me to Mallika. "I correct myself; I wish to speak immediately to Miss *Mallika* Das!"

"What?" Lucy shrieked, dropping her era-appropriate affectations. "No, this phone belongs to Eila!"

As Mallika shot me a terrified look, I stepped forward, stretching my hand out to grab the phone and bag from Lucy. "Yes, Lucy is correct. This bag and phone do belong to me!"

"No, milady," said Thomas courteously. "If you remember, this is the bag I saw you retrieving when your sister left it in the administrative area."

"She was found in the administrative area alone?" Lady Middleton's eyes looked like they were going to bug out of her head. "Why was this not reported to me immediately?"

"Well . . ." Thomas hesitated, biting his lip. I realized he must be fairly young; it was just the wig and uniform that made him appear older than he was. "Madam, I saw the young miss gather the bag myself and then leave the area immediately."

"Regardless!" Lady Middleton huffed.

"Maybe the bag is her sister's, but I know the phone is hers!" insisted Lucy, holding up my lock screen. It was, luckily, a picture of a tree and nothing more personal. Only Mallika and I would know that the photo was actually the last one our father had taken on his phone. To everyone else, it just looked like an ordinary tree.

"It is mine!" I repeated.

But then Mallika, that ridiculously noble ninny, stepped forward again. "My sister always sticks up for me; she's always trying to take responsibility for the things I do. The phone is mine."

"Mallika, stop!" I hissed. "What are you playing at?"

"Whoever's phone it is must leave this camp immediately!" announced Lady Middleton, her not-inconsiderable nostrils flaring. "These are our rules and they cannot be changed!"

"No! It cannot be!" wailed Will, beating at his chest dramatically. I noticed he'd conveniently unbuttoned a few of his shirt buttons. "My love to be taken away from me? I cannot bear it!"

Mallika rather prettily shed a tear or two, allowing Will to draw her into his embrace. "Our love will endure despite any obstacles!" she announced in a trembling voice.

Without me noticing, Rahul had stepped forward to stand next to me. "I'm afraid the phone is mine, Lady Middleton," he said. When I made a noise of protest, he reached out and squeezed my hand, hard, as if in warning. "I had asked Miss Das to put it in her purse because I don't have pockets in this suit."

Annie stuck her hand in the air to get Lady Middleton's attention, calling out, "Rahul's right! There is a shocking lack of pocket in that particular jacket. It's something I've been meaning to address with the team. I mean, it's a lovely cut and impeccable tailoring, in fact, the lines . . ."

Mallika gave her friend an almost-imperceptible shake of the head, as if to say, "Not now, Annie."

Everyone who'd been staring at me or Mallika was now staring at Rahul as he calmly took the phone.

"I'll show you it's my phone," Rahul said, punching in the code he'd obviously seen me use before, in his room. Then, quickly, he found and held up the picture of himself that I had taken, at close range, in the ballroom. It was so close it looked like it could have been taken by Rahul himself. "A selfie," he said shortly, before shutting the phone off again.

Lady Middleton, who had been only recently looking like a steam engine about to blow, now looked creepily calm and apologetic. "Well, of course, if it's your device, Mr. Lee," she demurred. "Exceptions can always be made."

I whirled around to look at the woman, sure I'd misheard. Had she actually just said that exceptions could always be made?! Wasn't this woman a stickler about rules, and about to kick either me or my sister out on our ears?

"I'm grateful, thank you, Lady Middleton," said Rahul. Then, to my dismay, he held out my phone toward her. "But I will of course be handing in my phone."

I let out a cry of outrage.

For the briefest of moments, Rahul glanced in my direction. Then he dropped the phone into Lady Middleton's outstretched hands. "Anything else would be unfair."

"Well, thank you, Mr. Lee," Lady Middleton murmured, tucking the phone into her sleeve. "Why don't we just let bygones be bygones and forget about this little misunderstanding?"

Hearing Lady Middleton's pronouncement, Will let out a

strangled yelp of joy, twirling my sister around and around in a dramatic arc before launching into another chorus of "Wallika."

I shot Rahul a shocked look. "Why . . . ?" I started, but he shook his head firmly, clearly not wanting to talk in public.

Lucy rounded on me even as the rest of the room joined Will in a joyous chorus of "Wallika." "This isn't over!" she hissed. Her beautiful face was ugly with spite.

"Lucy, please." Rahul turned on her, a strained look on his face. "Just stop with this petty power play."

Lucy was so outraged, and probably so unused to being put in her place, she didn't seem to be able to stand it. "As if!" she exclaimed, and swirled her way out of the room.

She would not wound the feelings of her sister on any account, and yet to say what she did not believe was impossible.

—JANE AUSTEN,
Sense and Sensibility

CHAPTER 20

"I DON'T THINK I can talk to you right now." Mallika approached me, flushed and furious after the entire dramatic mess in the music room. We had walked outside the manor and were standing a little bit away from where Will and Rahul were waiting for us. Not to mention Annie, Brandon, Penny, and John, who were all staring at us with avid curiosity on their faces.

"Go on to horseback-riding lessons! We'll meet you there!" I waved them all away, and they reluctantly retreated, much to my relief. My sister and I really didn't need an audience for this.

I didn't even try to pretend I didn't understand why Mallika was so angry. "Look, Mal, I know I should have handed in my phone, but I just couldn't give it up. I can't even tell you why."

"Well, I can!" said my sister. "You couldn't give it up because you can't give up any kind of control ever! You can't trust anyone!"

"But Lucy . . ." I protested.

"I don't care about Lucy! I care about you and why you lied to me! You were lying when I said all that stuff about how we'd handed in our phones, right? You were just laughing at me back then?" Mallika accused.

"No, please, try and understand," I begged, "I was just trying to protect you."

"What does that have to do with your phone?" She crossed her arms and stared me down with an unfamiliar expression. Disappointment.

I opened my mouth and closed it again as I fished around for an answer my sister would believe. "Well, I mean. What if something happened? What if there was an emergency?"

"Are you even listening to yourself? You sound unhinged!" The sun was high but there was a strong breeze whipping up from the Hudson River, making Mallika's hair dance around her face. "You do realize the camp is run by responsible people who would give us our phones back if something happened, or call Ma if they needed to? Or did you even forget that we have a mother, and that it's not you?"

That made me pause, my heart pounding painfully. "What did you say?"

"You're not my mother, Eila!" Mallika spat out. "And you're certainly not my father either!"

"I know that," I said weakly. "I would never try to take Baba's place."

Mallika looked pained as she rushed on. "And on a different point, why were you in the administrative wing to begin with? And throwing me under the bus besides, telling Thomas you were there to get my bag? When it was your bag and your phone all along?"

"You shouldn't have tried to take the blame," I said weakly. I looked out over the beautiful vista of the river and the Palisades beyond, rubbing away moisture from my eyes. "Obviously, I lied to Thomas then because it was a believable excuse when he saw me up there, but I didn't want you to get blamed for anything."

Mallika turned in a circle, trying to stop the wind and dust from getting in her eyes. She stomped her foot on the ground. "But that still doesn't answer the question as to why you needed an excuse to begin with!"

Desperate to explain, I barreled on. "I thought Lucy was going to try and sabotage your audition tape!"

Mallika looked at me for a full few seconds before responding. And when she did, her voice had risen by a serious few octaves. "How? How was she going to do that?"

"Unspool the tape?" I squinted against the whipping wind, which was lifting all sorts of dust into the air. "I don't know. I just had to make sure."

"Which brings us back to my original point." Mallika sounded more hurt and tired than angry now. "You're not in charge of me, Eila. You need to stop protecting me, or imagining you're protecting me, and live your own life already!"

"That's not fair!" I snapped. "You say that now, but do you know how much I've done for you, still do for you? How much of my carefree teen years I've given up to make sure you're okay and happy?"

Mallika's eyes shone with tears, but her mouth remained a stubborn line. "I do know, Eila. But you can't hold that over me, guilting me all the time. You need to smell the roses, live your life, be young, have fun!"

I remembered the older sister in the Austen novel I'd just read—the one who'd had to grow up too fast because of her responsibilities. Was I like that? Was I growing old before my time?

"I know how to have fun!" I crossed my arms over my chest defensively.

"Do you really?" Mallika scoffed. "You're the one who's always loved acting, not me, but I had to practically twist your arm to come here to Regency Camp, convince you that you were coming here for me when we were actually coming here for you!"

"What are you talking about? I came because of you!" I felt like there was steam coming out of my ears even as there were tears pooling behind my eyes. "And if you don't want to be here, what's all this over-the-top drama you're pulling with Will? I mean, running around falling into lakes and singing 'Wallika'?"

"What, are you mad that one of us knows how to have fun, take a chance?" Mallika's face was flushed and hair wild as she continued spitting out truths at me. "You're so out of touch with your own desires, you can't even admit that maybe you came because you wanted to see what might happen not for me, but for you, that you wanted to maybe give your acting career a shot! I bet, since we've been here, the only time you've stopped worrying about me and my chances to get cast in *Rosewood* are the times you've been with Rahul!"

I felt muddled by Mallika's accusations, distracted from what we really should be talking about, which was Lucy's plans to sabotage her.

"Mal," I said, my voice unsteady, "I just don't want Lucy to be able to pull another stunt like she did this morning. She clearly has it out for you, and thinks that it should be her getting close to Will."

"And so you figured, what, that in order to protect me from Lucy, you would just get us both kicked out of camp?" Mallika was practically yelling now. "Lady Middleton seemed about ready to catapult us out of the manor and straight into the Hudson River back there. If it wasn't for Rahul saving our butts, she probably would have. You think you're protecting me, but answer me this—do you think your behavior increases or decreases either of our chances of getting cast in any kind of walk-on role?"

Our friends had scattered, but I saw a little group of other campers gathering to listen to our very loud, very public argument. I turned away, making it a point to lower my voice.

"They didn't use catapults in the Regency era," I mumbled. "At least, not in that way."

"What are you talking about?" Mallika shouted, her beautiful face contorted in fury.

"I didn't mean to get us kicked out, obviously," I amended, pulling her even farther away from the curious crowd. I had never seen my sister this angry at me, and it was a terrible feeling. Especially as most of what she was saying wasn't entirely wrong.

"Whether you intended it or not, we would have both gotten kicked out if Rahul hadn't intervened." I could see unshed tears of frustration shining in my sister's eyes. "I mean, thank goodness for him!"

"But Rahul had no real need to hand in my phone. Lady Middleton looked like she was going to let him keep it!" I argued.

Mallika's mouth dropped open. "Are you actually serious right now? Have you completely lost any sense of reality?"

"Lower your voice!" I glanced over at our gathered spectators, before going on, "Did you notice how Lady Middleton didn't care at all when she thought it was his phone? Like the rules don't apply to him! That's only because he's a rich kid, like Lucy. Did you know that he has his own room—it's like a little mini-suite!"

That got my sister's attention. A slow smile spread across her face. "And when were you going to tell me that you were in his room?"

"It was nothing. He lent me a book," I mumbled, grinding my boot in the dirt.

Mallika raised that one cocky eyebrow, putting a hand on her curvaceous hip. "Is that some kind of dirty metaphor?"

"No! I was actually there because I was about to get caught by Lady Middleton up in the office area," I admitted.

Mallika's pretty face went from curious to furious in a matter of seconds. "What is wrong with you, Didi?"

"What?" I was sincerely confused.

"I mean, Rahul rescues us—actually you, for what sounds like the second time, besides lending you a book—and all you can do is spin conspiracy theories about why he has a single room and gets preferential treatment? And complain that he handed in your phone instead of risking his neck even more for you to keep it?" Mallika was pacing now, circling around a tree with a broad trunk next to where we were standing. Below us was the rushing Hudson, and beyond, the beautiful sheer cliffs of the Palisades. "You just said yourself his family's well off, like Lucy's. Okay, so what? I mean, were you born yesterday, Didi? Did you not realize this is how the world works?"

"But it's not how it should work." For the first time in my life, I felt like I was the younger sister and Mallika the elder. "I mean, privilege, class, and money shouldn't call the shots."

I thought of the Austen book that Rahul had lent me and the sisters in that novel who were also victims of those with more wealth. If the organizers of Regency Camp knew anything about Austen, they would know she was criticizing those stifling social realities, not asking people to re-create them.

"Stop being so ungrateful!" Mallika snapped. "Rahul saved us! He used whatever privilege he has to help us stay here!"

"He knew nothing would happen to him," I said stiffly. "I mean, it's not like he was exactly falling on a sword for us."

"You're impossible, Didi! You really are!" Mallika looked like she was about to spit fire and set the tree we were standing under ablaze. "I'm sorry I ever suggested you write your college essay about this place. But in the meantime, I do have a new topic for you: How Regency Camp ruined my relationship with my beloved sister!"

And with that, she whirled around and stomped away.

I have lost a treasure, such a Sister, such a friend as never can have been surpassed,—She was the sun of my life, the gilder of every pleasure, the soother of every sorrow, I had not a thought concealed from her, & it is as if I had lost a part of myself . . .

—LETTER FROM JANE AUSTEN'S SISTER
CASSANDRA TO HER NIECE
FANNY KNIGHT, *20 JULY 1817*

CHAPTER 21

A s MALLIKA LEFT me, I knew there was only one person I wanted to see, to speak to. Rahul.

If I had been a heroine in an Austen novel, I would have probably galloped dramatically on horseback across the manor fields to find him. Maybe even in the rain. At the very least, I might have run dramatically through a storm, if only to catch pneumonia and almost die.

As it happened, by the time I showed up at the stables, I couldn't even leave right away to find the others, who were already out riding. The first thing I had to do was report to a small stable-side costuming tent where Annie's aunt and her team fitted me in a riding habit. It was blue velvet and absolutely stunning, the hat with a little curving feather in it, but I really didn't have time for their fussing. Then came the actual picking of the horse.

"Are you a strong rider, miss?" asked an authentically dirty-looking stable hand. I gave a shudder, wondering at how far he'd gone for period authenticity by keeping his teeth quite that unbrushed.

"Define strong?" I said, attempting a joke.

Dirty stable hand dude didn't crack a smile, but stuck a piece of straw in his mouth to carefully chew on. "Have you ridden before?"

"Yes," I said briefly, eyeing a majestic dark brown horse who was snorting and prancing in his stall.

"On a horse?" he clarified, chewing some more.

"Yes," I answered. It felt like brevity was the way to go if I wanted any hope of riding a fast animal.

The man sighed. Deeply. He spat out his chewed-up straw piece. "How many times? In what context?"

Then it was my turn to sigh. I guess a fast horse was not in the cards for me. "Once or twice. At a local fair?"

And so instead of dancing across the fields on the back of an impressive steed, I was given a very gentle mare called Queen Mab, with a lovely disposition and dappled gray coat, who took me at a serviceable if less than romantic pace from the stable out to the fields where the others already were. It did not take me long to find Rahul, although far longer than if I'd been going at any sort of normal horsey pace. But Mab seemed content to waffle along, keeping me both safe and impatient.

Finally, I saw them. The riding instructors had set up some jumps in a wide green field and some more capable riders were practicing taking their horses over them. I saw Lucy in a sparkling green habit with two sharp feathers pointing out of her jaunty hat. She was riding astride, unlike the Regency era ladies, who would have ridden sidesaddle. Lucy called something to the instructor, and then she and her animal soared beautifully over a high green hedge. She made it with room to spare, laughing as she and her horse landed gracefully in the other side. Rahul was nearby on his horse, watching her and clapping along with the other campers. I felt like booing, but restrained myself.

Then Rahul took the jump just as Queen Mab and I were trotting slowly up. Lucy spotted me first, her eyebrows rising in disgust at both my elderly steed and my own awkward style of riding. But as soon as Rahul saw me, he left the jumping area and rode up to me and my slow-motion steed. His riding habit made him look even more dashing than usual, and face was pleasingly flushed from the exercise. "I was about to come looking for you! Everything okay?"

Trying to ignore Lucy's stare, I looked up at him, awkwardly gripping Mab's reins. "Is there somewhere we can go to talk?"

"Sure!" Rahul made a gesture that he'd be right back to the riding master and led me off to the right, toward a thicket of beautiful trees. Unfortunately, even though he thought he was leading me, and I thought he was leading me, Queen Mab seemed to have some other opinions. She chewed balefully on some grass as if it was the most delicious thing in the world, and let out a stinky horse fart, refusing to move.

"Giddyup, Queen Mab!" I jiggled my reins, pushing my heels lightly on her sides. I didn't dare look back, but felt Lucy's laughing eyes on me. I felt utterly defeated, and ridiculous. "Let's go, Your Highness!"

Realizing I wasn't behind him, Rahul had turned his horse back. "Having a spot of trouble?"

I frustratedly pushed some hair out of my eyes. "Apparently so."

Rahul reached out and lightly tapped Queen Mab, who put up her head obediently, neighed, and trotted off behind him.

"That felt like a setup," I scowled at my fickle horse.

"Mab and I have an understanding," Rahul said, his face entirely serious. "I'll be paying her in hay afterward."

We rode on for a few moments over the beautiful grounds, the thick trees and dewy grasses underfoot. The beauty of the scene almost made me forget my fight with Mallika. But I did remember how my sister had said that the only time I stopped mothering her and thought about myself was when I was with Rahul. As much as I hated to, I had to admit she was right. When I was with Rahul, I didn't feel like anyone's mother. I forgot my responsibilities. I felt young and free.

When we got to a protected little spot in the middle of two trees, Rahul dismounted and helped me do the same. He secured the horses, leaving them to graze as we walked on together into a scene as beautiful as a painting. The truth was, I could forget anything when I was with Rahul. I could almost believe we were back in another era, another time.

"That was a stressful morning; how are you doing?" he asked softly as we walked across the empty green field. He reached out for my hand. "Are you okay?"

"It was stressful. And I'm seriously not sure if I am, to tell you the truth." I thought I was being light and blasé, but my voice wobbled a little at these words.

Rahul's face grew concerned, and I let him pull me toward him. I buried my face in his shoulder. It felt good to be in his strong and capable arms and just let go. It had been so long since I'd just been able to let go. For years, I'd been the big sister, the capable sister, the one who was in charge, the one who had to push her own feelings down and take care of others. Now I felt like all those emotions were just bubbling forth to the surface, refusing to be denied anymore. Of course, the fact I'd hardly slept the night before helped the waterworks too.

I didn't cry on his shoulder long, but long enough to make his coat wet. Finally, I stopped, gave a couple of hiccups, and pulled away from him. As I did, Rahul's face was gentle with worry, the breeze rifling through his hair.

"You didn't need to hand in my phone, you know," I said, wiping my eyes. Then, immediately, I felt ashamed. Mallika was right; I should be thanking Rahul for saving us, not blaming him for not doing even more than he already had.

"You're welcome," Rahul said with a smile in his voice.

I cleared my throat. "Thank you. Mallika and I would have both been kicked out if it wasn't for you."

"It was my pleasure to help you both out. She wasn't like this when we were younger, but Lucy is really too awful these days." Rahul handed me a beautiful monogrammed handkerchief. I took it to wipe my face, wondering for a second if Annie and her aunt's team had supplied such a thing or if he was just the sort of boy who had a messy drawer jammed full of monogrammed handkerchiefs?

"She obviously really wants to get close to Will. Get cast on the show, whatever." I tried to sheepishly hand the wet handkerchief back to Rahul, but he waved it away, and I tucked it into my sleeve.

"She's the kind of person who wants a lot of things, but is never satisfied with whatever it is once she gets it," Rahul said.

"And now because of her, I've ruined my relationship with my sister," I said, amending honestly, "Well, because of Lucy and my own decisions too."

"Mallika's just frustrated right now. I'm sure she knows how much you love her," Rahul said as he played with a blade of grass he'd plucked.

"I do, you know." I rubbed my stiff neck as we walked along. I always held all my stress there. "But sometimes, since Baba died, it feels like I do all the giving and she does all the taking."

Rahul squinted at me thoughtfully. "I don't have any brothers and sisters, so I'm probably way off base here . . ." he began.

"Any advice at this point is better than what I've come up with!" I said ruefully. "Go ahead! Lay it on me!"

"I think Mallika is probably more capable than you give her credit for," Rahul said gently. "She's smart and funny and strong, and probably needs less protection than you think."

My first instinct was to argue, to explain to him how small and broken Mallika had been after we'd lost our father, how I'd had to be Ma's partner, help keep the family all together, help pick up my broken sister and put her together, piece by piece. But then I thought about how confident Mallika had been since we'd been here at Regency Camp, and realized that Rahul might be right. People changed. Some, like Lucy, for the worse. But maybe Mallika had changed when I wasn't looking, and changed for the better, into someone more capable. So maybe it was my turn to change as well.

"It's hard to stop shielding someone you've gotten used to protecting," I admitted.

Rahul nodded, bending down to pluck some more long grasses from underfoot that he began braiding together "But I wonder if, by doing so, even a little bit, you might be able to give yourself some grace as well?"

"Mallika said something like that too," I admitted. "She said I had to smell the roses, worry about myself and not just her."

"She's not wrong," Rahul said softly. "I know Lucy is a bit of a thorn, but there is beauty and joy here, if you just seek to find it."

I moaned, then laughed at myself. "I don't know why I'm always in a state of hyperalertness, waiting for things to go wrong, waiting for something . . ."

"Nefarious?" he suggested with a smile.

"Exactly," I agreed. "It's like I'm always waiting for the sky to fall down on me."

"It's because the sky did fall down on you," Rahul said, his face serious and intense. "You lost a parent. That's a trauma that doesn't just go away. Your entire body, your nerves are, like, permanently in a state of alarm, waiting for the next terrible thing to happen."

He sounded like he was talking from experience. But my instincts for self-preservation were too strong to let him in my carefully built defenses right away.

"You learn all that from your therapist?" I asked, immediately regretting the words as they left my lips.

But Rahul didn't look offended at all. "As a matter of fact, I did. That and a whole lot more." He handed me the little braided grass ring he'd been making. "Your father would want you to be happy; he'd want you to enjoy yourself and dream your dreams. As I'm sure your mother does too, as does Mallika."

"Thank you," I said, letting him slip the ring on my pinkie finger. I hoped he understood that I was thanking him not just for the ring but for the kind words he'd said, which had already planted themselves inside me and were taking root.

"I would have made you a crown of wildflowers, only the gardening staff seem a little too on their game." Rahul indicated the flowerless grass with a laugh that made his eyes crinkle.

"Thank you," I said again in a small voice. A breeze blew over the open meadow, sending a few bobby pins flying from my hair.

Rahul smiled, watching their flight. "I'm afraid those pins have escaped for good."

I grinned at him, remembering our first encounter in the ballroom, when he had handed me my fallen pins like they were a flower bouquet. I couldn't help but be embarrassed at how defensive I'd just been.

"This morning was awful," I said by way of an explanation for everything. "Getting caught out for the phone like that. Then having my sister get so angry with me. The only thing that saved me was you."

Rahul looked both startled and embarrassed at my words. "Hardly. I think you're pretty capable to saving yourself. I mean, those anti-attacker moves you broke out when I surprised you in the administrative wing!"

"Yes, it's true, I was pretty awesome back there," I laughed. "But seriously, hear me out. You have been the only person here who's kept me steady while I've been here, who's helped me see the forest for the trees."

Rahul laughed, putting a hand carelessly through this hair. "I'm not sure I'm an expert in that either."

"But you're not overreacting to a mean girl; you're not ruining the relationship with the person you most love. At least you're acting like a normal person." I shook my head ruefully. "That's what I value so much about you, that you're real and true. Not fake or superficial."

An unnamed emotion flicked across Rahul's face. "I wasn't going to come here, you know. It was a very last-minute decision. I was kind of manipulated into it," he said, reaching out to twirl the ring he'd just made me around my finger. "But I'm so very glad I came. I'm so very glad I've been able to meet you. It's meant . . . everything."

My breath caught. Rahul was staring into my eyes with an intensity I'd never felt before from another person. I could feel my heart thrumming in my throat as his fingers reached up to gently stroke the side of my cheek. I leaned into his hand, feeling dizzy and crystal sharp at the same time. His face was so close to mine, his lips only inches away. I felt the shivery thrill of anticipation shooting through me, the thought of finally feeling what it would be like to kiss him.

And then, like the last time we had been about to kiss, we were interrupted. Only this time, it was by the horses, whinnying nearby.

I laughed. "We'd better go make sure they're okay. That Mab seemed like she might just be a troublemaker."

"A real wild child, Queen Mab, running around late at night with a bad crowd, dealing in black-market hallucinogenic oats," Rahul said with a smile. But as I turned away from him, beginning to walk back toward the horses, he grabbed my wrist. "Eila?" he asked tentatively.

"Yes?" I turned, curious as to what he wanted to say.

Rahul cleared his throat, speaking faster than he normally did. "Tonight, after dinner, will you meet me by the front steps of the manor, the ones down to the Hudson River?"

"Why?" My pulse sped up a little.

"I want to take you somewhere, away from here, away from all this." He gently ran his thumb across the inside of my wrist like he'd done back in his room, then looked up to meet my gaze.

I gulped, feeling like there was little shivers of electricity climbing from where he was touching my wrist all the way up my arm to my neck and face.

"Should I bring normal clothes?" I asked, anticipating a restaurant or coffee shop out there somewhere in the "real world."

"Actually, you don't have to." Rahul indicated our Regency outfits with a flick of his hand. "Funnily enough, what we're wearing will be perfect."

"Okay," I said softly, wishing the hours would pass more quickly.

"Until then?" Rahul bent down and kissed the skin inside my wrist with warm lips. "My lady?"

It was all I could do not to faint. "Until then!" I agreed.

True Politeness:
A Handbook of Etiquette for Ladies (1847)

Let your dress harmonize with your complexion, your size, and the circumstances in which you may be placed: for instance, the dress for walking, for a dinner or an evening party, each requires a different style of both material and ornament.

Avoid the extreme *mode*; and, in adopting the style of your friend, be careful that it will suit your figure, your complexion, and stature: the dress which may be adapted to her may be absurd in you.

If your stature be short, you should not allow a superfluity of flounces upon the skirt of your dress: if you are tall, they may be advantageously adopted when fashion does not forbid them.

Perfumes are a necessary appendage to the toilet; let them be delicate, not powerful; the Atta of roses is the most elegant; the Heduesmia is at once fragrant and delicate. Many others may be named; but none must be patronized which are so obtrusive as to give the idea that they are not indulged in as a luxury but used from necessity.

🌹 CHAPTER 22 🌹

I N ANY OTHER situation, I would have told Mallika where I was going, but she hadn't been speaking to me all day, and actively left the room whenever I entered. So I had no option of telling her anything.

After dinner, when I returned to my room, I saw that Rahul had, true to his word, left the other Jane Austen books on my bedside. They were wrapped in a thick ribbon that had a simple card tucked under it. As I read the card, and its inscription (*Nefarious Purposes*), I gave a laugh.

Like the first book I'd finished, the volumes were beautifully bound and shining in elegance, with elaborate inside pages and gilded edges. I ran my fingers over the titles, filled with appreciation for Rahul's generosity and kindness.

I dressed for my mystery date with care. I wore the rani color deep pink gown that Annie had tried on me the first day we arrived. As someone with natural curls, it was easy enough to trail a matching ribbon through my partially upswept hair and call it Regency. In my ears were the small golden earrings my didu had given me on our last trip to India, and on my wrist was a golden bala also from my grandmother. I wasn't sure where we were going, but as I walked out across the still-sunny lawn after dinner, I felt ready for anything.

Rahul was waiting for me at the end of the front lawn. We were alone, since everyone else had gone to a voluntary extra dance class under the fairy-lit branches of the fruit orchard. From the excited way Annie and Mallika had been chatting about the lesson, I was sure it was going to devolve into a dance party as the evening wore on.

So no one could see my expression of sunny elation as I walked down the hill and saw Rahul for the first time. He was wearing a gray Regency suit jacket and dark breeches that he made look modern. Maybe it was the easy confidence with which he stood in them. Maybe it was just his air of comfort with himself—as if no piece of clothing could define who or what he was, whether from his culture or not, whether in this era or any other.

"You look amazing!" he breathed as he looked up to spot me.

"I was just about to say the same to you!" It was a new experience to be so open with someone, but I was realizing that with Rahul, I could be real.

"For you!" Rahul held out a flower that was, by some miraculous ESP coincidence, the exact same color as my gown. "O how much more doth beauty beauteous seem, by that sweet ornament which truth doth give!"

It was Shakespeare's Sonnet 54. Hard not to appreciate a guy who knew his sonnets.

"But how did you guess the color I'd be wearing?" I asked as he tucked the flower into my cascading curls.

"I'd like to say that I'm just good like that, but I've got to be honest, I had a spy helping me." Rahul grinned.

"Annie!" I guessed. "That saucy minx! She gave you a swatch or something of my gown. But how did she know I was going to wear this one?"

"Nope." Rahul shook his head. "Not Annie. It was someone even saucier, or, I guess, minx-ier."

"Mallika?" I asked. "But she's not even speaking to me."

"She may be temporarily angry, but I don't think it'll last too long." Rahul reached out to take my hand. "She seemed excited about our plans."

"Which are?" I prompted as I placed my hand in his proffered one. His skin was warm and soft against mine.

"You'll find out soon!" Rahul said mysteriously as he led me down a winding path I'd never been on before. It was graveled, with a few steps every couple of feet that wound down from the cliff-top manor grounds toward the river. There were arching trees overhead and a few evening blossoming vines somewhere that I could smell even if I couldn't see them. I held on to the rickety rope that had been placed by way of a railing. From the distance, behind us, came the music of the outdoor dance lesson under the trees. Basically, the evening already felt magical.

"Here we are!" Rahul said as we came upon a vine-covered gate. As he opened the gate and we stepped through, I saw that we were at a dock right on the Hudson River. And next to that dock, bobbing gently in the river, was a beautiful small speedboat.

"We're not going in that thing, are we?" I asked even as we walked down the wooden dock toward the boat. It was white with golden-brown wood trim, like something out of a James Bond movie. And its name, perfectly, was *Magic*.

"I know it's not exactly Regency appropriate, but I figured a rowboat wouldn't be the safest on this stretch of the Hudson," said Rahul with a grin. "Plus, unless you're some kind of a secret champion rower, maybe on an Olympic crew team, a rowboat would definitely take too long."

I shook my head. "Not an Olympic rower."

"Sadly, as I suspected," Rahul said with a laugh, ushering me before him.

"I've never been in something like this before," I admitted as Rahul helped me into the boat with its gorgeous leather seats. It was like something out of one of those rich-people reality shows, not the sort of thing an ordinary person like me should be riding.

"It's not mine, if that's what you're thinking," Rahul said quickly. "Just borrowed from a family friend for the occasion."

I settled into one of the seats, adjusting my dress and hoping that Rahul was as skilled driving boats as he seemed to be riding horses. "The occasion that is . . ." I prompted.

"Something you will discover very soon!" Rahul reassured with a smile as he powered up the boat.

The sun was warm, on its way to setting in the summer sky.

Little droplets of water hit my face, making me feel awake and alive. The waves crashing against the fast-moving boat and the roar of the engine made it difficult to talk, but I felt content just being there with Rahul, sitting next to him as he steered.

Soon, Rahul was guiding the sleek boat into another small harbor. Only, this dock had at least a few other boats already hitched there.

"Where are we?" I asked as he helped me out onto the shore.

"You'll see," he said mysteriously, taking a basket I hadn't noticed from behind one of the chairs with him.

We walked up a shorter gravel path from the dock to the cliff, this time passing a few other Regency-clothed couples. But they weren't from camp; they weren't teenagers at all. These were people of our parents' and grandparents' ages all decked out in Austen-era wear. I gave Rahul a look, to which he just did that tapping-the-side-of-his-nose thing again.

"Curiouser and curiouser," I muttered as a granny walked by me in full bonneted Regency attire.

And then we were at the top of the path, looking out over a grassy lawn not unlike Norland Manor's, with a very familiar-looking open-sided white tent set up out to the right. There were fairy lights crisscrossing the way to the tent, and the far-too-familiar sight of families sitting on the lawn picnicking.

Opening the basket, Rahul spread out a blanket. Then, with a smile, he pulled out some sparkling juice, grapes, berries, cheeses, and crackers.

"This is the new Shakespeare theater?" I guessed, taking

a seat beside him on the blanket. The golden sun was on the horizon and the lights overhead made everything seem otherworldly and magical. A few yards away, a little girl in modern clothes was doing cartwheels on the lawn.

"Yup. It's Barton Manor, the new home of the Hudson Valley Shakespeare Company," Rahul said. "I thought you might like getting away from everything and seeing a play."

"Not *The Tempest*?" I asked. It was amazing to be out here picnicking, like I'd once done with my parents, but the thought of seeing the last Shakespeare play I'd seen with my father was too much.

"No!" Rahul said, his expression making clear he understood why I wouldn't want to see that particular play. "A play about fairy revels in the woods!"

"*A Midsummer Night's Dream*!" I exclaimed. Only one of my absolute favorites—about magic spells and mixed-up lovers and naughty tricks that all get put to rights in the end. I took a drink of the lovely bubbly juice Rahul had brought—along with actual wineglasses!—and popped a raspberry into my mouth before asking, "But what's with our outfits?"

Rahul chewed and swallowed the piece of cheese he'd been eating. "In honor of the Regency Camp just up the road at their old location, they're doing the production in Regency dress, which is why they invited audience members to come dressed up as well." He sat up and looked at me intensely. "Tell me if you're not comfortable and we don't have to stay for the play. Your sister said you might enjoy it, but if it just feels too soon, let me know."

"No, I think it might be weird if it was the last play I saw with Baba, but honestly, just being in a different place makes it feel different too." I gestured to the beautiful setting, the overhead twinkly lights, the picnicking playgoers, the birds in the trees overhead. "I love it. I'm so glad we're here."

Rahul beamed at me as if I'd told him he had won some huge prize, and on impulse, I popped a grape into his mouth. He took my hand, lingering a second too long over my fingers, his eyes serious as they met mine. I felt my breath catch in my chest.

Regency Fun Fact

Regency-era audiences loved Shakespeare's works, although they often edited out words and dialogue that were considered "indelicate." (Including the word *body*!) In fact, a Regency-era Shakespeare lover, like Jane Austen herself, could not have attended a production of *King Lear* since that play was banned in 1810 for being too tragic and crass. Multiple Jane Austen books have Shakespearean references and themes, portraying characters performing Shakespeare's plays or reading his works aloud. Yet this might have been considered somewhat scandalous. Samuel Taylor Coleridge wrote, in 1815, "Shakespeare's words are too indecent to be translated . . . His gentlefolk's talk is full of coarse allusions such as nowadays you could hear only in the meanest taverns."

✿ CHAPTER 23 ✿

THAT BREATHLESS FEELING lasted the entire play as we sat close together, our hands first touching, then fingers intertwined for most of the rest of the first act. In our costumes, and under those magical lights, it felt like we weren't just watching but actually visiting Queen Titania's fairy bower in the woods. We laughed with the silly mechanicals—the tinkers and tailors putting on a ridiculous play within a play—as well as the young lovers confused by the impish Puck's magic. But when King Oberon cursed his queen to fall in love with one of the mechanicals, Bottom, who has had his head transformed into that of an ass, I couldn't help but feel irritated.

"Oberon claims he loves Titania, but he's humiliating her, making *her* into the ass," I said to Rahul during intermission as we were walking out on the lawn under the now-star-bedecked sky.

"The fairy king made a mistake, though; he admits it by the end of the play." Rahul's face was strangely unreadable, partially lit by the overhead string lights. "If she loves him, shouldn't she forgive him?"

"It doesn't matter if he admits it later. That kind of betrayal is seriously unforgivable." I waved away an annoying mosquito buzzing by my face. They made them big in the Hudson Valley.

"Yes, I would see how you would think so," Rahul said in a strangled voice. A little bit away from us, some fellow audience members were laughing with glee.

"You seem to be taking Oberon's side for no reason!" I teased, linking my arm through his as we took in the beautiful nighttime vista over the broad river. "Tell me the truth, are you a fairy king in disguise?"

Rahul reached over to brush a curl from my cheek. "No, but sometimes I feel just as trapped by my circumstances."

Poor little rich boy, I would have scoffed a mere day or two ago. But not now. Now everything was different.

"It's a beautiful night," I said, changing the subject. I stopped walking, turning him around to face me. I thought of what my sister had said about him. And how she was right about him rescuing me.

"Thank you, Rahul," I said. "For everything. For bringing me here tonight—the picnic, the boat—it's all been, well, a midsummer night's dream made real."

Meeting his eyes shyly, I reached up to kiss his cheek. His skin felt warm under my lips, his stubble a little scratchy.

Rahul's face was serious as he leaned toward me, brushing his lips against my cheek in return. "If we shadows have offended, think but this and all is mended. That you have but slumbered here, while these visions did appear."

I knew the lines, of course; they were the fairy Puck's famous last speech of the play, in which he apologizes to the audience for all his magic and mayhem. I tilted my cheek toward Rahul, feeling the heat of his lips against my skin. As he pulled back, I ran my fingers over his warm lips.

"And this weak and idle theme, no more yielding but a dream." Feeling bolder than I ever had, I leaned forward, brushing my own lips against his. He let me kiss him, and then, slowly, gently, began to kiss me back.

There were people milling about the lawn, but too far away to care about. Our closest companions, in fact, were the fireflies zooming around near us. I felt myself sway, caught up in the magic. Rahul reached out, steadying me, his hands warm around my waist. As he did so, I tangled my fingers through his hair, pulling him toward me again.

For a minute or two, we didn't speak. We almost didn't breathe. Instead, we inhaled each other's presence like fragrant blossoms, our lips and breath and selves intertwining.

It was only the oohing and aahing of the fellow audience members around us that made us break apart. I was breathless, and felt like I was shining all over.

"What's going on?" I brushed my tousled hair away from my face.

"Look up!" Rahul's face was was bright in the glow of the floating fire lanterns that the crew had set alight all around us.

Above our heads, the fleet of bobbing magic lanterns climbed slowly toward the dark sky. The lights danced in the darkness, shimmering with their inner fire. They were like little hopes and dreams made manifest, wishes from all us mere mortals that we were sending upward toward the fairy kingdom. What would my wish be? I wondered. Well, for one, that this night, and this feeling, would never end.

"Beautiful!" I breathed, leaning closer to Rahul.

"Yes, it is," he said, looking straight at me. The glow of the bobbing lights shone in his long-lashed eyes. He cleared his throat, as if searching for the right words. "Eila," he finally managed, "there's a lot I have to tell you."

But before he had a chance to say anything more, there came the bell signaling the end of intermission.

Rahul leaned his forehead into mine. "Gentle, do not reprehend. If you pardon, we will mend."

And with that, we returned to the magic of the dream within the tent.

I know a bank where the wild thyme blows,
Where oxlips and the nodding violet grows,
Quite over-canopied with luscious woodbine,
With sweet musk-roses and with eglantine:
There sleeps Titania sometime of the night,
Lull'd in these flowers with dances and delight

—WILLIAM SHAKESPEARE,
A Midsummer Night's Dream

CHAPTER 24

THE BOAT RIDE home was as if in suspended animation. I leaned my head against Rahul's arm as he took the boat slowly through the darkened water, like he couldn't bear to go back to camp after our little escape. I breathed it all in—the stars, the sky, the smell of the river flowing beneath us. I felt like I'd shed my skin and been reborn my true self back there among the flowers and fairies. I felt like tonight might be the first night of me finding out just how to be free.

As we got closer to camp, I made a sound of disappointment.

Rahul turned to me. "Everything all right?"

I gave a laugh. "No, I'm just being silly. I don't want this to end. I don't want to go back to Lucy and Lady Middleton and all that . . . artifice. I want to just stay in the amazingness that was tonight."

Without a word, Rahul shut off the boat engine, allowing us to float and bob upon the dark water, the stars our only lights overhead. "Then let's do that," he whispered, pulling me toward him.

To call our kiss an explosion of stars would not be an exaggeration. Because the moment our lips touched, tender and searching in the warm summer night, there was an unexpected flood of bright white light. Not metaphoric light, mind you. Actual, blaringly bright, artificial light.

"What's happening?" I pulled away from Rahul, throwing my hand up to shield my eyes.

"What in the blazes!" Protecting his eyes too, Rahul squinted toward the Norland dock.

I tried to understand what he was looking at, but my eyes hadn't adjusted to the onslaught yet. What was that? Outlines of people? Who were they? Maybe someone else with a boat? Some of the campers enjoying the beautiful night?

I heard a whirring and clicking noise, saw the popping of more lights.

"I don't believe it!" Rahul placed himself between me and the light, blocking it from my eyes, but also blocking me from view of whoever was on the dock. "Eila, I'm so sorry to say this, but I think those people might be here for me."

"Who's here for you?" I had never felt so confused. "What do they want?"

"There he is!" someone shouted. "Rahul Lee—in that boat!"

Finally, from around Rahul's protective back, I could make out what was going on, who had turned on that bright light like a search beacon. It was a group of reporters with cameras, lights, equipment, and everything.

I felt my heart beating wildly now in my chest. The evening had gone from ethereal to hard, surreal, and frightening. "Why are these people chasing you, Rahul? What's this about? Your father? The company?"

That's when one of the reporters shouted it out. "Rahul, how does it feel to be the next principal actor on such a hit show as *Rosewood*?"

"Wait, what did he say?" I grabbed at Rahul's arm, even as he kept standing, stubbornly, before me.

And then the man yelled out again. "Who's the girl, Rahul? Is she a young hopeful trying to get cast in *Rosewood* alongside you?"

"We've got to get out of here, they're filming my every reaction. And I don't want to let them get a shot of you," Rahul muttered, quickly backing the boat out of camera shot. The reporters on the dock were still yelling at us, their cameras unforgiving, but he backed up the boat around a bend of the shoreline with a quiet confidence laced with some serious anger. I, in the meantime, was just sitting there, my head spinning, while Rahul pulled out his own obviously nonconfiscated cell phone to call the camp administration.

"There are camera crews down at the Norland dock, please get rid of them as soon as possible," Rahul said in a voice of calm authority. "No, I have no idea how they found out about me."

They did as he asked. And why wouldn't they? Not only was he the son of a wealthy family, but he was actually the secret actor in our midst. Rahul was one of the stars of season two of the international hit television program *Rosewood*. Who had been lying about it this entire time. Who had been lying to me this entire time. I thought about all his denials—how he pretended he didn't know about there being an actor in our midst, how he'd acted like he didn't have a phone—and felt my hopeful lantern wishes burning to embers.

"Eila?" Rahul tried to get my attention several times as we were waiting for Lady Middleton's staff to clear the dock. "Eila, please, just let me explain."

But I couldn't meet his eyes, couldn't listen to his voice, couldn't feel like anything but a fool. I had thought I was a fairy queen, desired and cared for, but he had made me ridiculous with his lies. He had placed upon my shoulders a donkey's head. And now I felt like the only one who hadn't even been able to see the obvious, ugly thing before my face.

The water sloshing against the side of the unsteady boat felt like a perfect metaphor for our relationship. I sat there in the semi-darkness, my shock slowly being replaced with hurt and righteous anger.

"You told me," I finally managed in a choked voice. "You told me all the magic was just pretend. Since the first time I met you, you've been trying to tell me it's all an illusion, it's all fake. And here I was, going on about how real you were. When all along, you were the biggest pretender of all!"

"No!" Rahul grabbed my hand, but I pulled away. "This isn't fake. Please believe me, this, with you, it's the only real thing I have right now."

I couldn't fully make out his features in the dark, but I could hear the sincerity in his voice. Then I remembered him dancing with Lucy, and how right they'd looked together. Boy, was I fool. "How am I supposed to believe you? I mean, you must be a very good actor, right? To get cast on a show like *Rosewood*?"

"I'm not acting! Eila, I was never acting with you!" Rahul's voice was thick.

"Oh, really?" I shot back, my hurt turning to a slowly growing fury. "Not that time you pretended you hadn't seen the Insta post, or didn't have a cell phone? The time you acted shocked to hear there was an actor in our midst, when the whole time, it was *you*?"

Rahul cleared his throat, so carelessly pulling loose his white cravat that it flew from his hands and into the river. He didn't even notice its loss. "I can understand why you feel hurt . . ."

"You could have told me, you know," I interrupted with a harsh sob. "I would have kept your secret safe."

Rahul was quiet for a moment, as our boat bobbed and swayed upon the dark waters. We could hear the scuffle at the dock between the camp administration and the reporters. Then in a voice so low I almost missed his words, he murmured, "I almost told you so many times."

"But you didn't." How could I have been so stupid to finally let down my guard and open up to someone who was just *acting* this whole time? And I thought Mallika was the naive one.

"I'm so sorry, Eila." Rahul reached out for my hand, but I pulled it back like I'd been stung. "I'm so sorry."

"So what's the story with the camera people? Is that like some kind of publicity stunt?" My voice sounded harsh even to my own ears. I pulled the shawl I was wearing tighter about my shoulders. "Like, all publicity is good publicity or something?"

"No, nothing like that! I have no idea how they found out." Rahul rubbed angrily at his face. "But believe me, I'm going to get to the bottom of it. I didn't like the deception, but I came to Regency Camp only when the producers promised my identity would be secret the whole time."

"Hollywood isn't a normal place." I touched my cheeks, surprised to find them wet. "Maybe they double-crossed you, just like you double-crossed me."

"Eila, please." Rahul was half kneeling at my feet now. "You have to believe me when I tell you that I never meant to lie to you. I wanted to get you away from this place because—"

"Why should I believe you?" My voice was rising with emotion, but I consciously spoke more softly, aware of how well sound travels across water. "I mean, every time I think I can, you do something else that makes it obvious how untrustworthy you really are."

"I understand why you're so angry. I know you have no reason to forgive me for lying to you," Rahul said miserably as a wave made the boat go up and down. "I see that now. You probably don't want anything more to do with me. And believe me, I'd understand if that's the case."

"You're right," I said, kicking myself for being so gullible. For saying yes when I should have been smart and safe and said no. "I don't want anything more to do with you. Ever."

Sources tell this reporter that Regina Rivera-Colón and the team at *Rosewood* have already started casting for season two of their international hit television show. While it is public knowledge that the Rosewood Foundation has created a Hudson Valley Regency Camp at Norwood Manor, to scout for young and unknown talent, what the producers have not wanted to make public is that they dropped, unannounced and incognito, an already cast actor amid the hopefuls attending these camps. A reliable source at the Hudson Valley, NY, location at Norland Manor, who is identifying herself only as "the Heiress of Rosings," tells this reporter that the actor at the Norland Regency Camp is none other than a Rahul Lee, son of international business tycoon James Lee and his socialite wife, Farah Joardar Lee, recently deceased. But who is the mystery girl he was kissing on this illicit midnight boat ride? Is it a hopeful *Rosewood* actress unaware of his identity, or someone in on the secret? Watch this space for more *Rosewood* news as it breaks!

Dearest Aficionados of *Rosewood*:

Please be apprised that certain heiresses contradicting rumors about the secret season two casting are utterly and totally wrong.

(Right back at you, Heiress of Rosings—IF THAT IS YOUR REAL NAME.)

Which is why I, your humble servant, am pleased to inform you that the secret actor in your midst is none other than **Mr. Will Allen,** who is currently attending Norland Manor Regency Camp. He is the principal actor in question, not any other dude named by some informant who clearly doesn't know what she's talking about.

Your real insider and revealer of truths,

The Heir of Allenham

Dearest Aficionados of *Rosewood*:

We, the producers of your favorite program, are appalled at the multiple anonymous sources who claim to have inside knowledge of our casting for season two but are undoubtedly simply seeking their own notoriety.

We categorically deny that any season two principal actor is attending any of the many Regency Camps created by the Rosewood Foundation to not only scout for talent but foster a love of Regency manners, customs, and habits.

Kindly ignore any so-called heirs or heiresses and their bits of scandalous, and false, on-dit.

Yours as ever,

The producers of *Rosewood* season two

CHAPTER 25

LADY MIDDLETON, RED-FACED and furious, called an all-camp meeting the next morning to reiterate the position of the *Rosewood* producers. She was in one of her usual pink dresses, her blue hair looking even more azure today, piled high and decorated with an abundance of roses.

"There is no principal actor among us!" she announced to the assembled campers. By now, everyone had seen the *New York Tattler* story as well as the series of conflicting Insta posts from the administration and the Heir of Allenham. "This is a blatant and patent falsehood!"

As Lady Middleton said this, she pointing her finger skyward for emphasis. Yet despite her denials about there being an incognito actor among us, everyone's head swiveled toward either Will or Rahul. But I noticed that most people were looking toward Will, who, to be honest, better looked the part. Noticing everyone's eyes on him, Will did a little subtle toss of his hair, then cracked his knuckles with a fakely unselfconscious air. I was worried he would take off his shirt and start juggling his biceps up and down or something, but he thankfully didn't. I couldn't help but feel a flash of fury at the preening boy. He'd lied to my sister, and convinced her that he was the actor in question, probably just to get her to like him. The only question was, how was I going to tell her about his betrayal?

As if sensing my concern, Mallika threw me a questioning look. Even if no one else knew who the mystery girl in the boat with Rahul was, my sister knew it was me.

Lady Middleton was going on, "And we condemn these rumormongers, who appear to be right here in our Norland Manor Regency Camp! If we discover that any of you are this Heir of Allenham or so-called Heiress of Rosings, you will be out on your ear, you can believe that! In addition, since none of you are supposed to have your phones or other contact with the outside world, how are you reading these trashy newspapers, hearing from these false online heirs and heiresses anyway?"

No one was willing to answer that.

It went on like that for a few more minutes, Lady Middleton practically frothing at the mouth in her fury. But ultimately, besides some idle threats, there was really nothing else she could do.

Rahul came up to me after the meeting, trying to speak with me, but I quickly fobbed him off. "How can you even try to talk to me?" I hissed.

"Can we speak later, then?" he asked, his eyes soft.

"I don't want to talk to you anywhere, anytime." I walked quickly in the other direction. I should hate Rahul, I knew, and part of me did. Just not all of me.

That's when I saw her. The bane of my existence. Lucy. I

squared my jaw and headed straight toward her. It was time to stop reacting to the mean girl and go on the offensive.

Lucy stopped short when she found me blocking her path. The girl tugged at her long gloves and raised her eyebrows at me. But before she had a chance to say anything, I jumped in. "Did you enjoy that stunt you pulled last night?"

"What are you talking about, you pathetic little social climber?" Lucy's lip curled in derision.

"At the dock last night, I'm sure you're the one who called the reporters?" I felt like ripping her ridiculous ringleted curls from her head. "After your discover-the-cell-phone plan failed, I'm sure you were psyched to call the press!"

But that's when I realized my mistake. Because Lucy's amber eyes lit up with this new information. Information she clearly hadn't known until I foolishly revealed it.

"So it was you with Rahul in the boat?" She shook her head like she was a schoolteacher going *tsk, tsk*. "Of course it was. I should have guessed."

I felt like I was losing ground. "Don't even pretend you didn't know that, 'Heiress of Rosings'!"

"Could you be any more ridiculous, you silly, naive, boring girl?" Lucy pretend-yawned in my face. "How do you not understand how this game works? I'm not the blasted Heiress of Rosings! I don't need to be, if only because I'm an heiress in my own right, but more importantly because revealing such information doesn't exactly serve me!"

"What are you talking about?" I felt like the room was

spinning with my confusion. I was sure that it had been Lucy who had called the reporters to the dock last night. But if not her, who?

"Why don't you use that little plebian brain of yours and figure out who might benefit from newspaper coverage like that? Not me, that's for sure!" Lucy sneered, tossing her hair over her slim shoulder. "Why would I benefit from images of someone who is clearly not me being seen with Rahul?"

"What are you saying?" I knew I should walk away from this conversation but didn't seem to be able to. My skin was tingling with a realization that I didn't want to acknowledge.

"Ever hear the expression 'all publicity is good publicity'?" Lucy gave me a near-feline smile. "How else would those reporters know when you were due back to the dock?"

I felt my insides freeze, remembering how I had accused Rahul of the same thing last night. But no, I'd been angry then. I'd been reaching at straws. And yet, here Lucy was, getting to the exact same conclusion.

"Rahul told me it wasn't him who called the reporters. I can't believe . . ." I trailed off, not sure how to finish my sentence.

"He's able to lie effectively to one so emotionally discerning and attuned to the universe as you?" Lucy rolled her eyes. "Rahul is a very good actor, you know. That is precisely why he was cast in *Rosewood*."

I felt myself deflating, crawling back into my brittle emotional shell. I didn't want to believe Lucy, but after everything, I couldn't help but do so. "You've known about him being cast this entire time?"

"You poor, pathetic little thing." Lucy patted my arm in mock sympathy. "You're really way out of your league, you know."

And with that, she swept away, leaving me wallowing in the truth bombs she'd just dropped.

"Are you all right? I saw Lucy talking to you." Rahul was at my elbow, a look of undoubtedly false concern on his face.

I was suddenly aware of the depth of our differences. Rahul was the son of a wealthy businessperson who'd been brought up all over the world. I was an ordinary, upper-middle-class girl from the northern Jersey burbs. He was handsome and charming; I was studious and serious. He was an about-to-be-famous actor, and I was a hopeless wannabe who couldn't tell the difference between the glow of artificial stage lights and the light of the sun.

I felt the eyes of my fellow campers on me, the curious stares of the staff, the invisible attention of all those cameras, greedy for juicy drama. "I changed my mind, actually. Let's go outside. I need to talk to you," I choked out.

All the world's a stage and all the men and women merely players, Shakespeare had written. I'd never felt the truth of those lines until now, as I made a great gesture of taking Rahul's arm and letting him escort me out of the building. It was all an artifice. It was all fake. It was all a lie. And that was the only truth I could hang on to.

Rahul's face looked hopeful as we walked outside and down the broad steps of Norland Manor, but then fell again as I dropped his arm as if it was a burning coal.

"Don't read too much into my walking out with you; I didn't

want anyone to hear what I had to say," I snapped almost as soon as we were outside.

"I want to talk, to explain," said Rahul. "I know you have every right to be angry at me after everything that happened last night."

We were standing before the manor on an open expanse of grassy lawn. Just in case we were overheard, I kept walking farther, all the way out to the edge of the grass overlooking the water, with Rahul following me. Finally, I turned to him. I wasn't going to confront him about the reporters. I'd already been lied to once and couldn't stomach being lied to again about it.

Instead, I kept my facial expression neutral as I asked the only question that mattered. "So you really are the actor that's been cast in season two?"

Rahul looked at his boots, the breeze from the river ruffling his hair. "I told you how I loved the summer Shakespeare academy. Well, I've always wanted to act. Be Kenneth Branagh, Denzel Washington, Riz Ahmed, something like that. But I also know that it's not such an easy road for actor of color. When the chance came to be cast as Lord Rosewood's detective assistant on *Rosewood*, I couldn't help but jump at it."

His words sounded far too familiar, like what I'd told Mallika those many months ago. But the fact remained, I couldn't forgive him for his many betrayals.

"Well, then, it's a good thing I was faking it too," I declared firmly.

Rahul's head snapped up, his eyes round with hurt. "What do you mean?"

As I had done with Lucy, I was going to follow the policy of the best defense being offense. It was the only way to regain some of the dignity I'd lost. Lucy was right, I'd been a pathetic, naive fool, gullible and eager to believe anything a cute guy told me. I'd been an idiot to listen to Mallika and Rahul, be more vulnerable and let my guard down. But that was ending today.

"You wanted to be a Shakespearean actor? Well, me too!" I tried to sound airy and carefree. "I told you it was all for Mallika, but this Regency Camp was a chance I couldn't give up on either. A chance to act. At whatever cost."

"What are you saying?" Rahul looked confused, his dark eyes wide.

I rushed on, looking out over the cliffs to the Hudson, then back to the manor, anywhere but directly at him. "I've been acting this whole time. You didn't think I actually liked you?"

"Eila, I know your pride is hurt, but . . ." Rahul's voice sounded rough and scratchy.

"How dare you!" I held up my hand, stopping his words. "How dare you assume you know the first thing about me because you lent me some books that your rich daddy bought you?"

Rahul's eyes flamed and his face flushed. "Is that what you think of me?"

"Have you showed me any reason to think otherwise?" I was on a roll now, having found a verbal spear with which to poke him. I wanted him to hurt as much as he'd hurt me. There was a slight breeze coming up over the river, but it didn't cool me down. All I could feel was the beating heat of the sun overhead, the flames of the fury within me. "I mean, you're such a cliché! What with the single room, the fancy extra-specially tailored clothes you can't even bother to fold right, the expensive boat you just borrowed conveniently to impress me? And named *Magic* of all things—as if all the magic isn't false and idle dreams!"

"But what we had between us was real!" Rahul reached out, trying to take hold of my hand. "That magic was real!"

I brushed him off. My words were rolling out of my mouth now as if on their own power. "Was it, though? We were both faking it, right? Acting is your job, isn't it? You're not here as a camper, you're on the clock! As for me, I might not have known you were the already cast actor, but I knew that all the sparks between us would draw the casting crew's attention."

"You're not that calculating!" Rahul protested, again trying to reach out and touch my cheek.

"Aren't I?" I made a half-scoffing, half-choking sound, pushing away from him. "They do call it acting for a reason!"

I saw something harden and shift in Rahul's expression, and felt my own heart sink. "So where does that leave us?" he said finally, his voice low.

"Us?" I scoffed, all my pain and anger and hurt making my words sharp as a sword. "There is no us." And then I walked away from him, not looking back.

A Regency Etiquette Lesson

In Regency times, to "cut" someone was to socially snub them. The worst, the "cut direct," was to stare someone you knew in the face and then pretend not to know them. The "cut indirect" was to look away and pretend not to know someone. The "cut sublime" was to occupy yourself admiring the top of a building or a cloud in the sky until the person had passed, while the "cut infernal" was to bend down to adjust your boots until the person had gone by.

CHAPTER 26

AFTER LUNCH, I threw all of Rahul's Jane Austen books into a bag with the full intention of dumping them into the lake. I wanted nothing more to do with him, or his over-the-top presents.

Unfortunately, by the time I made my way down to the empty lake and got into one of the metal rowboats, I started to lose my nerve. I remembered Baba, who had taken Mallika and me out in a similar boat on this very lake so many years ago. I thought of how much he loved books, how he would read to us every night before bed, doing all the funny voices. He loved stories so much, he taught me to love them too. I took out one of the beautifully bound Jane Austen volumes and ran my finger over the spine. The thought of damaging it, allowing it to sink, its gilt-edged pages waterlogged and smearing, was enough to turn my stomach. I might hate Rahul, but I just couldn't do that.

Which was why I found myself sunbathing as I read another Austen novel in a floating boat on the lake. I was wearing a completely impractical navy-and-white-striped Regency dress and tiny boots, but felt, for the first time in a full day, actually like myself. It was amazing to be alone, away from the lies and make-believe of Regency Camp. But I hadn't been out there all of fifteen minutes before I heard another boat being taken out of the boathouse, and oars slapping through the water toward me.

At first, I thought I might make a run for it, but then I saw who was in the boat: Will and Mallika. She was wearing a beautiful yellow dress and carrying a matching parasol over her shoulder while Will rowed in his shirtsleeves and breeches. They made a stunning couple, that was for sure. But there was no way I would ever forgive Will for lying to my sister in the same way that Rahul had lied to me.

"What is going on, Didi? Why are you out here?" my sister called from her boat. Her beautiful brows drew together over her forehead. She'd seen me come in the night before, exhausted and upset, but we still hadn't really talked.

"I'm not going to throw myself in and make a dramatic fuss, if that's what you mean," I said, glaring at Will.

"That's not fair." Mallika twirled her parasol on her shoulder as Will put down his oars.

"If you did fall in, I'd definitely jump in after you!" Will declared with a grin. His hair was attractively mussed, and despite his size, there was something about him that gave the air of an impish toddler.

"I really wouldn't want you to bother!" I snapped at him.

Will looked confused, his grin failing. He scratched his thick hair, staring at me as if trying to decipher an encrypted code on my face.

"Rahul told me all about your Shakespeare date last night," my sister said. "I showed him your favorite rani color dress and he kept asking me if I thought you'd be upset, since we used to go to Shakespeare plays with Baba before he passed away. I mean, Rahul really went to a lot of trouble to make sure you'd enjoy it. And even if he hadn't told me, I would have known it was you in that newspaper picture!"

"Sounds like a nice time," Will added, his voice unsure. "Dude went to a lot of trouble."

"You realize that women don't owe men anything based on how much trouble they go to or how much money they fork out on a date or whatever, right?" I said in a heated voice. Then I couldn't help but add, "Besides, all that trouble he went to was just to make sure we got photographed."

"What do you mean?" Mallika frowned at my words.

I thought again about just rowing away from the two. I didn't have the energy for this conversation. I shielded my eyes against the sun with my book as I asked, "Why are you here, Mal? Why do you care? I thought you were mad at me because I hung on to my cell phone."

"I was, yeah, but I'm not going to abandon you in the middle of this . . ." Mallika waved her hands over the landscape of the lake. ". . . crisis."

"The only crisis I'm having is that I almost fell for an actor who is, unsurprisingly, a publicity hog." I looked over at Will critically. "A guy who's the real actor for season two." I looked back at my sister. "You do realize Will's been lying to you, right?"

For a minute, Will looked defensive. "There could be two of us already cast actors here at Regency Camp."

I felt myself losing control of my temper. I couldn't stand to see Mallika lied to just as I had been. "Enough, Will! If you really like her, Mallika deserves to know the truth! You're not the actor who's been cast for season two! You never have been! It's always been Rahul!"

There was a few minutes of silence while our boats kind of bopped into each other as an invisible ripple crossed the lake. Mallika's face twisted into that look she always got when she was little and trying not to spill a big secret. "Should we tell her?" she finally asked Will.

Will didn't seem to be able to meet my sister's eyes, but instead studied what appeared to be a very fascinating bird on the shore.

I squinted against the too-bright sun. "What do you need to tell me, Mal?"

"Well, you're wrong about Will. He hasn't been lying to me at all." Mallika cleared her throat a couple of times. "You see, Will and I might have met before that day when I fell in the lake."

"That first day, outside the dressing tents," Will admitted, shooting my sister an appreciative grin.

"When you disappeared for a while, remember?" Mallika reminded me.

Of course I did remember. The ballroom, the bobby pin bouquet, the magic, the Shakespeare. That was the first time I met Rahul, and danced in his arms.

"So we met, and your brilliant sister here came up with the

idea to let people believe I was the actor cast in *Rosewood* season two," Will said, reaching out to adjust Mallika's parasol for her.

"Wait, *what?*" I practically shouted.

Mallika looked around the empty lake in alarm. I'd startled a family of squawking ducks and possibly a bullfrog who jumped with a large splash into the lake, but luckily there were few others to overhear my exclamation.

"There had been rumors already circulating all over Instagram for weeks about it, that the *Rosewood* producers might try to sneak some unknown season two actors in among us," Mallika said, her eyes sparkling. "So I just figured, why not set up the Heir of Allenham account and go for it? Frame the situation to my own advantage? All I needed was an actual actor."

Will pointed proudly at his chest. "That's where I came in."

"So you two decided to fake this whole thing?" I felt like my entire life was becoming revealed as a series of lies. But I did feel a weight of relief lifted from my chest at the thought that Will hadn't been deceiving my sister, after all. I licked my lips, carefully clarifying, "So, Will, you decided to pretend to be the principal actor and, Mal, you decided to pretend to be in love with him?"

"Something like that," my sister agreed, smiling brightly from beneath her parasol.

"It was all her idea." Will beamed at Mallika. "She's brilliant."

"And devious!" I couldn't believe what I was hearing. My sister—not a naive and sweet innocent, but a mastermind criminal! "So you wrote those Heir of Allenham posts, Mal?"

"Just the first one," Mallika admitted.

Will sheepishly flexed and unflexed his impressive biceps.

"That last one was me kinda going rogue. I should have let Mallika proofread it before I posted it."

"It's okay." Mallika patted his arm like a mother hen. "You were trying to show initiative."

I nodded. That made sense. It also explained the use of the word *dude* and other not-Regency-appropriate language in that latest post.

"So, are you going to blow the lid on us, Didi?" Mallika's brows were furrowed and face pinched with worry, but she still looked like something out of a painting as she twirled her parasol over her shoulder. "I wouldn't blame you if you did."

I studied my sister and Will, who, for all his over-the-top performativity, was actually kind of endearing. So he hadn't been lying to my sister at all, just following her instructions on how to lie to everyone else! Will might look like Gaston from *Beauty and the Beast*, but the truth was, he was more like the gentle Beast to my sister's surprisingly clever Belle.

"Of course I'm not going to blow the lid on you," I finally said, rubbing at my neck. It really was hot out here. "I was just worried that Will was lying to you!"

Mallika laughed in relief. "I can see that. But he wasn't!"

"I really shouldn't have underestimated you, sis!" I ran my hand over the surface of the water and splashed some on my neck. "But, okay, fine! I mean, let people be confused, keep believing whatever they want to believe. We're only here for two weeks anyway, right? And if in the time we have left, either of you a chance to catch the attention of the *Rosewood* producers, who am I to stop you?"

"Oh, thank you, Didi!" Mallika gushed. She squeezed Will's broad arm. "I told you she wouldn't tell anyone if we let her in on the secret."

And of course my sister was 100 percent correct. No matter how much we were disagreeing, or even fighting, I'd never side with anyone but her. She was my family. She was my best friend. She was my everything. And I'd never turn my back on her.

"You were right, Mals!" Will gave my sister a high five that rocked their boat a little from its force. "Eila's a good egg."

I wasn't sure how I felt about that descriptor, but didn't say anything.

"So . . ." Mallika gave me a speculative look from the rocking boat. "What's going on with you and Rahul?"

I gritted my teeth, turning my gaze away from my sister's inquiring eyes. "There is no me and Rahul."

"Say what?" Will scratched his head again. "But you two have been looking pretty tight." He turned to my sister for confirmation. "Haven't they been looking pretty tight?"

My sister pursed her lips, studying me. An unreadable expression crossed her face, and finally, she let out a sigh. "You're mad at him for not telling you he was the principal actor. You're mad at him for lying to you. Which is why you were so furious when you thought Will might be doing the same thing to me."

"Obviously," I agreed. "But I'm also mad at him for calling those reporters last night. I mean, it must have been him. There's no one else who could have done it!"

My sister looked uncomfortable. "Are you sure it was him? Why would he do that?"

"Haven't you ever heard the expression 'all publicity is good publicity'?" I asked bitterly.

Mallika was quiet for a moment, twirling her parasol as if it was helping her think. Finally, she said, "Well, even if there's nothing between you and Rahul anymore, you've got to make sure it seems like there still is."

"And why in the Regency world would I do that?" I tried not to shout again, but it was very hard.

Regency Romance Trope

FAKE DATING: A popular story line in which
two characters pretend to be in a relationship, and
therefore get increasingly thrown together, able to
explore their hitherto-hidden feelings for each other.

CHAPTER 27

WHY SHOULD YOU fake date Rahul?" Mallika repeated. "Because if you don't keep up romancing Rahul, someone else will. Like that awful Lucy." My sister's rosebuds lips were firm as she said this, and I knew she was right. "I don't think I could stand to see her getting cast opposite Rahul in season two of *Rosewood, and* gloating as she gets together with your man."

"Not my man," I interjected in a singsong tone. "Anyway, I thought you were the one who wanted to be cast?"

"I wanted to have fun and dress up and do a walk-on role," confessed Mallika. "Or maybe be a beautiful murder victim."

"Same." Will high-fived her again. "I mean, I'm a jock in school, not really a drama nerd."

"Hey!" I protested. "Nothing wrong with drama nerds."

"No offense!" Will said in such an endearing way, I couldn't be offended.

"Neither of us is interested in real acting," said Mallika with a funny twist of her mouth. "In fact, Annie's shown me how I'm much more into costuming. She's been showing me how to design properly, and I've even gone down to her aunt's shop and done some sewing. It's actually been pretty awesome."

"You two are always talking about history and clothes and stuff," observed Will.

"Also gender and its relationship to costuming," said Mallika.

"And you do seem to really dig each other's company," Will added with a smile.

"Okay, okay, I get it. Costuming is important." I ran my fingers over the water's surface, letting the cool liquid run over my palm. "So what is it you're both suggesting I do?"

"We're suggesting you pretend date Rahul to get back at him." Mallika twirled her parasol behind her head. "And maybe get something cool out of it besides, like a role on *Rosewood*!"

"I am all about a fake-dating trope," said Will matter-of-factly. "After 'there's only one bed,' it's the best trope there is."

"What's 'there's only one bed'?" asked Mallika, her eyes round.

"Just what it sounds like." Will jiggled his eyebrows. "There's only one bed and the people in the movie or story have to share it."

"Oh!" Mallika's eyes got rounder, but she smiled.

Will cleared his voice, fidgeting uncomfortably on his seat in the boat. "It's very hot out here, isn't it?"

I thought about my sister's suggestion. Rahul had once suggested I fake date him, so he could shake off Lucy. I'd turned him down then. But now I'd realized he was a lying rake of the worst kind. He had lied to me about who he was. I didn't know if he had ever felt anything for me, but there was no way, under pain of torture, that I would ever admit I had felt anything genuine for him. So what better way to rub that into his face than to convince him to be my fake boyfriend?

"Eila, you should come up with a song—like we did—and sing it at the showcase!" Will suggested ebulliently. "Put your names together, like we did. 'Reila' or maybe 'Eilahul'!"

"Maybe." Mallika's eyes were sparkling and her parasol twirling faster than ever. "But our rendition of 'Wallika' was really a phenomenon unto itself. I'm not sure anyone could replicate it!"

"For sure," I muttered under my breath.

"Just a suggestion," said Will in a small voice.

"And a really good one that I appreciate!" I enthused, making the giant boy smile again. "But Mal's right, I'm just not as good of a songwriter as you are. I don't think I could pull off a ballad called . . . um . . . 'Eilahul'!"

Mallika and I exchanged an amused look.

"So no song, but you've got to convince Rahul to pretend to be your fake boyfriend!" Mallika mused.

"How?" I squinted against the unforgiving sun. My head was starting to pound and I was wishing I'd also brought a parasol. Or an umbrella. Or a new head.

"With your sister and me pretending to buy it, the *Rosewood* people will definitely believe it." Will beamed at me.

"And then Eila gets to salvage the situation to her advantage," added Mallika with a nodding smile. "Come on, Didi, you've got to love a little self-serving feminist subterfuge. I know you're a fan of playing the patriarchy against itself."

She definitely wasn't wrong on that score.

"But won't Rahul's feelings be hurt?" Will softly stroked his chin.

My sister whirled on him, practically upsetting their boat. "Doesn't he deserve to have his feelings hurt a little? I mean, if he lied to my sister and was leading her on?"

"No, you're right, Mals." Will pumped his fist in the air again. "Eila, girl, you gotta break his heart. And get that role you deserve!"

Almost as soon as Will said this, we heard yet another boat sloshing its oars on its way toward us. I looked up to see John, Annie, Penny, and Brandon in a third boat. Annie and Penny were sitting in pretty pastel floral dresses, each with matching parasols over their shoulder, while the two boys—who'd all abandoned their Regency jackets as Will had—rowed them over. I grimaced at how we'd all gotten so used to the restrictive, old-fashioned gender roles in such a short time.

"What's going on with Eila? Is she jumping into the lake so she can be rescued?" called Sir John. His light brown cheeks were flushed from the exercise.

"I am not jumping into the lake!" I practically shouted. I looked with jealousy at everyone's parasols. Why hadn't I brought one? It was boiling out here in this tin tub under the sun, and I was starting to sweat like a piglet. It was really not cute.

"If you were to fall, however, I would happily and verily rescue you, my lady!" declared Will. The handsome boy looked down at the water, as if he was contemplating jumping in just for good measure. Now that the others were here, he'd obviously gone back into performance mode.

229

"No need to rip off your shirt just yet, lover boy!" said Annie dryly. "No one seems to be falling into the lake!"

"Besides which, women don't need rescuing, you know," I added. "We are perfectly capable of rescuing ourselves."

"Right on!" Annie grinned at me.

My sister clearly felt differently. As all three boats kind of bumped one another now, like a giant game of bumper cars, Mallika turned dramatically to Will, hamming it up to impress the others. "But it was very noble when you rescued me! I am forever grateful!"

"Oh, my lady, it is I who am grateful that you gave me such an opportunity!" Will practically capsized the boat again in his attempt to kiss Mallika's arm.

"Watch it!" Brandon cautioned as water sloshed into their boat.

"Or we'll all be falling into the lake with no one left to rescue us!" added Penny with a laugh. She held out her parasol like a high-wire acrobat seeking balance.

"It's not actually that deep, you know, the water," muttered Annie.

"All right, so what were we talking about?" asked Sir John.

"How much Eila and Rahul are in love!" announced my sister in a loud voice. "You all must know that was her in the *New York Tattler* picture!"

"I knew I recognized that dress!" Annie snapped her fingers. "I'd know my own seam work anywhere!"

"So romantic!" squealed Penny. She looked at Brandon and let out a dramatic sigh.

"Very romantic!" Brandon put down his oar to hold the small redhead's hand.

"Mallika!" I admonished, feeling more than a little overwhelmed at this bizarre three-boat interchange on the water.

"What? They would have found out anyway," Mallika protested with a grin and a wink.

"They would have found out . . . from you!" I splayed my hands in irritation.

"Well, *obviously*," agreed my sister with a grin. "So now they've found out. From me."

I pinched the bridge of my nose. I really was getting a terrible headache. And I wasn't sure it was just the sun to blame. "There is nothing going on—" I began.

But Will interrupted me. "Don't be shy, Eils! We know you're in love!"

I rolled my eyes at him but stayed quiet when Mallika shot me a look of warning. I guess the first part of fake dating Rahul was getting everyone else to believe I was too. Starting with our friends.

"So are you going to elaborate on that kissing picture?" asked Annie with a grin.

I grunted, but said nothing.

"But," said Penny, biting her lip a little, "is the Heiress of Rosings right? I mean, is Rahul the incognito actor after all?"

We all turned to look at Will, who had the grace to look shamefaced. Before he could say anything, however, Brandon jumped in, saying in a ridiculously eager voice, "Why can't there be two actors in our midst? I mean, what if the Heir of Allenham and the Heiress of Rosings are both right?"

I exchanged a look with Mallika, who gave a tiny, almost imperceptible shrug. If we could get people to believe that, it might be the answer to everything. Maybe Will, Mallika, and I could all land roles on *Rosewood*, while I'd still get to enact some serious revenge on Rahul.

"I honestly don't know if Rahul is the actor." I dragged my hand through the water again and spread it over my forehead and neck. Man, it was hot out here.

John nodded from over on his boat. "That Rahul guy is nice enough, but he seems kind of quiet, uptight. Not the Regina Rivera-Colón type."

I felt like roaring in annoyance, correcting John's assumptions, but of course didn't.

"Really?" Annie scrunched up her face as if it was helping her put the pieces of a puzzle together. "When I heard about that *Tattler* story, it all kind of made sense to me. I mean, he did come early to camp, hang around with us staff . . ."

I thought about how Rahul had repeated that nose-touching gesture of Annie's, how he'd known things he shouldn't have, and was amazed it had taken me this long to realize the truth.

"Well, I'm glad it's you that's spending time with him, and not that Lucy," said Will with a suggestive eyebrow waggle, trying to be subtle but being anything but.

"That Lucy girl is the absolute worst!" My sister groaned dramatically. "I know you said she had it out for me, but she's been hating on you since day one."

"Me?" I started. Mallika's words, and my new knowledge about Rahul's identity, made me reconsider all of Lucy's actions. Had she been talking about getting rid of not Mallika but *me* that day to Lady Middleton? Well, if it was Rahul and not Will who was the real *Rosewood* actor she wanted to get close to, she must have been! This new reality really was making everything I thought I knew seem upside down and backward, like through a looking glass.

"You don't see the way that girl looks at you." Annie pointed her parasol at me now in emphasis. "Like she'd love to push you into the Hudson River and then run off into the sunset with Rahul."

"She seems smitten," agreed Brandon.

"And what's worse, the first day, Lucy made me hold her croquet mallet like I was some kind of . . ." Penny pursed her lips, searching for the right word. ". . . croquet mallet holder!"

We all looked over at Penny and laughed.

"Turns out Lucy's and Rahul's families know each other, are in business or something," I told my motley crew of friends. "So whether or not she's the Heiress of Rosings, she really is a real-life heiress."

"All the best evil villains are." John had pulled out what looked like a bottle of lemonade and was taking luxurious sips. I felt my parched throat tighten in thirst.

"You are very silly, you know that, John?" said Will, grinning.

John grinned back, and I was struck by the chemistry between the boys. I studied my sister's complacent face, and remembered how I'd first thought she might have a crush on Annie. Huh. Will had said fake dating was one of his favorite tropes. I wondered if he and Mallika were speaking from experience.

Then John dramatically stood up in his boat and began serenading us with a ringing rendition of "Wallika." Only he'd forgotten the little fact that he was on a floating boat on a lake, and promptly overturned the boat with him, Annie, Penny, and Brandon in it. All of them went straight into the lake.

"Help!" a very bedraggled Penny cried. She was hanging on to the side of the upside-down boat, clearly in no actual danger, but all the same, Brandon scooped her up.

"I've got you, my lady!" Brandon announced. Penny sighed contentedly in his arms, despite the fact that he was holding her a little lopsidedly and looked like he was about to drop her into the water again.

"Help!" John cried, his hair having gotten all tangled over his face.

"I'll save you!" cried Will dramatically, promptly capsizing his and Mallika's boat in his attempts to reach John.

Then they were all in the lake, laughing and joking, splashing one another with water. And it really was so very hot that afternoon. I don't think anyone can blame me for accidentally leaning too far over the side and landing myself in the water as well.

The summer lake was cool and lovely, and the friendship was lovelier. Besides, I knew now how to get back at Rahul for all his lies, and it felt delicious to have a plan.

- FROM -

The Young Lady's Book:
A Manual of Elegant Recreations, Exercises, and Pursuits (1829)

ON ARCHERY: When all the party have shot at one target, they walk up to it, gather their arrows, and shoot back to the one they came from, to which they again return when their arrows are expended . . . so that, not merely the arm, but the whole frame, enjoys the benefit of salutary exercise in the open air, while the mind is interested, and the spirits elevated, by the sport. The attitude of an accomplished female archer . . . at the moment of bending the bow, is particularly graceful; all the actions and positions tend at once to produce a proper degree of strength in the limbs, and to impart a general elegance to the deportment.

CHAPTER 28

Aᴀ ꜰᴛᴇʀ ᴡᴇ ᴀʟʟ dried off and changed, my sister and I spent a night of planning together. So when I approached Rahul the next morning at archery practice, I had a plan in mind. It seemed the perfect place to propose my little scheme to him, since we were learning to launch deadly sharp arrows, hitting them squarely at a target. A pretty on-the-nose metaphor, I thought.

The first thing I did was march right up to Rahul, across the long line of other archers. I did it without looking around, but I could feel everyone's eyes on me. But I had no reason to hide. In fact, to do so would be antithetical to my plan. As I passed Lucy, John, Brandon, and Penny played defense, preventing her from getting to me. They cornered her in such a way, much to her frustration, that there was no way for her to move closer to Rahul and me without making a huge scene.

"Gold digger," she hissed as I passed.

I ignored her, my eyes locked on my target. I walked up to Rahul in my forest-green archery dress, feeling and looking every bit the huntress. He gave me a surprised if guarded look, but waited for me to speak first.

"I have a proposal for you." I nocked my arrow back in the bow the way that Sir Reginald, the archery instructor, had just shown us. We were lined up and spaced out along the great lawn of Norland, overlooking the river, each with a target bull's-eye out a number of feet before us. Because of my friends blocking Lucy, I was in the spot next to Rahul.

He turned toward me, his face hopeful. "Oh? What is it?" Rahul's arrow was nocked as well, but he hadn't seemed like he needed to pay too much attention to the lesson to know how to wield his weapon.

"You once asked me to fake date you, and I refused. Well, I've changed my mind." After a moment of trying to eye my target, I let my arrow go. It hit, but at the outermost corner of the wide straw bull's-eye, only to kind of hang there limply. Gah. Not my strongest performance.

"You want us to fake date? Now?" reiterated Rahul. "Why in the world would you want to do that?" He let his arrow go then, hitting in the second circle near the center. "For that matter, why would I?"

I seethed a little, not sure why his accuracy was so annoying to me. "Because after lying to me and making me into a damn fool . . ." Rahul winced at my words. I barreled on. "You owe me the chance to fulfill my dreams and get cast on *Rosewood*." I picked up another arrow, nocking it. "It's the very least you can do after being such a scoundrel."

"And how do you figure that?" Rahul's voice was tight as he

too picked up another arrow from the quiver placed between us. "That I'm a scoundrel?"

People were watching us now, pretending not to as they practiced shooting their own arrows up and down the line. I edged closer to Rahul.

I lowered my voice, lacing it with sharp edges and spikes. "You didn't tell me you were the actor among us, you pretended not to know anything about those Insta posts, you gaslit me about my sister, telling me how I needed to let her grow up and smell the roses myself. You fake romanced me, piling it on thick—what— just to get back at Lucy, or your father for forcing you to date her?"

"That's not true, and not fair," Rahul spat out. "Lucy and my father have nothing to do with it. He wanted me to date her, romance her, bring her to the notice of the *Rosewood* producers so that her mom would be more generous during the upcoming merger. And I thought I could do it at first, but I couldn't."

"So you're telling me what you felt for me was real?" I asked carefully, trying not to betray myself.

"What I felt for you was always real." Rahul agreed immediately. "Even if you were faking it."

The hurt in his voice hit me hard, like my chest was a target and his pain an arrow. But I couldn't worry about that now. I had a plan to follow. Plus, there was no way he was going to catch me off guard again, assuming that which was glittering to be gold. In Hollywood, nothing that glittered was gold; it was all artifice. I'd learned that now, the hard way.

"Well, good, then, I'm glad you genuinely liked me; it'll be easy for you to tap back into those feelings and bring me to the attention of the producers." I let go another arrow toward the target. This one went even worse than the previous, kind of bouncing harmlessly off the bull's-eye and falling onto the grass.

"Try not to kill anyone, my lady!" called Will good-naturedly from a couple of bull's-eyes down.

"I'm not making any promises." I fobbed him off with a smiling wave.

"Why do you want to do this?" Rahul was asking in a lower voice. "After everything that's happened?"

I turned back to him, all business. "You said it yourself: It's really hard for brown actors to break into the business. So you're going to help me take a shot at it, and get cast."

"Why do you even want to be on *Rosewood*?" Rahul sounded genuinely confused. "I thought all this Hollywood stuff wasn't for you?"

I thought of what would happen if I just faded away, going into the West like Galadriel at the end of the time of the elves. As soon as I backed off, in would saunter Lucy, winding her spindly Sauron arms through Rahul's, parading a sickly-sweet relationship around for the casting directors. The idea made me sick. I couldn't bear it.

"If I don't take advantage of the situation, then someone else will," I said shortly.

Rahul said nothing for a few moments, but nocked and shot one arrow, then another. The first one hit near the bull's-eye, the second right on it. He answered through clenched teeth. "Then by all means, you should take full advantage of the situation. For what am I but a situation to be taken advantage of?"

I wanted desperately to yell out that he was misinterpreting me; that wasn't what I meant. But I couldn't. More importantly,

I wouldn't. He was hurt at the thought of being taken advantage of? Well, good, he deserved to be hurt. Because so was I.

"We're going to build up our relationship, make a serious show of it until the culminating point of the final ball, when Regina Rivera-Colón and all her team will be back here for their final look at all of us," I told him. "You're going to fawn over me and say sweet nothings loudly and publicly at every chance."

"Oh really?" Rahul snapped. "Why don't we just kiss at every public opportunity?"

This made me pause for a moment, fiddling with my third arrow. But as I nocked it, I steeled myself. This was no moment to be missish or mealymouthed. "Yes," I finally agreed, loosing my arrow toward its target, "that's probably a good idea."

"Really?" Rahul let an arrow fly, but strangely enough, it went wildly wide of center. I guess the thought of kissing me was doing something to his aim. The thought filled me with not a little bit of satisfaction.

"Yes, really." I let my arrow fly as well, this time hitting decently close to the bull's-eye. I gave a little fist pump of delight, much to the chagrin of a passing helper.

"Miss, I'm afraid to say that Regency ladies did not fist-pump in the air," said the footman in a monotone.

"Terribly sorry," I called to him. "Won't happen again! I'll make sure to remain voiceless and agency-less, happy to have my life, voice, and future circumscribed by others."

The man gave me an odd look, then nodded and moved on to help other campers.

"Well, then, maybe we should start now," said Rahul.

240

"Now?" I asked, a little bit startled. "What do you mean?"

"You should kiss me now, in front of all these people." Rahul turned his body toward me, his eyes dark with a hidden emotion as he closed the distance between us. "That is your plan, after all."

I squirmed, fiddling with my bow and arrow. I tried to keep my gaze from his lips, but wasn't too successful. "No one's watching us and there aren't any casting directors here," I hissed uncomfortably. "What would be the point of kissing you out here if there was no one to see?"

"All these gentlemen and ladies of the ton out here would see, and probably make immediate Insta posts about it." Rahul indicated the rows of campers and staff with a casually held arrow. "And as you said, you've been faking it this whole time for their benefit anyway."

"I just don't want to waste any extraneous kissing energy for substandard returns." I edged closer to him as if pulled toward him by a magnet.

"You sure there? Sure you're not just scared to do it?" Rahul taunted, raising an eyebrow.

"You don't scare me." My fury and frustration coiled out of me as I leaned even closer.

"Are you positive about that?" Rahul stepped so close, we were right up against each other now.

I knew we must be drawing other people's attention. But I had no energy for anyone but him in that moment. Him and my own, rabbit-fast beating heart. I licked my suddenly dry lips, looking up at Rahul's face. His eyes were dark and unreadable, looking down at me. He, like all the guys, was just in his shirtsleeves and cravat, since it was impossible to shoot an arrow with those tight coats on. And I must say I appreciated the view of his shoulders and arms through the thinner material of his Regency-era shirt. I made a mental note to thank Annie and her team for that one. There was a wave of hair kind of hanging down over his forehead in a sexy way, and it was all I could do not to fix it for him. I saw him gazing at my lips, even as I gazed at his, feeling unsure and angry and off balance.

"You know," I said, my voice almost cracking, "Artemis the huntress had the right idea, forsaking the company of men."

Rahul raised an eyebrow in the direction of my target, and my hardly perfect markswomanship. "Artemis, huh?"

That, for some reason, made me see red. "Don't even insult my bow and arrow skills! Not all of us had the money for riding instruction and comportment classes and archery lessons."

Rahul was silent for a moment, as if taking in this accusation. Then he took in a big breath and let it out in a gust. "You seem to be doing perfectly fine aiming your barbs at me without any archery lessons."

"It's because you're such a big, annoying, giant target," I snapped. And then, for unknown reasons, I felt my face twitch in laughter.

"You're laughing." Rahul's face slowly split into a smile.

"I'm not!" I protested. "And if I was, it's just at the thought of putting you back in your rightful place!"

"What place is that?" said Rahul in far too suggestive a way. "That you're putting me back into?"

"You're intolerable, you know that?" I muttered through gritted teeth.

"Careful," Rahul leaned on his bow, the picture of nonchalance. "I thought you wanted to convince everyone we were in head over heels."

"Oh, my little buttercup!" I said in too loud a voice. I fixed a simpering, goofy look on my face. "I do adore you!"

A bunch of people turned to stare, some giggling a little. I felt the heat climb up under my skin.

"A good first attempt, but maybe a little too much? Anyway, I think our relationship is better compared to a thorny rosebush than a field of buttercups." Rahul reached out to tuck an errant strand of my curly hair behind my ear, and it was all I could do not to flinch from his touch. "Your beautiful hair, it has a mind of its own!" He projected his voice, but didn't shout as I'd done.

"All the better to turn you to stone, my dearest." I turned my face into his hand and tried to surreptitiously bite it.

"How about you keep your fangs to yourself, Medusa." Rahul tried to snatching his hand away without looking like he was snatching his hand away.

"How can I?" I gnashed my teeth at him. I saw him studying my mouth. "You're such a tasty little treat."

"Please, less talking and more archery practice!" called Sir Reginald from somewhere down the line.

And although we returned to our arrows and targets, our bows and quiver, there was something that had shifted between us. We were enemies now, for sure, but both in this thing together.

Say that she rail; why, then I'll tell her plain
She sings as sweetly as a nightingale:
Say that she frown; I'll say she looks as clear
As morning roses newly wash'd with dew.

—WILLIAM SHAKESPEARE,
The Taming of the Shrew

CHAPTER 29

A T THE ALL-CAMP meeting the following morning, there were, thankfully, no Insta posts to discuss or dissect. Instead, Lady Middleton had an announcement.

"As you know, not only is there to be a ball on the last day of camp, at which Queen Regina will make another appearance, but there is a whole day of festivities to be planned before," she said in sonorous tones. "And this is where you campers come in!"

"This is about the talent show!" Penny was crossing her fingers in eagerness. "Oh, please let this be about the talent show!"

The rest of us exchanged amused glances.

"I think they called it a showcase in that opening letter," said Mallika even as Brandon gently asked, "What's your talent, Pen?" The boy's face was so filled with tender attraction, it was obvious he was besotted.

"Well," Penny confessed breathily, "I'm an excellent breakdancer. I'm not being braggy, I really, really am! I won the competition at my middle school a few years ago!"

We all exchanged amused glances again. "Someone's got to tell her," mumbled Annie.

"Well, it's not going to be me," returned Mallika with a grin. "Make Eila do it."

I rolled my eyes. Of course it should fall to me. Responsible Eila. Mature Eila. Boring Eila. Well, I scolded myself, I saw what happened when I lost touch with that responsible older sister persona. So I uncomfortably put it back on, like an outgrown costume.

"I'm not sure there was a lot of break dancing in the Regency era, Penny," I said gently.

When Penny's face fell, Will quickly added, "But I'm sure you're terrific! Why don't you show us later?"

"For the showcase, we welcome instrumental ensembles and dance performances, individual playing and singing"—at this, Lady Middleton gave a small shudder in Will's direction—"poetry reading, archery, fencing, or perhaps even horseback-riding displays." Lady Middleton looked at us all with her hawklike eyes, pursing her unnaturally red lips. "But remember, only volunteer to participate in those events that will best showcase your skills. We want to impress Ms. Rivera-Colón, not frighten her."

The showcase was on everyone's lips that morning during "flower class"—a session with a Regency-era historian of flowers named Dr. Palmer who was an expert in the language of flowers in the Regency and Victorian eras.

"Who can tell me where the phrase 'the language of flowers' first originated?" asked the crusty historian. Annie's aunt and her team had outfitted the old gentleman in Regency-era clothes that looked like they had been distressed. I could swear the jacket and breeches weren't new, but rather an old outfit he'd been wearing forever.

When no one answered his query, Dr. Palmer waggled his not-inconsiderable gray eyebrows at us and intoned, "For the flowers have their angels . . . for there is a language of flowers. For there is a sound reasoning upon all flowers."

"For elegant phrases are nothing but flowers," said a voice to my right.

It was Rahul, of course. With an effort, I melted my stern expression into an over-the-top lovey-dovey one. I knew everyone was watching us. But just in case he got the wrong impression, I made sure my whispered words did not match my appearance. "In your case, those blossoms would be lying, rotten flowers. Roses which by any other name would still smell as bad."

Rahul seemed strangely unfazed. "Oh, my sweet silly chickadee!" he said loudly, for all to hear. "Why, that poem is by Christopher Smart, somewhere in the mid-1700s. Of course, the Regency folks really went crazy for the meanings behind flowers when in 1819 a book called *Le Langage des Fleurs* was published."

"Did you memorize all that to impress me?" For show, I patted his face, but made sure to do so a little too hard. "What a thoughtful, thoughtful thing to do. But you're always thoughtful and kind and truthful, aren't you? So opposed to lying, such a good guy."

"Maybe tone it down a little?" muttered Rahul. "You look like you're about to let down your fangs."

"All the better to murder you with, my dear," I muttered back.

"How do you know so much about the language of flowers?"

asked Penny, looking from Rahul to me with a bit of awe in her face. "I'm impressed."

"Thank you, but no need to be," said Rahul, elegantly bowing to Penny and making her blush. "I was simply reading from the professor's book." He held up a small, elegant volume that had Dr. Palmer's name on it. "He writes about the importance of planting very tall trees at the edge of one's property."

"This is clearly going to be a fascinating morning," yawned John sarcastically.

"You will insist on being droll," I quipped.

"Always, dear lady," said John, performing an over-the-top bow.

Mallika gave him a swift kick in the shin, which John took with equanimity. "Come, William, let us walk closer to the good professor and hear what he has to say," he said, offering his arm to Will.

When Will didn't take it, John's face fell.

"What's the flower that says 'I can't live without you, my darling dearest dear'?" asked Will dramatically. He fell before Mallika's feet as he asked this, making her titter.

"Morning glory," supplied Rahul with a snort, looking up from his book.

"I hate those flowers," I sniffed.

"Well, what's your favorite flower?" asked Annie. "Mine's the water lily."

"Which means pure of heart," supplied Rahul after flipping through his book.

Mallika gave Annie a smiling glance. "That works."

Up in the front of the formal outdoor gardens, Dr. Palmer was speaking in a wheezy, hard-to-hear voice, about how the violet represented faithfulness, and why the delicate violet was such a favorite flower of the Regency set.

"I like lavender," I supplied, curious as to what that might mean.

Rahul looked up from his book, his eyebrows raised. "Ah, well, that's very interesting," he said cryptically.

"What?" Penny bounced on her toes in eagerness.

"Maybe it's better if I don't say." Rahul shut the little volume with a dramatic snap. "I wouldn't want to offend anyone's delicate sensibilities."

"Oh, get off it," I growled.

"What does it say?" persisted Mallika, reaching for the volume. "Tell us!"

"Lavender is the flower of distrust," Rahul answered, even as he laughingly held the book out of my sister's reach.

Everyone in our little group let out a little "ooh" and then, as if there had been a signal preplanned between them, all headed forward to better hear the professor. Will escorted Mallika, John escorted Annie, and Brandon brought up the rear with Penny on his arm.

"Alone at last," said Rahul in a way-too-loud voice. "Alone with you, my sweet petunia plumcake."

"You are completely terrible at this," I mumbled, adjusting the little shawl I had draped over my shoulders. It was a gray and windy morning, and felt like it might rain later. "You should try and look up some better endearments."

"May I?" Rahul crooked his arm toward me. I wasn't going to take it at first, but he must have seen the stubbornness in my face as he added, "Remember, we are desperately in love."

"How could I forget." I placed my hand gingerly upon his forearm.

"Your plan to convince everyone of that won't work if you look like a stalk of lavender every time you're with me," said Rahul through clenched teeth.

His words made my temper snap. "I'm no flower, but a wasp within it," I countered.

"Then I'd best beware your sting." Rahul raised a dark eyebrow to sardonic effect.

I glared at him. There he was, doing it again, quoting Shakespeare to me. Only this time, it was from *The Taming of the Shrew*—the same play I'd written a feminist adaptation of and that Mallika had sent in for our audition. Well, two could play at that game. I hated Rahul for lying, but still, the matching of our wits always felt like sparklers going off inside me.

"You best beware my sting, because you shall not pluck it out," I muttered. "You could not find where it lies."

Rahul's eyes sparkled. "Who knows not where a wasp does wear her sting? In her tail."

"In her tongue," I shot back, digging my nails into his arm a bit for good measure.

"Whose tongue?" asked Rahul, drawling out the words. His eyes were hooded as he gazed at my mouth.

That made me pause, my feet stumbling a little on the gravel of the garden path. The rich scent of an invisible flower wafted over me from somewhere to my left. "The rest of that argument between Petruchio and Katharina," I muttered, averting my eyes from his. "It gets dirty."

"Oh?" Rahul grinned like a cat. "I don't remember. Enlighten me."

"You wish." It was, of course, a line about tongues in tails that had caused a great deal of scandal when I'd written it into my own student show.

"Then kiss me, Kate," said Rahul, like he was taunting me. Of course, I knew it was another line from the play, but I also knew he was referring to our conversation during archery class.

"What, in the midst of the street?" I instinctively pulled away from him.

I could feel the curious eyes of our fellow campers on me from all over the ornamental garden. I could hear their whispered speculations and giggles, and suddenly felt unprepared to put myself on such display.

"No, pray thee, love, stay." Rahul pulled me back toward him again. His voice lowered to a growl as he said, "Come, my sweet Kate, better once than never, for never too late."

By now, most of the class, including Dr. Palmer, were watching us. As if to kiss him, I leaned toward Rahul. In the end, however, I jammed between our faces a little fistful of lavender I'd just picked from the garden.

"Still distrustful, then?" Rahul shoved the flowers from his face.

"You've given me cause to be nothing but, my sweet flower bud," I reminded him in between clenched teeth. Then I gave him my cheesiest smile, and bopped him none-too-gently on the nose for the crowd who I knew was still watching.

Regency Fun Fact

Wealthy men in Regency England fenced for sport, but it is unlikely women were allowed to do so except in secret, getting training from fathers or brothers. Certainly, no matter what we see in certain Austen adaptations (zombies, cough, zombies), it is unlikely that women could comfortably wield a sword while wearing Regency-era gowns.

CHAPTER 30

THAT AFTERNOON, THE sun came out again, shining and
strong.

Our afternoon's activity was an outdoor fencing class.
Even though women wouldn't have participated in the sport in the
Regency era, the camp had allowed this small anachronism since
everyone of every gender was dying to learn. This was including
me, as fencing was something I actually had a little bit of skill in.
Not only did they teach it in my gym class at school (because one
of the gym teachers had been a former college-level fencer), but of
course I'd had plenty of chances to hone my sword-fighting skills
as part of the Young People's Shakespeare Company.

I don't know how Rahul had managed to avoid getting paired
with Lucy, but when I arrived at the lawn, I saw that Monsieur
Florimond (the dance teacher who was also the fencing master)
had me matched with Rahul in one of the first rounds.

"Have you held a sword before?" drawled one of Florimond's
helpers. I recognized the same stable boy who had saddled me,

literally, with Queen Mab. Clearly, Lady Middleton was getting the most out of all her workers.

This time, I had the confidence to grin at him. "I have."

He coughed, raising his eyebrow skeptically. "In what context? A Renaissance fair?"

"No," I said, choosing a foil carefully from the ones available for weight and grip. "From fencing lessons, and stage combat lessons in my Shakespeare company." For additional emphasis, I gave the sword a little zinging flourish through the air.

Florimond's dirty-toothed assistant had the grace to give a little bow. "Madam, I wish you only luck, then, against your opponent."

I stood across from Rahul in our outdoor practice area. The costume department also had gone anachronistic for this activity and given us all almost-identical white fencing costumes. It would have been foolish, not to mention dangerous, to expect half of us to fence in skirts and shawls. I waited impatiently for Florimond to finish a little demonstration and speech regarding the safe handling of our already blunt-tipped weapons before turning and facing Rahul. We raised our weapons in salute to each other, and as soon as Florimond called out "fence," I initiated a simple attack, lunging at Rahul.

Rahul clearly knew what he was doing, because he countered with an easy parry-riposte. Then, as if we were still strolling through the gardens learning the language of flowers, he said, "What if I offered you an idea—for the showcase?"

Rahul feinted, forcing me to parry, our blades ringing out as they clashed. "Okay, what is it?" I moved up to try to shorten the distance between us.

"We put on a play." Rahul parried my blade again. He licked his lips in concentration, throwing me entirely off my stride.

I tried not to get distracted and refocused on my technique. "You and I will put on a play?" I asked as I thrust my blade. "Aren't we doing that already with all our fake dating ploy?"

Rahul was a good fencer, and almost got in a touch at that moment, before I parried and used some footwork to regain my position. "A fake dating ploy that no one believes."

I danced backward out of the range of his blade. "Well, then we should try harder."

"Aren't you going to ask me about the play?" Rahul initiated a compound attack with a feint.

Wow, I really had to keep my head in order to stay in the game. Rahul was a better fencer than I was, and I hated the sneaking suspicion that he was going easy on me.

"Fine! Please, please, do tell me about your play idea," I said, panting only a little. "Since you have come up with it, it must be nothing less than absolute genius!" I tried out some fancy footwork I'd learned during a combat workshop last fall at my Shakespeare company, almost getting the better of Rahul.

"I was thinking of the play within a play from *A Midsummer Night's Dream.*" Rahul met my complicated footwork with his own fancy steps, now going on the offensive himself. "Your friends could be in it, and you could write it. Didn't you say that you'd adapted *The Taming of the Shrew* for a high school theater festival?"

"I did. It was a feminist tour de force," I declared a little too fiercely.

For a few moments, our blades spoke alone, meeting and parrying, clashing and kissing.

That's when Rahul said the thing that clinched it for me. "It would be a chance to tell Regina Rivera-Colón and all the *Rosewood* producers what you think they could make better, change in their show."

I dropped my guard, at which point Rahul got in an easy touch. "Darn it!"

We cleared the fencing arena for the next pair as we continued to talk. "So tell me more," I said.

Rahul looked around at all the people watching us, then reached out to play with my sweaty curls. "Only if you put some effort into this dating pretense."

I gave him a sickly sweet smile. "Oh, of course, my darling!" I singsonged too loudly, then wound my fingers into his hair, way too hard.

"Oh, you naughty little suet pudding," returned Rahul, trying to disentangle my fingers from his hair without looking like he was.

"Are you two planning on doing any more fencing?" I looked up to see Lucy staring at us with a frozen expression on her face. "I'm afraid I find myself without a partner. Rahul?" She snapped her fingers at him like she was telling a dog to sit.

I saw Rahul's jaw tighten in irritation, but still, he gave Lucy a gentlemanly smile. "Why not spar with Eila here?"

"I imagine they didn't have too many fencing lessons in the

public school systems," Lucy was saying to Rahul. "I really don't want to embarrass the girl."

"I'm a quick learner," I said. "Rahul's given me a few pointers."

Rahul gave me a curious look, like he was trying not to laugh. "Yes, indeed," he coughed. "Eila's a promising, erm, beginner, Lucy. Just go gentle on her. Be kind, won't you?"

"I'm always kind," purred Lucy, running a hand way too slowly down Rahul's arm. Then the girl turned to me, a nasty look on her face. "If you're as good a fencer as you are a rider, you'll need more than kindness, I'm afraid."

I remembered with some embarrassment my bumpy, awkward ride on the back of Queen Mab. "Well, as you said, there aren't really a lot of opportunities for horseback-riding lessons in the New Jersey public school systems." At least that was 100 percent true.

Lucy and I faced each other and held up our swords in salute. At the call of "fence," we began sparring.

"So you've decided to forgive Rahul? After he deceived you and lied to you, called the reporters on you?" Lucy initiated a compound attack. "Honestly, I'm surprised. I figured you'd just have more pride than that."

I'd been planning on pretending to be a worse fencer than I was, but her words upset me enough that I didn't need to pretend. I parried her attack clumsily, fumbling my footwork and almost stumbling backward. "Maybe I'm just more calculating than you thought?"

"I see that you are," sneered Lucy, attacking again with more aggression than finesse. "Kudos to you for having a limited set of morals, I guess!"

I defended with some parries and then attacked with a thrust. "Maybe you're wrong. Maybe we're just in love!"

"Don't make me laugh." Lucy lunged toward me, fencing from a position of anger rather than strategy. From her facial expression, I could tell she was figuring out, a little too late, that I was a worthier opponent than she thought.

"I have no intention of making you laugh." Rather than parry, I stepped smartly aside, almost making her fall on her face.

"Well, then, maybe I can make you laugh." Lucy turned and attacked without mercy. Our swords clashed as I parried again and again. "By letting you know that there's something more at stake in Rahul's and my relationship. My mother, whose company is about to make a huge deal with Rahul's father's company, is not going to look too kindly on the situation if Rahul doesn't make every effort to have me be cast in *Rosewood*."

"Yes, I know about that," I said. "Rahul told me."

Lucy narrowed her eyes. "Well, did he also tell you that his father's promised to disinherit him if this deal with our company falls through? Kick him out of the family?"

"What?" I faltered, misstepping and almost letting her get in a touch.

"He didn't tell you about that, did he? Isn't that interesting?" Lucy purred, now more confident in both her attacking and attitude. "Just one more omission in rather a long list of things he hasn't told you, isn't it?"

"His father wouldn't be so cruel!" I said, feeling flustered.

"Actually, he would." Lucy grinned, obviously delighted at my reaction to this piece of news. "And you know his mother died.

Wouldn't it be such a shame to ruin his relationship with his one remaining parent? And for what? A little fling?"

I parried, then went on the attack myself. "We're not having a fling! We're not even involved!"

As soon as the words were out of my mouth, I regretted them.

"Isn't that interesting you say that? When I thought you were so in love!" Lucy gave a feint, and then thrust, getting in an easy touch. She blew a piece of brown hair out of her face with a lazy gesture. "Or is that all an act? Fake dating to catch the attention of the casting directors?"

I practically threw down my sword in frustration. I was so angry at myself for my unguarded words I could spit.

"I knew you were faking it, princess," sneered Lucy. "After all, you're not that good of an actress."

She gave me one last, triumphant look before sauntering off. And as she did, I had a deep, inappropriate desire to throw a sword at her.

Regency Fun Fact

Jane Austen, like many Regency-era people of her social class, often performed in at-home theatricals, where everything from adapting a play, casting roles, crafting scenery and props, to creating costumes was done by the family members and close friends involved in the production. However, Austen and other Regency writers also portrayed home theatricals as fraught with danger, a space where dangerous entanglements and hidden desires might find free expression.

CHAPTER 31

WE ARRANGED TO have our first play meeting in the orchard. The trees were heavy with late summer growth, and the hanging fruit was bathed in the glow of the waning sun. It was that golden light when summer refuses to let the afternoon go but holds on tight with both hands to its beauty.

We'd brought out blankets and gathered under the trees, bathing ourselves in the gentle sunlight: Will and Mallika, John and Annie, Brendan and Penny, plus, of course, Rahul and me. I had to keep pretending I was in love with him, because only Will and Mallika knew the truth about us fake dating. But there was something new now in my feelings toward him, a protectiveness. By blowing off Lucy, he was risking his relationship with his one remaining parent. And even though his father was being a jerk, the thought of Rahul being cut off from his family was almost too much to bear. Having lost a parent myself, I couldn't imagine it.

"Don't feel like you have to overdo it," I muttered in a low voice to him as we reached the orchard.

Rahul turned to me, a ridiculous smile plastered on his face. "Look at how the sunshine settles like drops of brightness on your lashes," he said, reaching out to touch my face.

Penny stopped shaking out a blanket to look at us and sigh. It was all I could do not to swat Rahul's hand away. But instead I too plastered a fake smile on my face.

"That was you not overdoing it?" I asked out of the corner of my mouth.

"Just trying to play my part," Rahul said breezily. "Do my duty. Keep calm and soldier on."

"Right, I forgot. You're a very good actor." At my words, Rahul's expression faltered, cracking open to reveal the hurt underneath. But I couldn't feel pleased. Instead, I felt was tired and confused. For all my acting skills, I was really not very good at lying.

Mallika's keen eyes seemed to take in my discomfort. As she settled herself onto a blanket, she called out, "All right, what's the brilliant idea you lovebirds came up with to impress Queen Regina?"

"We're going to put on a play!" announced Rahul.

"A play?" Annie wrinkled her nose. "Aren't we already kind of in a play?"

"The Regency folks loved referring back to classical times," I said by way of introduction to my motley crew.

But no one was really paying attention. Penny and Brandon had just unpacked some snacks, so everyone was busy stuffing their faces. Mallika was actually holding a bunch of grapes for

Will to eat as he lay on her lap. I anticipated a need to do the actual Heimlich fairly soon.

"Anyway," I went on in a louder voice, giving Mallika a frown that she ignored in the manner of all younger siblings toward their wiser elders since time immemorial, "it will be a double reference sort of thing. We'll be doing the play within a play they do in Shakespeare's *Midsummer Night's Dream*. It's called *Pyramus and Thisbe*."

"Or, as the characters call it in the play," added Rahul with a flourishing hand gesture, "a tedious brief scene of young Pyramus and his love Thisbe; very tragical mirth."

I turned to our friends, expecting a big laugh. Instead, Brandon just kept spreading jam on his scone, while Penny, John, and Annie continued arguing about the best flavor of macaron.

I waved my hands in explanation. "Which is ridiculous, right? Because something can't be both merry and tragical, tedious and brief."

"That is, hot ice and wondrous strange snow," added Rahul, quoting from the play.

"How shall we find the concord of this discord?" I said dramatically, not to be outdone.

But turning to our little band, I found each person's face blanker than the next. Mallika, maybe the most used to my Shakespeare obsession, paused in her grape feeding and raised her eyebrow. "So we're supposed to laugh now, are we?"

"Please don't tell me we're going to be wearing *Handmaid's Tale* red cloaks or whatever," said Annie, her mouth full of raspberry macaron. I felt a flash of embarrassment. She'd obviously been filled in by my sister on my reinterpretation of *The Taming of the Shrew*.

I shot Mallika a dirty look as John gave a sarcastic laugh. "I do hope your version of the play will be merrier, or more tragical, or whatever, than the little schtick the two of you did just now."

"Come on, it's very sweet how they're both so into Shakespeare," said Penny sincerely. Not so sincerely that she looked up from her slicing of a giant wheel of brie. "It's very important that people in a relationship share common interests."

"Like you and I both like Brie," said Brandon, who seemed equally invested in the breakdown of that wheel of cheese.

Mallika shot me a not-so-subtle look. Obviously, this was my opportunity to convince our friends that Rahul and I were together.

"It was actually Shakespeare that brought us together," I said, not looking at Rahul.

"*The Tempest*, in fact," Rahul added from my side. "The first time we met, we recited lines from Prospero the magician's famous speech. Didn't we, my dove?"

"And danced," I added, remembering our first meeting in the ballroom, when all had seemed possible and hopeful.

"And danced," Rahul confirmed, his eyes dark and unreadable.

There was a moment's awkward silence, which my sister broke by dramatically announcing, "Some are brought together by cheese, some by Shakespeare."

"Some by cheesy Shakespeare," said John with a hand flourish.

Everyone laughed and the spell was broken. I tore my eyes away from Rahul.

"Wait, so you guys are talking about Shakespeare?" said Will, the light bulb finally going off in his head. He was still sprawled out, lying across Mallika's lap as she played idly with his hair. "Like, the play guy, right?"

"Yes, Will, we're talking about Shakespeare, the play guy," I confirmed, trying not to laugh.

"Hey, we have the same first name!" Will said, as if this had just occurred to him. "Like, that's cool! Will Allen—Will Shakespeare," he went on.

I caught Annie rolling her eyes, and couldn't help but let out a giggle.

"To get back to what we were talking about," Rahul jumped back in. "The play we'll do for Regina Rivera-Colón: It'll be fabulous. Eila is a talented playwright who will adapt the Shakespeare for us, and we've already started thinking about casting. Will and Mallika, you'll be the lovers, Pyramus and Thisbe."

"Obviously!" Penny gave a bright smile only slightly tinged with jealousy.

"We could be their understudies," suggested Brandon with a shy look at the little redhead.

"I actually thought you and Penny could play the lions who eventually make Pyramus think Thisbe is dead, which then makes him kill himself," I said cheerfully.

"Like a Romeo-and-Juliet situation? He thinks she's dead and so he kills himself for no reason?" asked Brandon. "I never understood how that was supposed to be a romantic gesture. It seems pretty awful to me."

"Depressing, really." Penny jammed some Brie and a cracker into her mouth. "Not to mention impulsive."

"But the thing is, you're not playing a lion, you're playing a character who's playing the lion. Get it? That's the play within a play within a play aspect of the whole thing. In the original, the lion is played by a joiner named Snug," began Rahul by way of explanation.

"So we're both called Snug?" asked Penny, a slow smile spreading over her face.

"Snugs, Snuggles, Snuggums," spitballed Brandon as he stared with goofy admiration at Penny's reddening face. "Snuggalicious, Snugacious, Snug-Snug-a-Nug-Nug."

I shot Rahul a look of concern. This was not going as smoothly as I had thought it would.

Will's hand shot into the air. "Will, you don't actually need to raise your hand," I sighed.

I'm not sure if he heard me, because he kept his hand raised, and now added an urgent wave.

"Yes, Will?" I felt my patience growing very, very thin. I rubbed at my temple. "You had a question?"

"What's a joiner?" asked Will. "You said this Snugalicious guy was a joiner?"

"Kind of like a carpenter," explained Rahul.

"What's the difference?" Will persisted. "Why don't they just call him Snuggles the carpenter?"

"Yeah, Snug the joiner sounds like the guy is, like, a follower," Mallika suggested. "Like he doesn't have leadership potential."

"I suppose he doesn't," Rahul said, obviously wanting to move on.

"But is that a fair commentary on Brandon and Penny?" asked Annie.

"Kinda harsh, amirite?" added John, his mouth full of scone.

"No one is saying anything about Brandon and Penny," I hurriedly explained. "Or their leadership skills."

Rahul rushed on before anyone could add anything else. "Anyway, Snug is very concerned about scaring people with his lion costume and gives this hilarious speech when he first comes onstage."

I made a show of clearing my throat and then taking on a meek and bowed appearance. I made my voice childlike as I began Snug's speech: "You, ladies, you, whose gentle hearts do fear the smallest monstrous mouse that creeps on floor, may now perchance both quake and tremble here, when lion rough in wildest rage doth roar."

Rahul picked up where I left off. He went for more of a Cowardly Lion from *Wizard of Oz* direction, but it still worked. "Then know that I, one Snug the joiner, am, a lion-fell, nor else no lion's dam; for, if I should as lion come in strife into this place, 'twere pity on my life."

"You're my lion," sighed Penny to Brandon, who gently put a macaron in her mouth, with a muttered "Rawr!"

"And you call Jane Austen anti-feminist because she writes about marriage and courtship!" Mallika pointed an accusing finger at me. "But Shakespeare's not sexist? I mean, ladies being scared by monstrous mice and all that? How are you not outraged by that, Didi? Hypocritical much?"

"Okay, none of this is the point!" I practically bellowed, both hands on my aching head now. I wondered if the bard had so many issues with his players. Maybe this was why Austen wrote novels and not plays. As a novelist, you didn't have to deal with anyone else's idiotic opinions but your own. "Go on, Rahul, will you?"

"Anyway, long story short. It's very funny because the actors are actually terrible and break out of character all the time, forget their lines," continued Rahul. "Case in point, the lion taking off his mane for a minute to reassure people he's just an actor."

"So the two of you thought the best way for us to show off our acting talents for Regina Rivera-Colón and the *Rosewood* producers was for us to play bad actors?" John raised his eyebrows.

"It takes a lot of talent to act like you act badly," said Will, creating an awkward pause, during which everyone seemed to feel the need to look in all sorts of different directions.

Clearing his throat and obviously trying not to laugh, Rahul nodded. "Absolutely, it does. Bad acting is hard."

"Actually, we thought that we might use those same moments to maybe make some commentary on how we might like to see *Rosewood* season two go down." I tried to be patient. "Like maybe less with the sexy stuff."

This comment generated a number of boos and thumbs-downs from my friends.

"We love the sexy stuff!" shouted Will.

"It's empowering to see people who look like us doing those

sorts of, um, things." Annie ended her sentence with an embarrassed look at Mallika.

I sniffed. "All right, what would you all suggest to Regina Rivera-Colón if you had the chance?"

"More queer couples!" shouted out John, eliciting several cheers.

"More couples of all derivations and combinations!" Brandon added, to more cheers.

"Women's lives explored outside of courtship and marriage," said Annie firmly. "We do have our own interests, hobbies, passions, talents, no matter what era we're from! I mean, look at Jane Austen, who wrote all those brilliant novels!"

Mallika gave her an inscrutable look. "But those things don't have to exist outside of romance, do they?"

There was another uncomfortable silence among the company, and a few secretive exchanged smiles.

"So what roles do the rest of us have?" asked John through a mouthful of scone.

"We figured you would be Snout the tinker, who plays the wall that separates the ill-fated lovers." I held my fingers in an "OK" sign. "He makes his fingers like this to indicate the chink in the wall through which Pyramus and Thisbe can speak, and pretend to kiss each other by kissing the wall."

"Kissing the wall, huh?" John shot Will a look that made me pause. Then, appearing to collect himself, he muttered, "Is this Snout thing some kind of a commentary on my nose?"

"You're gorgeous, Sir John, and you know it!" Will said, bopping him gently on the arm.

"I am, aren't I?" agreed John with a blushing laugh.

I looked curiously from one boy to the other, then finally said, "A snout is a sort of a kettle spout, apparently. Something tinkers fixed."

"Still," sniffed John.

"And me?" Annie asked.

"You're Robin Starveling, who plays Moonshine by holding up a lantern to light up the stage," Rahul explained. "He also has a dog, but that seemed beyond our capabilities right now."

"All that I have to say is to tell you that the lanthorn is the moon," I said, quoting the moon's speech, "I, the man in the moon. This thorn bush, my thorn bush, and this dog, my dog."

Annie frowned. "Can I ask a follow-up question about this thorn bush?"

"No!" I said definitively.

"Fine, fine, no need to be defensive," Annie said lightly. "I mean, I'm just the moon, controller of tides and moods and menstrual cycles, don't mind me, I'm not super powerful or anything."

"I don't know if that menstrual cycle thing is true," I couldn't help but say.

"I feel like we might be on a tangent again," Rahul muttered.

"What about you two?" Mallika asked. "What are your roles?"

"We're sharing the role of Peter Quince, the playwright and director," I said. "But we'll also be Hippolyta and Theseus, who are watching the theatrics."

"Queen of the Amazons," said Annie unexpectedly.

I narrowed my eyes at her. "You know the play? Why didn't you say so?"

"You didn't ask," said the girl, exchanging a smiling look with Mallika.

"Is it only me, or does this seem confusing?" asked Will, straightening up finally from Mallika's lap. "I mean, I'd totally be psyched if we just all sang together or something."

Another pregnant pause ensued, since we all knew what song Will was on the verge of suggesting we all sing.

"But the thing is," said John gently. "'Wallika' is such a special song, you wouldn't want all of us singing it with you and messing it up."

Will nodded, taking Mallika's hand and looking into her eyes in a very affected way. "Then Mallika and I will sing it after the play."

"Just not during the play," I muttered.

"It could be very funny," countered Rahul. "Pyramus and Thisbe could sing it over the wall to each other. Only it would have to be 'Pisbe' or 'Thyramus' or something."

"Don't even give them any ideas," I whispered back, trying not to laugh.

"I can see he's not in your good books," said the messenger.
"No, and if he were I would burn my library."

—WILLIAM SHAKESPEARE,
Much Ado About Nothing

CHAPTER 32

THE DAYS LEADING up to the final showcase were a whirlwind. There were the regular events of Regency Camp: horseback riding, elocution, music, archery, needlepoint, croquet, and drawing classes. But the class that took up most of our time was dance. Monsieur Florimond was in an absolute tizzy about our footwork and our formations, our turns and our trippings. Everything but everything had to be perfect for the final ball, when Regina Rivera-Colón and her team would preside over us all, judging not only how appealing and castable we campers were, but what kind of a job our teachers had done. Lady Middleton seemed in a permanent state of flushed adrenal frenzy, screaming at the least provocation and calling emergency meetings about such things as a torn petticoat that had been visible during class, or a gentleman who had forgotten to properly button his breeches. Annie was constantly being pulled away to help her aunt's team tailor our final ball outfits, and an entire extra team of cooks had been brought in to start preparing our after-dancing feast. I just prayed it would be less veal soup and more chicken tikka masala, but I also knew my stomach's prayers weren't going to be answered.

After our long, exhausting days, we were given free time to rehearse our showcase events. For us, that meant not only rehearsals, with writing and rewriting of the script on my part, but frenetic costume making by Annie and Mallika, as well as set design and painting by the rest. We were to be dressed in Greek style, as many Regency plays seemed to harken back to, but creating flowing white gowns for us all was taking the two girls longer than they'd anticipated, especially as certain players, like John and Will, kept complaining about the fit of their togas. The sets were simple painted wood; one side was the outline of two castles—Pyramus and Thisbe's parents' homes—and the other side was a tomb by which the lovers plan to meet, only to have Thisbe meet the lion first.

During this entire time, Rahul and I kept up our fake dating. It was actually kind of fun, not that I would admit that to him.

One afternoon, during another fencing class, he raised his saber and loudly announced, "By my sword, Eila, you love me."

At first I was startled, but then realized he was just holding up his end of the bargain, and doing it through Shakespeare, as usual.

"Don't swear like that and then go back and eat it later," I said, lightly parrying his sword with a flick of my blade. I was paraphrasing the line that Beatrice tells Benedick in *Much Ado About Nothing*. I had to give Rahul credit where credit was due. The play wasn't a bad choice for us, as the characters are bickering lovers who engage in a merry war of wits.

Rahul made a feint, then an attack. "I'll swear by my sword

that you love me, too, and I'll make any man who says that I don't love you eat it."

I had to keep on my toes to parry his sword. "But you won't eat your words?"

Our blades clashed and Rahul loudly declared, "Not with any sauce they could provide for them. I swear, I love you."

The other campers around us actually stopped fencing to watch us banter, our wits clashing just as much as our blades. Rahul lifted his sword, hilt to nose, before giving it a dramatic swish through the air as he bowed to our adoring fans. Then, facing me, he made the same gesture, only gave his sword prettily to me.

Everyone clapped, and I gave a little awkward curtsy in my fencing gear. I was beginning to realize that the hardest thing about fake dating was remembering that all the words that Rahul was saying—whether his own or quoted—were not things he actually felt, but rather, that he was playing the role of the besotted lover. And unfortunately for the state of my nervous system, he was playing the role really well.

The next evening, as we were all painting some set pieces together, Penny turned to me, her paintbrush raised.

"You and Rahul seem meant for each other," she said softly.

I dipped my brush in the gray paint—she and I were painting the tomb—to buy myself some time. "I might say the same about you and Brandon."

"He's kind and gentle." Penny blushed prettily as she dabbed at the set. "But you and Rahul, your love of theater, and your knowledge of Shakespeare . . . your tastes seem to coincide on every point. And you've known each other for such a short time!"

I paused, exchanging a look with Rahul, who was within earshot. "It's not time or opportunity that determines intimacy. Seven years would be insufficient to make some people acquainted with each other, and seven days more than enough for others."

He looked up and met my eye. I was, of course, quoting from Jane Austen, and I realized that, like Shakespeare's, her words had found their way into my heart and mind, becoming a way for me to engage with and understand my own life.

Penny's question had come from naivete about Rahul's and my real relationship, but my sister, who should have known better, seemed to have just as many. That night, in the darkness of our room. Mallika's voice came floating over to me from her bed.

"I know you say you hate Rahul, but are you still really faking it?" she asked.

I didn't answer for a moment, but let her words hang in the dark air between us. Finally, I cleared my throat. "What do you mean?"

"Just that it doesn't seem like you're fake dating as much as just trying not to let on to the other how much you each like each other," Mallika said. It was annoying when she was so observant.

Rather than answer, I turned her words around. "Well, I could ask the same of you and Will. I mean, that scheme you came up with! I still can't believe you created that whole Heir of Allenham account and masterminded that entire plan to have him pretend to be the actor."

I heard Mallika turn over, adjusting the pillows and covers around her. "Maybe I'm more devious than you thought I was."

"Not devious," I disagreed. "Just more ambitious and willing to go out there on a limb to get what you want."

"But not just for me. I want to help you fulfill your dreams too, Didi."

We sat in silence in the dark, listening to the sounds of the quieting manor around us. There were campers still getting to their rooms, and downstairs, the remains of our dinner being cleaned up. Outside our window was the tap-tap of a branch knocking to be let in, its motion guided by the summer wind.

"Do you really like him?" I asked. "Will, I mean. You say you do, but there's something that always makes me think that you guys are the ones actually faking it for the cameras."

"I like Will a lot," Mallika admitted. "Just not in the same way you like Rahul."

"I don't like Rahul." Even to my own ears, my voice sounded thin and strained. I really was terrible at lying.

"You liked him once; don't you think you could like him again?" My sister's voice was measured and even, as if she were the older sister guiding her younger sibling to realize something about herself.

"I liked a different version of him, an untrue version," I said with a sigh. "He lied to me, Mal, about being the actor, about calling the reporters. I mean, how can I trust someone who would do that?"

Mallika didn't say anything for long enough that I wondered if she'd actually drifted off to sleep. But then I heard her voice again in the darkness. "Are you sure he did? Call the reporters, I mean?"

"Who else could have known what time we were due back at the dock?" I said, repeating the words that Lucy had said to me. "Just imagine, Mal, to arrange such a perfect evening, Shakespeare under the stars, the picnic, everything. And then to ruin it like that. I mean, all those other plans were just serving the publicity he ultimately wanted."

"But Rahul doesn't seem like he's the sort of person who likes publicity, does he?" Mallika asked.

"He doesn't seem like that, I know." I sighed in the darkness. "But actions speak louder and all that. How can I trust him after such a stunt? He's obviously just like these other Hollywood types, in it for the fame."

"What if he did it for you?" There was a note of urgency in my sister's voice. "Not because he wanted the publicity for himself, but because he wanted to give you a chance to shine and then get cast?"

I thought about it before answering. "I don't think so. I mean, when the reporters turned their cameras on us, he blocked me, then backed the whole boat up so they wouldn't get a good shot of me. That doesn't seem like the behavior of someone who had called up a bunch of reporters to give me exposure."

Mallika gave a funny snort. "No, you're right. I suppose it doesn't."

There was another significant silence. Finally, my sister said, "What if I were to tell you that Rahul wasn't the one who called the reporters?"

"What?" I sat up in bed, letting the sheet fall off me. I clicked on my bedside lamp. "What do you know that you're not telling me?"

But Mallika had already turned over and wouldn't answer.

"Mallika?" I prompted.

I sat for a few moments like that, wondering what she'd found out. Then I heard her soft, even breathing and turned out the light.

It had been a long day, and any more revelations could wait until morning.

It is not what we say or feel that make us what we are. It is what we do, or fail to do.

—ANDREW DAVIES,
Sense and Sensibility [screenplay]

CHAPTER 33

THE SHOWCASE WAS scheduled for Friday morning, prior to the evening ball. Regina and her casting staff were on campus, and as Lady Middleton put it, when a queen is in attendance, she must be entertained!

We were in the same grand hallway in which we had first been introduced to the *Rosewood* director. She was on her throne, like last time, but the sparkling white wig she wore was even higher than the last one she'd had on. In fact, there were little birdcages woven into it, not to mention little birds as well. And on the top, maybe something that might just be . . . a tiny nest in a tree? As opposed to the Empire-waist dresses most of us wore, she was attired in an elaborate gown with broad panniers on the hips, which gave her the appearance of a giant ship. Her ears and neck were dripping with jewels and she honestly looked like she was having an absolute blast.

"Let the games begin!" she announced, having her footman crew actually "toot-toot-toot-toot" some horns like old-fashioned court heralds.

Unfortunately, the first few acts were absolutely horrendous. There were jugglers and acrobats; there was a ventriloquist and a painter who looked like they might be coloring by numbers. A few couples tried to re-create the success of "Wallika" by singing little ditties with names like "Jenda" (Jay + Brenda) and "Felipicity" (Felipe + Felicity). Most of them stuck to rhymes of the moon-June room-bloom variety and stole their tunes from popular musical sources. I actually thought Regina's eyes glazed over at one point when Felipe started coming up with things that rhymed with "Felicity": "I feel so much bliss-ity and specificity to your domesticity." And who could forget the classic line "My heart expands with elasticity, I am awash with authenticity and electricity for my darling Felicity!" It made "Wallika" seem like it was written by a great, like Austen or Shakespeare.

And soon it was our turn to put on our little production. When Rahul and I came out, appropriately toga-attired, to introduce our play, I saw that Regina sat forward, giving Rahul a little wink.

"Gentles, perchance you wonder at this show, but wonder on, till truth make all things plain," I began, keeping close to the original text.

"Our friend Will here is Pyramus, if you would know, this beauteous Mallika Thisbe is certain," continued Rahul, gesturing to Will and my sister. He dragged out the last syllable of *certain*, making it rhyme with *plain*.

"I represent the wall which did these lovers sunder." John walked in with a purposefully homemade-looking brick signboard hanging over his front and back. He was speaking in a weird monotone as he held up his fingers to represent a hole in the wall, and the audience all laughed at his obviously contrived bad acting. "Through this wall's chink, poor souls, they are content to whisper."

"Have you ever heard a wall speak better?" Rahul asked, leaning against my shoulder with a casual hand.

"It is the wittiest partition I ever heard speak," I agreed.

Regina gave a snicker from her throne.

But then there was a significant gap, during which Will tossed his hair a good deal, but unfortunately said no actual lines, as he was supposed to. We all exchanged alarmed looks and the audience shifted in their seats at the overly long pause. Finally, I couldn't take it anymore.

"Will," I hissed, "you're up!"

The handsome boy looked askance, first at me, and then at John. "I am?"

I realized that the thing we'd all been worrying about during rehearsals was coming true. Will, who had been total crap at memorizing any lines, had forgotten everything we'd all worked so hard to help him learn. Honestly, how I'd ever thought he was the *Rosewood* actor was beyond me. The guy had a memory like a sieve.

"Oh, grim-look'd night!" I hissed, and Will obediently repeated the words, causing Regina to whoop with mirth.

"Oh, night with hue so black!" I continued.

"Oh, night with . . . black!" repeated Will with a confused grin. Despite us coaching him, he'd clearly forgotten what the word *hue* meant.

I decided it wasn't worth prolonging this agony anymore, and so skipped the next line and went on to "Oh, night! Oh, night! Alack, alack, alack!" Which Will obediently repeated.

Then, just as I was about to sigh in relief, having delivered Will through his first set of lines, Mallika began to speak. She was in full operatic, overacting mode, making the most of her comic role. She beat her chest in an honestly painful-looking way, crying, "Oh, wall, full often hast thou heard my moans, for parting my fair Pyramus and me!"

But then Will, for unknown reasons, suddenly joined in, saying her next line with her, but a little off-tempo, so that he sounded like her echo: "My cherry lips have oft kissed thy stones! Thy stones with lime and hair knit up in thee."

But with that, rather than mock-kissing the stones of the wall, as both lovers were supposed to do, Will reached up and gently kissed John.

Then Pyramus did something decidedly not in the Shakespearean original. With an apologetic look to Mallika, Will stole another one of her lines. However, he delivered it directly to John, peering into his eyes. "My love thou art, my love I think."

The entire audience was heart-stoppingly silent, everyone mesmerized by this new happening. Even Regina looked transfixed, sitting on the edge of her throne. When nothing happened for a few seconds, she called out imperiously, "Well, Wall, what say thee to this unexpected turn of events?"

John, startled and blushing, then stole one of Pyramus's lines. Reaching around his ridiculous signboard costume, he grasped Will by the shoulders. "Oh, kiss me through the hole of this vile wall!"

And Will, his face equally transformed by pleasure and embarrassment, returned, "I kiss not the wall's hole, but your lips and all."

The noise that followed was room-shattering as everyone whistled, hooted, and clapped in decidedly non-Regency fashion at Will/Pyramus kissing John, who had hitherto been his wall.

The two boys joined hands and bowed shyly, acknowledging the positive reception of the community. Rahul and I exchanged bemused looks. "I *knew* he and Mallika had been fake dating!" I exclaimed.

"I knew those two had chemistry!" agreed Rahul with a grin.

"But what happens to fair Thisbe, abandoned by her lover *and* her wall?" exclaimed Queen Regina in loud tones.

"She comes, my queen, anon! Anon!" I improvised, using Pyramus's unsaid lines. "I see her voice, I hear dear Thisbe's face. Oh, Thisbe, dear!"

"I'm right here, no need to shout!" Mallika complained, making Regina scream with laughter.

I poked Rahul in the ribs, and he spontaneously jumped forward in the scene. "Now is the barrier down between the two neighbors."

"No helping it, my queen, when walls are so willful to fall in love without warning," I said, curtsying with mock apology.

"At this unexpected junction, now is perhaps the time for Moonshine to appear, that controller of tides and moons and menstruation!" announced Annie, coming out of the shadows in her moon costume, which was nothing more than a silvery toga, a lantern, and a cardboard crescent affixed to her forehead.

"You don't come on until the second act!" Rahul whispered, waving her back, but I held out my hand and stilled his protests.

"No, I think she comes on now. Truly, the moon shines with a good grace."

Annie held up her lantern to shine on Mallika's face. And I saw, there, in my sister's expression, what else I had suspected all along.

"Sweet moon, I thank thee for thy sunny beams," laughed Mallika, her eyes shining with joy. "I thank thee, Moon, for shining now so bright. For, by thy gracious, golden, glittering gleams, I trust to take of truest Thisbe sight."

Everyone watching gasped again as the Moon reached out to embrace Thisbe, declaring, in a watery voice, "What beauty is here? Eyes, do you see? How can it be! Oh, dainty duck! Oh, dear!"

And then the two girls exchanged the sweetest of kisses. I felt my own heart expand with joy for my sister's happiness. Of course it had always been Annie and not Will she was interested in!

"We fly! From this heteronormative story, we flee!" announced John, ad-libbing some lines.

"We make our own stories of joy, for we are truly free!" added Mallika, grinning at me.

And with that, the two lovers ran offstage with their own true love interests: Will with John, Mallika with Annie.

"I am heartily entertained!" Queen Regina cried. "But I need a conclusion to this play! It cannot end so abruptly! Two sets of lovers is half enough!"

"More lovers! More lovers! More lovers!" chanted the audience.

I poked Rahul. "I think we're up!" I said, running onstage, and switching out the scenery from Pyramus and Thisbe's homes to the tomb.

"This is old Ninny's Tomb!" I called in a high-pitched voice, taking over my sister's role of Thisbe. "Where is my love?"

"Hey, lions!" Rahul called. "That's your cue!"

As soon as Penny and Brandon ran on, roaring rather enthusiastically, I screamed.

"Oh no, a pair of amorous lions in love!" I ad-libbed, making our two lions blush in delight.

Hooting with laughter, Regina shouted, "They have tails and manes and teeth enough between them!"

I recognized the line as adapted from another of Jane Austen's novels, the one I'd been reading on the lake, and so I ad-libbed back, "Aye, aye, and two of the silliest lions in Norland!" Then with another bloodcurdling scream, I ran offstage, Brandon and Penny forgetting to give chase.

"Well run, Thisbe!" called Regina Rivera-Colón.

"Well roared, lions!" added Rahul, to which Penny and Brandon not only each gave a bow, but then threw back their manes and gave each other a kiss.

"Well kissed, lions!" called one of Regina's entourage, causing another peal of laughter from the famous director.

"Pyramus, you're up!" I hissed from offstage, nearly hysterical from all that had just happened. Our play was running away from us like a wagon losing its wheels on a hill, but it was clearly time to give it some kind of satisfying ending.

"Right!" Rahul had obviously forgotten that he had to take over Will's role in all the excitement. Now, with little further delay, he skipped onstage. "Aren't I supposed to see Thisbe's bloodied cloak?" he called.

Penny, who still had the cloak in her lion paws, threw it back onstage, much to the amusement of all the onlookers, who exploded with laughter.

"Eyes, do you see! How can it be?" cried Rahul in an incredibly false voice of shock, sending Regina into spasms of laughter. He held the red paint-bloodied cloak to his toga-ed chest. Unfortunately, the paint wasn't entirely dry, so it left an ugly red stain that made Rahul come out of character for a second, grimacing. "Yuck!"

Then he remembered to get back into the scene, intoning, "Oh, dainty duck! Oh, dear! They mantle good, what stained with blood!" Only, Rahul pronounced the word "blood" so it rhymed with "good" making the entire thing all that much more ridiculous.

When Rahul looked lost as to what to do next, I called from offstage, "Now you're supposed to die!"

"Oh, right!" Rahul muttered, looking around. "But where's my sword?"

Brandon the lion for some reason was in possession of that particular weapon and, being a responsible person and not wanting to toss a sword onstage, walked back on with it. He handed it back to Rahul hilt first, as we had been taught in weapons class.

"This lion roars and returns thy sword!" announced the boy, looking quite pleased with his spontaneous rhyme as he handed Rahul his weapon. Then he looked out at the audience, saying in a serious voice, "When handling weapons, even theatrical ones, always remember that safety comes first!"

"Well done, lions! Safety first!" called Regina's entourage, and Penny dashed onstage to hold Brandon's hand and give some spontaneous bows.

"I'm still supposed to die!" announced Rahul dramatically. "If you could save your applause until then?"

"Apologies, Pyramus the Second!" called Regina merrily from her throne.

There was a small pause, during which Rahul stared at his sword, obviously not remembering what to do. "Go ahead and die now!" I called out encouragingly.

"Right!" he called back, giving me a thumbs-up of appreciation. Then, picking up the sword and holding it to his chest, he called out, "Out, sword, and wound the pap of Pyramus!"

"The pap?" asked Penny from backstage.

"I honestly have no idea," I replied with a laugh.

"Thus die I, thus, thus, thus," cried Rahul, pretending to pierce his chest over and over.

"He's surely dead!" cried out one of Regina's assistants.

"Not yet!" I called loudly. "He still has more lines, I think!"

"Now I am dead, now I am fled," pronounced Rahul in ringing, melodramatic tones. "Now die, die, die, die, die."

Finally, after all that energetic pretend stabbing, Rahul lay in an exhausted heap upon the floor, his chest visibly rising and falling as the sword stuck out of his armpit. The crowd went wild.

I ran out, hand over forehead, gathering Pyramus/Rahul's still form into my lap.

"Asleep, my love? What dead, my dove?" I cried rather hysterically. "Oh, Pyramus, you're quite dead, dead!"

"Kiss! Kiss! Kiss! Kiss!" cried the hooting and stomping crowd.

And then for who knows what feverish theatrical reason, I leaned down over Rahul's head in my lap, and did just that. And, reader? He kissed me back. Enthusiastically, energetically, rising up like a man risen from the dead by love. Which, of course, was what he was.

"A kiss that brings even the stabbed pap to life!" announced Regina.

"You kiss by the book!" I accused Rahul mock angrily, covering up my own embarrassment with a line from *Romeo and Juliet*. The audience was laughing so loudly by now I had to shout my lines.

"Teach not thy lips such scorn," Rahul cried, pretending to be hurt. "For they were meant for kissing." Then Rahul met my eye, sat up, and kissed me again, rather enthusiastically, I might add.

There were things we had to discuss. There were things I didn't understand. There were arguments still to be had. But for the moment, the magic of theater had made all of that fall away, and all I knew was how to let my emotions lead me. Because the best magic is woven in the theater with the truest threads.

The crowd went wild at our terrible play. We managed to find all our lost lovers—Will and John, Annie and Mallika—and bring them back onstage, flushed and bright-eyed, for their final bows. Brandon and Penny, still in their lion costumes, got wild cheers of "Safety first! Safety first!" Finally there was Rahul and me, our hands joined, taking bow after flushing, near-hysterical bow.

"That was the absolute worst play I've ever been in!" said Rahul as the crowd continued to roar and hoot.

I nodded in agreement, wiping my streaming eyes. "You'll probably get fired from *Rosewood* after that horrible death scene."

Rahul grinned, squeezing my hand tight in his. "Well, if so, it will definitely have been worth it."

I couldn't help but agree.

Regency Fun Fact

The dance floor of a ball was much like a stage. It was a chance for young men and women to perform, in their best finery, for their communities. And they weren't only performing the steps of dances, but the status and breeding of their families, their attractiveness and eligibility as potential spouses. A ball or assembly was a rare chance for men and women to speak, touch, flirt, and, if Jane Austen's novels are to be believed, fall in love.

CHAPTER 34

THE REGENCY CAMP ball was, predictably, over the top and absolutely fabulous. There were lights strung up through the garden and into the ballroom so that the party could spill through the French doors and out onto the balcony and lawn. Waiters were circulating with drinks and the musicians were tireless in their exertions. There were flowers everywhere, and their scent filled the air with heady delight, not to mention quite a few pollen-allergic sneezes.

The campers were dressed in their finest. Ms. Park and her team had outdone themselves. There were flowing dresses and perfectly tailored jackets, long gloves, and silken breeches. The colors reminded me of a butterfly garden, vivid and spectacular.

Annie and her aunt had taken my love of the rani color dress and expanded on it, making me an outfit of vivid pink and orange—like a silk sari converted into Regency dress. Mallika was in a sapphire-blue silk that had an almost transparent silver overdress. Both of us had our hair up and our necks and ears adorned with Indian jewelry we had brought from home.

As we were getting ready in our room, I had turned to her, asking, "So you really like Annie? You're happy?"

Mallika laughed. "We're only in high school, Eila—it's not like we're getting married!"

I grabbed her hand, making her understand the seriousness of my question. "But still, she's the one?"

"Annie is the best." Mallika grinned at me. "Beautiful, funny, smart. Everything I could ask for. Plus, she has some mad sewing skills!"

I kissed my sister tenderly on the cheek. "Then I wish you very happy."

Mallika tilted her head in my direction. "Did you actually think I like-liked Will? Did you not realize that was all pretend?"

"I wasn't sure," I admitted. "But now that I understand, it all makes perfect sense."

"You've got to admit, he and John are adorable together," Mallika said as she pulled on her long gloves.

"That they are," I agreed with a grin.

As we entered the ballroom, we saw that all our friends were outfitted in colors that enhanced their good looks. Annie was in a light pink dress of varying shades and Penny in a deep green. John wore a blue velvet coat and Will a black one. Brandon's military dress uniform was tailored impeccably, with the shiniest of gold buttons. And Rahul, well, he looked, as usual, like he had been born in his black coat and white breeches.

"May I have this dance, my lady?" he asked as soon as I entered the packed ballroom.

I made a show of looking at the dance card dangling from my gloved wrist. "It does appear that I am free, sir. You may, indeed."

He put out his arm to escort me into the middle of the dance floor. I felt suddenly shy, unsure of what to say to him.

"The play was a disaster," Rahul said with a smile. "And a complete delight."

"Did you get fired because of that death scene?" I asked as we lined up with the other couples for the next folk dance.

"I'm not sure, but I did hear that 'Queen Regina' wants to speak to us." The orchestra began the quick notes of the dance and we were almost immediately separated in our respective directions. So it wasn't until we came back together that Rahul was able to add, "Regina wants to speak to all of us."

I looked around at the dance floor, where Brandon, Penny, Annie, Mallika, Will, and John were dancing in a group, now together with their respective love interests, now trading partners as the dance required. Everyone seemed flushed and bright-eyed, clearly all where they needed to be. I looked at their happiness and felt a jolt of disappointment that I couldn't experience the same. Our ridiculous performance of *Pyramus and Thisbe* had been a little respite, a vacation from real life, as the best theater always is. But what I felt for Rahul during the confines of the play couldn't translate into our real lives.

"The play was fun. It was wonderful fun, to be honest," I confessed as Rahul whirled me by the hand. "But I'm not sure if that changes anything between us. I'm not sure it can."

His face grew serious, his eyes soft and sad. "I understand. You can't forgive me for my lies before. But let's at least just have this dance."

"No, I don't think you do understand," I insisted as I looked around the ballroom. I spotted the person I was looking for, who was glaring at me, angry-faced. "You should be dancing with Lucy, not me."

"What are you talking about?" Rahul looked flabbergasted.

"She told me how your father threatened to disown you if you didn't date her, or at least give her a chance to get cast in *Rosewood*." I couldn't see his face at first after I said this, because the steps of the dance had whirled me away from him. When I turned back toward Rahul, however, I was startled to see him laughing.

"Did Lucy actually say that?" Rahul looked shocked. "That girl's audacious, I'll give her that! I mean, talk about a saucy minx!"

I felt a heavy weight lifting from my heart. "It's not true?"

"My dad's not the most warm and fuzzy, but he's not a monster!" Rahul said, laughing even more. "I mean, that lie of Lucy's is straight out of some strict Asian dad stereotype!"

I opened my mouth, wanting to ask him about his other lies, but then it was time for all of us to visit Queen Regina up on her dais.

"I would like to offer all of you roles on *Rosewood* season two, some small, some perhaps a bit bigger, if you would like to consider them," Regina Rivera-Colón said quickly. "I appreciated your play so much, and you all clearly have the kind of chemistry and joy that leaps off the screen and right into people's hearts— which is ultimately the formula for *Rosewood*'s success."

Mallika raised her hand, as if she were in a schoolroom. I was reminded of Will doing the same to me in the orchard.

"Yes?" Queen Regina raised an imperious eyebrow.

"Majesty, I think I wouldn't like to be cast after all," Mallika confessed.

I let out a little squeak of surprise and my sister shrugged in my direction.

"I think what Regency Camp has made me realize is how much I don't enjoy acting," Mallika went on. "I think my real passion is for costuming instead."

She looked at Annie, who held her hand enthusiastically. "If it was possible, I'd love for Annie and me to get some sort of student internships in the season two costume department."

Regina leaned toward one of her assistants, who whispered something in her ear. After a few seconds' consultation, she straightened back up. "Well, it would be ultimately up to Ms. Park and her team, of course, but I don't see that being a problem. In consultation with your school schedules, and your families, of course."

Annie and Mallika hugged each other happily.

"And if there aren't other objections—" began Queen Regina, only to be cut off once again by John giving a little cough. She gave a grin, gesturing magnanimously to him. "Yes? Do you have some other concern or request? Would you like to take over my role and direct, possibly?"

"Well, maybe eventually," said Will before John cut him off.

"Even if we're to be extras," said John in a slightly nervous voice, "Will and I would like to be cast as a couple. We'd like to make sure that *Rosewood* has more on-screen queer representation."

Again, Regina leaned toward one of her assistants. They had

a brief, whispered conversation, after which the queen straightened up. "Done!" she announced loudly.

Finally, she turned to me once again. "And now, Eila, as you have probably guessed, we did indeed want to see if our Rahul here had chemistry with any of the Regency Campers. Which, if my spies are to be trusted, you have in spades. A modern-day Beatrice and Benedick, I hear!"

Our friends went "oooh," and I exchanged an embarrassed look with Rahul, who smiled and nodded.

Regina went on, "But, Eila, what you are is so much more than a good match with an already cast actor. What you *have* is so much more."

"More?" I squeaked, not sure how to react.

"Yes! It's a light and an energy completely unique to you," the queen of streaming shows said, her voice ringing with enthusiasm. "What you have is the ability to improvise like some of the most experienced comedic actresses I've ever seen."

I felt my knees give way and thought I would pass out. Wait, Regina Rivera-Colón thought *I* was good at improvisation? Me, who hated saying yes in any improv, who hated saying yes in life? Me, the girl who preferred the safety of a written script to the spontaneous chaos of playing a scene? I shook my head, convinced I'd misheard her. "I'm sorry, Your Majesty?"

"How can you be surprised?" Regina chuckled. "This morning, in that disaster of a theatrical, it was you who thought on your feet when everything was going wrong, you who helped those who had forgotten their lines"—here she raised her eyebrows at Will, who had the grace to look embarrassed—"you who spontaneously drew from Shakespeare and Austen and who knows where else to keep us howling with laughter; even you who reminded Rahul to dramatically kill himself when he forgot. It was your vision, humor, and spontaneity that made that disaster into a triumph!"

Our friends cheered and clapped for me even as my head spun. "Safety first! Safety first!" they chanted inanely.

"But really, Your Majesty," I couldn't help but say, raising my voice to be heard over the chaos, "that's hardly an accurate likeness of my character."

"Another adapted line from Austen! See? You're brilliant at spontaneous humor!" Regina Rivera-Colón let out a hoot. "So, let me hear your answer! Will you do it? Will you come work on *Rosewood* season two with Rahul? And with me?"

I felt warmed all over by her compliments, her ability to see in me what I had never been able to recognize in myself. "Thank you, I'm forever grateful." Then I cleared my throat, thinking through my next words carefully. "Only, the thing is, I'm not sure I can work with Rahul."

"Oh, what's wrong now?" groaned the director, not without good humor. "Honestly, I have never met a group of teenagers with more issues and demands!"

Well, then she couldn't have met too many teenagers, I thought. But I kept the comment to myself.

"With all respect, ma'am, you said I'm spontaneous. And I thank you for that compliment, but you said I have good chemistry with Rahul and that's just not true." I bit my lip, giving Rahul a regretful glance from under my lashes. "It was all pretend. You see, we were faking it, our relationship, our chemistry, all of it."

"Indeed? What horrors!" said Regina Rivera-Colón, arching an eyebrow. She put a jeweled hand to her chest. "Faking it? Pretending? How shocking! Do you mean to actually say you were *acting*?"

Our friends burst into laughter, but Rahul's face remained serious. "No, Your Majesty," he volunteered over the ruckus. "I think what Eila is trying to say without saying it is that she doesn't think she can trust me."

I felt my heart plummet, even though I wasn't sure why. But now wasn't the time for cowardice. I nodded, making my voice firm and resolute. "He's right, Ms. Rivera-Colón. I am afraid I can't accept any role that would require me to be on-screen with Rahul. He lied to me, and I just can't forgive that."

Love, however, cannot be forbidden. The more that flame is covered up, the hotter it burns. Also love can always find a way. It was impossible that these two whose hearts were on fire should be kept apart.

—EDITH HAMILTON,
MYTHOLOGY, "Pyramus and Thisbe"

CHAPTER 35

OH, TISH TOSH! Pish posh!" Queen Regina exclaimed as one of her assistants fanned her with a giant white-plumed confection. "It was written into Rahul's contract that he couldn't reveal his identity to anyone here at camp. That's not lying."

"That's not the only thing, Majesty," I said firmly. I didn't want to throw Rahul under the bus, but I had to get her to see, to understand why I couldn't accept her offer even though every cell in my being was screaming for me to say yes. "You see, Rahul called a bunch of reporters and had them take pictures of us as we boated into the Norland dock. You must have seen some of the shots in the *New York Tattler*."

Queen Regina held up her hand, halting the motion of the fanner. "Is this so, Mr. Lee?" she asked, her brows furrowed. "Because if you did that, it does break your nondisclosure clause."

The birds in her hairdo seemed to be peering down at us, as if they wanted to know the answer too.

My heart was plummeting down a rabbit hole and into the

recesses of my gut. I hated that I'd gotten Rahul in trouble with his boss. But I felt like I didn't have a choice. Or did I?

Rahul opened his mouth to answer, only his was not the voice that responded.

"It's not true, Majesty." It was Mallika, leaving Annie's side to approach the throne.

"Care to clarify, young miss?" asked Regina Rivera-Colón, one of the birdcages in her wig rattling dangerously.

"I'm afraid it was me who called the reporters," confessed Mallika, twisting her fingers around themselves. "I'm the Heiress of Rosings. And also the Heir of Allenham. It was me all along."

"Excuse me?" I demanded. I glanced at Rahul's face, but the expression there told me nothing. I whirled back to my sister. "Why would you do that?"

"For you, Didi." Mallika ran up to hold my hand, her eyes earnest and expression pleading. "I knew what time you'd be coming back from the play, and so I called the press. I didn't realize the reporters would be so awful and scary. I just wanted to give you an opportunity to shine, to be discovered."

I glanced from her to Rahul in confusion. "Are you letting my sister take the blame for something you did?"

But Mallika shook her head. "It's the opposite, actually." Her voice held a little wobble in it and her eyes were filling with tears. "He kept wanting to cover up for me. Rahul told me not to tell you it was me, that he'd rather take the blame so your and my relationship didn't get damaged."

I wanted to be furious with Mallika. I wanted to shake her and yell. But if I'd learned anything during Regency Camp, it

302

was to accept my sister as she was—an impulsive, joyous, loving dreamer—and not how I wanted her to be, or how society said she should be.

"Do you forgive me?" Mallika begged. Her beautiful face was wrinkled with worry. "Please, Didi? I couldn't bear it if you didn't forgive me!"

I nodded, unable to put to words all the complicated feelings in my heart. I simply reached out and took her in my arms. "You are my other self. I couldn't live without you."

"Does this then change your answer to me, Miss Eila?" asked Regina, clearly amused at all the confusions and confessions. It was as if we were putting on a second theatrical only for her.

I gave Rahul a shy look as I tried to process all I'd just learned. But I couldn't say yes to Regina, not yet. And so I said the only thing I could.

"Perhaps," I whispered, feeling everything shifting and resettling inside me. I was like an origami sculpture unfolded and smoothed out into its original square paper, once again able to become anything I wanted. "Perhaps."

Later that night, after all the dancing and eating and drinking of fizzy punch, after the sore feet and the stumbled steps and the racing hearts and soaring music, we were all gathered on the fairy-lit lawns of Norland Manor in the velvet promise of the night.

"Why are we here?" Will asked, yawning.

"It's too early to be sleepy!" John scolded, wrapping an arm around Will's shoulders. "The music's still playing inside! Let's go back in and dance!"

"Just wait," said Rahul, reaching out to hold my hand. Even

under the dim lights overhead, I caught his expression and guessed his plan.

"What are we waiting for?" asked Mallika. Her arm was linked through Annie's and they were both flushed and happy.

"Just wait a minute," I said, looking up. I felt Austen's words inside me, guiding me: "You want nothing but patience—or give it a more fascinating name—call it hope."

"There! Look!" cried Penny, her voice bright as a child's. She pointed upward, to the sky. "Look up! Look up!"

"It's magic!" Brandon laughingly swung her around in his arms.

And it was magic—the glowing lanterns that Rahul had somehow arranged the Norland Manor staff to release—just for us—into the dark night sky. They rose like hope and dreams and ambition; they floated and bobbed like laughter and friendship; they reached out for the sky like hearts reaching out for a future just beyond the horizon of today. They were the love of those we had lost, urging us to go on doing what the living do, dancing on the cusp of all things beautiful and bright, blazing up into the night.

I reached out for Rahul's hand, and found it, warm and real and solid in mine. Unlike my sister, I had always assumed magic and reality to be two different states of being—one ephemeral and fleeting, one hard and fast. But what if they were a choice? What if we could make our own realities as we desired—full of flowers and beauty and power and grace? A reality where we all belonged and we were all celebrated like the pieces of sparkling magic we were? What if right here, right now, was just the first step in creating that future for us all?

I felt Rahul's arms around me then, his breath on my cheek, his voice in my ear, as he whispered, "Are you ready for *Rosewood*?"

And I, floating up and up like the lights glowing fiercely in my eyes, said the only thing I could.

"Yes," I said.

Yes.

Yes.

Yes.

Dearest Aficionados of *Rosewood*:

Please be apprised that season two has found a new leading lady from its Norland Manor Regency Camp.

The talented Miss Eila Das will be playing the lady-detective love interest of Mr. Rahul Lee.

A circumstance of art imitating life, perhaps? And do remember, dear viewers, to stop and smell the roses, Or, in the words of the Persian poet Rumi,

Come out here, where the roses have opened. Let soul and world meet.

Yours, as ever,

The producers of *Rosewood* season two

AUTHOR'S NOTE

For many years, my midsummers have been full of magic. There's nothing more I enjoy than going to an outdoor Shakespeare performance and being transported into an imaginative world far greater than my own—a world of kings and fairies, lovers and villains. It's the same transformative feeling I get when I lose myself in the novels of my favorite author, Jane Austen.

I wanted to infuse this romp of a story with all the midsummer joy and giddy firefly romance I feel when I see outdoor theater. I wanted to cast it with the same inclusivity that color-conscious directors are using to transform Regency adaptations on the small screen. Unlike *Debating Darcy*, which is a fairly faithful reimagining of *Pride and Prejudice*, this novel is far more loosely based on *Sense and Sensibility*, with hearty doses of many Shakespearean plays—from *The Taming of the Shrew* to *The Tempest* to *A Midsummer Night's Dream*—thrown liberally in.

I wrote this story because representation matters. Because no matter our ethnicity, sexuality, background, or body, we all deserve to see ourselves as beautiful, magical, and desirable. I never did as a little brown-skinned immigrant daughter, but I vehemently want a different, self-loving happy ending for my own children and all those younger people coming up after me. For this world to be a fair and just place, our stories must center us all as protagonists, heroes, and love interests.

I hope that this tale sweeps you into a world of dreams and fancies from which you will awake transformed. Because now, more than ever, books make things fictional so that they can be made real. Stories help us dream new worlds we would imagine into being. Let this new future we are creating together—in story and in practice—be more just, inclusive, loving, and true.

Let us together dream such a world into being. Let us awaken from our dreams and fight for it.

For love is always, *always* enough. Radical love and joy can be revolutionary.

♥

Sayantani

ACKNOWLEDGMENTS

I want to thank Jane Austen and William Shakespeare for being the best, even though there aren't admittedly lot of brown girls in their stories. I want to thank Julia Quinn and Shonda Rhimes for coming up with the Bridgerton universe and then casting it to reflect our actual universe. I also thank Kate Sharma—fellow dark-skinned, firstborn immigrant daughter (if fictional)—for being unapologetically beautiful and smart and setting the world's imagination on fire.

Thank you to my agent, Brent Taylor, who believed in me when few others did, and keeps tirelessly cheering me on. Thank you to my editor, Abigail McAden, for her razor-sharp wit and her merciless sarcasm. Half of the jokes in this book, and any of my books, are for her.

Thank you to the cover design team of Elizabeth Parisi (*cough* artistic genius *cough*) and Muhammed Sajid. Gratitude to Melissa Schirmer, my production editor, Jessica White, my copyeditor, and to the rest of my Scholastic family including Ellie Berger,

David Levithan, Rachel Feld, Lizette Serrano, Emily Heddleson, Seale Ballenger, and Lia Ferrone!

Thank you to all those author friendships I've made on this journey—especially those who've seen me through these last difficult years of the pandemic—including my We Need Diverse Books, KidLit Writers of Color+, and Desi Writers families. Thank you to the librarians, teachers, parents and readers who have enjoyed and shared my stories.

Endless love to my beloved parents, Sujan, who can't get enough of Bangladeshi romantic films, and Shamita, who first introduced me to Austen, Heyer, and Regency romance in general, and who I mercilessly hooked on Bridgerton. Thanks to my husband-slash-one-man-publicity-team, Boris, and my darling pup, Khushi. Particular love and thanks to my collaborators and co-conspirators Kirin and Sunaya, who helped me be brave enough to write this book full of giddy, unadulterated joy. How did I get so lucky to be your mama?

IT IS A TRUTH
UNIVERSALLY ACKNOWLEDGED THAT LEELA BOSE
PLAYS TO WIN

Don't miss bestselling author Sayantani DasGupta's
reinterpretation of the beloved classic *Pride and
Prejudice*—imaginative, hilarious, thought-provoking,
and truly reflective of the complex diverse world of
American high school culture.

★ "Studded with references to U.S. and South Asian pop culture
as well as Jane Austen–related Easter eggs, DasGupta's astute,
buoyant comedy of manners employs witty, rat-a-tat dialogue
alongside social commentary about subjects including classism,
colorism, and sexism. —*Publishers Weekly*, starred review

"A delight." —*Kirkus Reviews*